MEG CABOT

AVALON HIGH

HARPER TEEN
An Imprint of HarperCollinsPublishers

HarperTeen is an imprint of HarperCollins Publishers.

Avalon High
Copyright © 2006 by Meggin Cabot

Library of Congress Cataloging-in-Publication Data
Cabot, Meg.
    Avalon High / Meg Cabot.— 1st ed.
      p.   cm.
    Summary: Having moved to Annapolis, Maryland, with her
medievalist parents, high school junior Ellie enrolls at Avalon
High School, where several students may or may not be
reincarnations of King Arthur and his court.
    ISBN 978-0-06-075588-1
    [1. Reincarnation—Fiction. 2. Arthur, King—Fiction.
3. Identity—Fiction. 4. Secrets—Fiction. 5. High schools—
Fiction. 6. Schools.] I. Title.
PZ7.C11165Ava 2006   2005014558
[Fic]—dc22   CIP
                                                   AC

Typography by Sasha Illingworth
❖
First HarperTeen paperback edition, 2007

For the two Barbara Cabots,
Bad Mommy and Aunt Babs

Many thanks to Beth Ader,
Jennifer Brown, Barbara M. Cabot,
Michele Jaffe, Laura Langlie,
Abigail McAden, and especially
Benjamin Egnatz.

AVALON HIGH

She knows not what the curse may be,
And so she weaveth steadily,
And little other care has she,
The Lady of Shalott.

—Alfred Lord Tennyson

CHAPTER ONE

And by the moon the reaper weary,
Piling sheaves in uplands airy,
Listening, whispers
"'Tis the fairy Lady of Shalott."

"You are so lucky."

Trust my best friend Nancy to see things that way. Nancy is what you would call an optimist.

Not that I'm a pessimist, or anything. I'm just . . . practical. At least according to Nancy.

Apparently, I'm also lucky.

"Lucky?" I echoed into the phone. "In what way am I lucky?"

"Oh, you know," Nancy said. "You get to start over. In a whole new school. Where no one knows you. You can be whoever you want to be. You can give yourself a total personality makeover, and there won't be anyone around to be all, 'Who do you think you're kidding, Ellie Harrison? I remember when you ate paste in first grade.' "

"I never thought of it that way," I said. Because I hadn't. "Anyway, you were the one who ate paste."

"You know what I mean." Nancy sighed. "Well. Good luck. With school and everything."

"Yeah," I said, sensing even over the thousand-mile difference between us, that, it was time to hang up. "Bye."

"Bye," Nancy said. Then added, "You're so lucky."

Really, up until Nancy said this, I hadn't thought there was anything lucky about my situation at all. Except maybe the fact that there's a pool in the backyard of our new house. We never had a pool of our own. Before, if Nancy and I wanted to go to the pool, we had to get on our bikes and ride five miles—mostly uphill—to Como Park.

I have to say, when my parents broke the news about the sabbatical, the fact that they were quick to add, "And we're renting a house with a pool!" was the only thing that kept down the vomit that started coming up in my throat. If you are a child of professors, *sabbatical* is probably about the dirtiest word in your own personal vocabulary. Every seven years, most professors get offered one—basically a yearlong vacation, so they can recharge and try to write and publish a book.

Professors love sabbaticals.

Their kids hate them.

Because would you really want to uproot and leave all your friends, make all new friends at a whole new school and just be getting to think, "Okay, this isn't so bad," only to have to uproot yourself again a year later and go back where you came from?

No. Not if you're sane, anyway.

At least this sabbatical isn't as bad as the last one, which was in Germany. Not that there's anything wrong with Germany. I still exchange e-mails with Anne-Katrin, the girl I shared a desk with in the weird German school I went to there.

But come on. I had to learn a whole other language!

At least with this one, we're still in America. And okay, we're outside Washington, D.C., which isn't like the rest of America. But everyone here speaks English. So far.

And there's a pool.

Having your own pool is a lot of responsibility, it turns out. I mean, every morning you have to check the filters and make sure they aren't all jammed up with leaves or dead moles. There's almost always a frog or two in ours. Usually, if I get out there early enough, they're still alive. So then I have to conduct a frog rescue expedition.

The only way you can rescue the frogs is to reach down into the water to pull the filter basket out, so I've ended up touching all sorts of really gross stuff that floats in there, like dead beetles and newts and, a few times, drowned mice. Once there was a snake. It was still alive. I pretty much draw the line at touching anything that is capable of sending paralyzing streams of poison into my veins, so I yelled to my parents that there was a snake in the filter basket.

My dad is the one who yelled back, "So? What do you want me to do about it?"

"Get it out," I said.

"No way," my dad said. "I'm not touching any snake."

My parents aren't like other parents. For one thing, other people's parents actually leave the house to go to work. Some of them are gone for as many as forty-five hours a week, I've heard.

Not mine. Mine are home *all the time*. They never leave! They're always in their at-home offices, writing or reading. Practically the only time they come out of their offices is to watch *Jeopardy!* and then they yell out the answers at each other.

No one else's parents know all the answers to *Jeopardy!* or yell them out if they do. I know, I've been to Nancy's house and seen the evidence for myself. Her parents watch *Entertainment Tonight* after dinner, like normal people.

I don't know *any* of the answers on *Jeopardy!* That's why I sort of hate that show.

My dad grew up in the Bronx, where there aren't any snakes. He completely hates nature. He totally ignores our cat, Tig. Which of course means that Tig is crazy about him.

And if my dad sees a spider, he screams like a girl. Then my mom, who grew up on a ranch in Montana and has no patience for spiders *or* my dad's screaming, will come in and kill it, even though I've told her a million times that spiders are extremely beneficial to the environment.

Of course, I knew better than to tell my mom about the snake in the pool filter, because she'd probably have come out and snapped its head clean off right in front of me. In the end, I found a forked branch, and pulled it out that way. I let it go in the woodsy area behind the house we're renting. Even though the snake didn't turn out to be that scary once I finally got the guts to save it, I kind of hope it doesn't come back.

There's other stuff you have to do if you have your own pool, besides clean out the filter baskets. You have to vacuum the pool floor—this is kind of fun—and you have to test the water all the time, for chlorine and pH. I like testing the water. I do it a few times a day. You put the water in these little test tubes, and then add a couple drops of this stuff, and then if the water in the test tubes turns the wrong color, you have to drop some powder into the filter baskets. It's a lot like chemistry, only better, because when you're done, instead of a stinky mess like the kind I always ended up with last year in chem class, you get beautiful clear blue water.

I spent most of the summer that we moved to Annapolis messing around with the pool. I say "messing around with." My brother Geoff—he left for his first year of college the second week in August—put it a different way. He said I was "acting like a freak about it."

"Ellie," he said to me so many times I lost count, "relax. You don't need to be doing this. We've got a contract with a pool company. They come every week. Let them do it."

But the pool guy doesn't really *care* about the pool. I

mean, he's just doing it for the money. He doesn't see the beauty of it. I'm pretty sure.

But I guess I can see where Geoff was coming from. I mean, the pool did sort of start taking up a lot of my time. When I wasn't cleaning it, I was floating on top of the water, on one of these inflatable rafts I made my mom and dad buy for us over at the Wawa. That's the name of the gas stations here in Maryland. Wawas. They don't have any Wawas back home in Minnesota. Just, like, Mobils and Exxons or whatever.

Anyway, we filled them up at the Wawa, too—the rafts—with the air hose meant for people to use on their tires, even though you aren't supposed to use an air hose to fill a raft. It says so right on the raft.

But when Geoff pointed this out to my dad, he just went, "Who cares?" and filled them up anyway.

And nothing bad happened.

I tried to keep the same routine going for the whole summer. Every day I got up and put on my bikini. Then I grabbed a Nutri-Grain bar and headed down to the pool to check the filter baskets for frogs or whatever. Then when the pool was all clean, I got onto one of the rafts with a book and started floating.

By the time Geoff left for school, I was so good at floating that I could do it without even getting my hair wet or anything. I could go all morning without a break, right up until my mom or dad would come out onto the deck and say, "Lunch."

Then I'd go inside and Mom and Dad and I would

have peanut butter and jelly, if I was the one cooking that day, or ribs from Red Hot and Blue down the road if it was one of my parents' turn, on account of them both being too busy writing books to cook.

Then I'd go back out to the pool until my mom or dad came out and said, "Dinner."

I didn't think this was a bad way to pass the last few weeks of summer.

But my mom did.

I don't know why she had to go and make it her business how I spend my time. I mean, she's the one who let Dad drag us out here in the first place, on account of the book he's researching. She could have written her own book—on my namesake, Elaine of Astolat, the Lady of Shalott—back home in St. Paul.

Oh yeah. That's the other thing about having professors as parents: They name you after totally random authors—like poor Geoff, after Geoffrey Chaucer—or characters from literature, such as the Lady of Shalott, aka Lady Elaine, who killed herself because Sir Lancelot liked Queen Guinevere—you know, the one Keira Knightley played in that King Arthur movie—better than he liked her.

I don't care how beautiful the poem is about her. It's not exactly cool to be named after someone who killed herself over a guy. I have mentioned this several times to my parents, but they still don't get it.

The name thing's not the only thing they don't get, either.

7

"Don't you want to go to the mall?" my mom started asking me every single day, before I could escape to the pool. "Don't you want to go to the movies?"

But now that Geoff had left for college, I had no one to go to the mall or the movies with—no one except my parents. And no way was I going with them. Been there, done that. Nothing like going to the movies with two people who have to dissect the film to within an inch of its life. I mean, it's Vin Diesel, okay? What do they *expect*?

"School's going to start soon enough," I'd say to my mom. "Why can't I just float until then?"

"Because it's not normal," my mom would say, when I'd ask her this.

To which I would reply, "Oh, and you would know what normal is," because, let's face it, she and my dad are both freaks.

But she wouldn't even get mad. She'd just shake her head and say, "I know what normal behavior for a teenage girl is. And floating in that pool by yourself all day is not it."

I thought this was unnecessarily harsh. There's nothing wrong with floating. It's actually pretty fun. You can lie there and read, or, if your book gets boring or you finish it and are too lazy to go inside and get a new one or whatever, you can watch the way the sunlight reflects off the water onto the backs of the leaves of the trees above you. And you can listen to the birds and cicadas and, off in the distance, the rat-tat-boom of gunnery practice down at the Naval Academy.

We saw them, sometimes. The middies, I mean, or "midshipmen" as they preferred to be called, the student officers. In their spotless white uniforms, walking in pairs downtown, whenever my parents and I went to buy a new book for me to read and coffee for them at Hard Bean Coffee and Booksellers. My dad would point and say, "Look, Ellie. Sailors."

Which isn't that weird, really. I guess he was trying to make girl talk. You know, because I can't get any of that from my mom, the spider killer.

I guess I was supposed to think the middies were cute, or something. But I wasn't going to talk about cute guys with my *dad*. I mean, I appreciated the effort, and all, but in a way it was just as bad as Mom's "Why don't you let me take you to the mall?" thing.

And it's not like my dad spent *his* days doing anything all that exciting. The book he's writing is even worse than Mom's, on the boredom barometer. Because his is about a sword. A sword! It isn't even a pretty sword, with jewels or gold or anything. It's all old and has these rust spots and isn't worth a dime. I know because the National Gallery over in D.C. let my dad bring it home so he could study it closer. That's why we moved here . . . so he can look at this sword up close. It's sitting in his office—well, the office of the professor whose house we're renting while he's in England on his own sabbatical, probably studying something even more worthless than Dad's sword.

Museums let you borrow stuff and bring it home if it's

of academic interest (in other words, not worth any-thing) and if you're a professor.

I don't know why my parents had to choose medieval times as their field of study. It's the most boring era of all, except possibly prehistoric times. I know I'm in the minority in thinking this, but that's because most people have this really messed up idea about what things were like in the Middle Ages. Most people think it was like what they show in the movies and on TV. You know, women floating around in pointy hats and pretty dresses saying "thee" and "thou," and knights thundering up to save the day.

But when your parents are medievalists, you learn at a pretty early age that things weren't like that at all. The truth is, everyone back in the Middle Ages had totally bad B.O. and no teeth and died of old age at, like, twenty, and the women were all oppressed and had to marry people they didn't even like and everybody blamed them for every little thing that went wrong.

I mean, look at Guinevere. Everyone thinks it's all her fault Camelot doesn't exist anymore. I'm so sure.

Except that I discovered at an early age that sharing information like this can make you kind of unpopular at Sleeping Beauty birthday parties. Or at that Medieval Times restaurant. Or during games of Dungeons & Dragons.

But what am I supposed to do, remain silent on the subject? I genuinely can't help it. Like I'm really going to sit there and go, "Oh yeah, things were all really great back then. I wish I could find a time portal and go back to, like, the year 900 and visit and get lice and have all my hair frizz out because there was no conditioner, and oh, by the way, if you got strep throat or bronchitis you died because there weren't any antibiotics."

Um, not. As a consequence, I'm not at the top of anybody's list when it comes time to send out invites to the Renaissance Fayre.

But whatever. I ended up giving in to my mom in the end. Not about the mall. About running with my dad.

I didn't want to go, or anything.

But this was different than going to the movies or the mall. I mean, exercise is supposedly very good for middle-aged men, and my dad hadn't gotten any in a long time. I'd won the district's women's two hundred meter back home just last May, but Dad hadn't exercised since his annual physical, which was last year, when the doctor told him he needed to lose ten pounds. So he'd gone to the gym with my mom twice, then gave up, because he says all the testosterone at the gym makes him crazy.

My mom was the one who was all, "If you take him running, Ellie, I'll get off your back about the floating thing."

Which pretty much clinched it for me. Well, that and the fact that it would give Dad a chance to get his heart rate up—something I knew from what they're always saying on the *Today* show that old people badly need.

Like a good academic, Mom had done her research.

She sent us to a park about two miles from the house we were renting. It was a very fancy park that had everything: tennis courts, baseball diamond, lacrosse field, nice, clean public restrooms, two dog runs—one for big dogs and one for little ones—and, of course, a running path. No pool, like back home in Como Park, but I guess people in our new upscale neighborhood don't need a community pool. Everyone has their own in their backyard.

I got out of the car and did a few stretches while I surreptitiously watched my dad prepare for his run. He'd put away his wire rims—he's blind as a bat without them. In fact, in medieval times, he'd probably have been dead by the age of three or four from falling down a well or whatever; I'd inherited my mom's twenty-twenty vision, so most likely I'd have lived a bit longer—and put on these thick plastic-rimmed glasses that have an elastic band he can snap behind his head to keep them from sliding off while he runs. Mom calls this his Dork Strap.

"This is a nice running path," my dad was saying, as he adjusted his Dork Strap. Unlike me, who'd spent hours in the pool, Dad wasn't a bit tan. His legs were the color of notebook paper. Only with hair. "It's exactly one mile per lap. It goes through some woods—a kind of arboretum—over there. See? So it's not all in the hot sun. There's some shade."

I slid my headphones on. I can't run without music, except during meets, when they won't let you. I find that rap is ideal for running. The angrier the rapper, the better. Eminem is ideal to listen to while running, because he's so mad at everyone. Except his daughter.

"Two laps?" I asked my dad.

"Sure," he said.

And so I turned on my iPod mini—I keep it on an arm strap when I run, which is different than a Dork Strap—and started running.

It was hard at first. It's more humid in Maryland than it is back home, I guess on account of the sea. The air is actually heavy. It's like running through soup.

But after a while, my joints seemed to loosen up. I started remembering how much I'd liked to run back home. It's hard and everything. Don't get me wrong. But I like how strong and powerful my legs feel underneath me while I run . . . like I can do anything. Anything at all.

There was hardly anyone else on the path—just old ladies, mostly, power-walking with their dogs—but I tore past them, leaving them in my wake. I didn't smile as I ran by. Back home, everybody smiles at strangers. Here, the only time people smile is if you smile first. It didn't take my parents very long to catch on to this. Now they make me smile—and even wave—at everyone we pass. Especially our new neighbors, when they're out in their yards mowing their lawns or whatever. Image, my mom calls it. It's important to keep up a good image, she says. So people won't think we're snobs.

Except that I'm not really sure I care what people around here think about me.

The running path started out like a normal track,

with closely cut grass on either side of it, snaking between the baseball diamond and the lacrosse field, then curving past the dog runs and around the parking lot. '

Then it left the grass behind, and disappeared into a surprisingly thick forest. Yeah, a real forest, right in the middle of nowhere, with a discreet little brown sign that said WELCOME TO THE ANNE ARUNDEL COUNTY ARBORETUM by the side of the path.

I was a little shocked, as I ran past the sign, at how wild the undergrowth on either side of the trail had been allowed to get. Plunging into the deep shade of the arboretum, I noticed that the leaves overhead were so thick, hardly any sunlight at all was allowed to get through.

Still, the vegetation on either side of me was lush and prickly looking. I was sure there was also a ton of poison ivy in there, too . . . something that, if you contracted it badly enough back in medieval times, could probably have killed you, since there wasn't any cortisone.

You could barely see two feet beyond the path, the brambles and trees were so close together. But it was at least ten degrees cooler in the arboretum than it was in the rest of the park. The shade cooled the sweat that was dripping down my face and chest. It was hard to believe, running through that thick wood, that I was still near civilization. But when I pulled out my headphones to listen, I could hear cars going by on the highway beyond the thick growth of trees.

Which was kind of a relief. You know, that I hadn't accidentally gotten lost in Jurassic Park, or whatever.

I plopped my earphones back into place and kept going. I was breathing really hard now, but I still felt good. I couldn't hear my feet striking the path—I could only hear the music in my ears—but it seemed to me for a minute that I was the only person in these woods . . . maybe the only person in the whole world.

Which was ridiculous, since I knew my dad wasn't that far behind me—probably not going much faster than the power-walking ladies, but behind me nonetheless.

Still, I had seen too many TV movies where the heroine was jogging innocently along and some random psychopath comes popping out of thick growth, just like the stuff on either side of me, and attacks her. I wasn't taking any chances. Who knew what kind of freaks were lurking? I mean, it was Annapolis, home of the U.S. Naval Academy and the capital of Maryland, and all—hardly an area known for harboring violent criminals.

But you never know.

Good thing my legs were so strong. If someone did jump out at me from the trees, I was pretty confident that I could deliver a good kick to his head. And keep stomping on him until help came.

It was right as I was thinking this that I saw him.

CHAPTER TWO

Willows whiten, aspens quiver,
Little breezes dusk and shiver
Thro' the wave that runs for ever
By the island in the river
Flowing down to Camelot.

Or maybe I just thought I did.

Still. I was pretty sure I saw something through the trees that wasn't green or brown or any other color found in nature.

And when I peered through the thick leaves around me, I saw that there was someone standing at the bottom of a pretty deep ravine to one side of the path, near a large cluster of boulders. How he could have gotten through all that vegetation without a machete, I couldn't imagine. Maybe there was a path I'd missed.

But he was there all right. Doing what, I went by too quickly to tell.

Then I was out of the woods, out into the blazing

sunshine, and sprinting past the parking lot. Some women were getting out of a minivan and heading toward the dog run with their Border collies. There was a playground nearby, on which some tiny kids were swinging and going down the slide, their parents watching them closely in case of accidents.

And I thought to myself: Had I really seen what I thought I'd seen? A guy standing at the bottom of that ravine?

Or had I just imagined it?

There was a park employee with a weed whacker by third base over at the baseball diamond. I didn't say hi to him. I didn't smile, either.

Nor did I mention the man at the bottom of the ravine. I probably should have. What about those kids on the playground? What if he was a child molester?

But I didn't say anything to the guy with the weed whacker. I blew past him without making eye contact.

So much for Image.

I could see my dad, in his bright yellow shirt, way on the other side of the track. He was three-quarters of a lap behind me. That was okay. He's slow, but he's steady. Mom always says Dad will never make it there fast, but at least he'll always make it, in the end.

Mom's one to talk. She can't even stand running. She likes to do aerobics at the Y.

Which, given the freak-out I'd gotten from passing that guy in the woods, was starting to sound like it wasn't such a bad idea.

This time around, when I headed into the trees, I scanned the sides of the path for signs of a trail, something the man could have used to make it down to that ravine without getting all scratched up by the undergrowth. But I didn't see anything.

And when I went past where I'd seen him before, I saw that the ravine was empty. He wasn't there anymore. There was nothing, in fact, to indicate that he'd been there at all. Maybe I really had imagined him. Maybe Mom was right, and I really should have spent less time in the pool, and more at the mall this summer. Maybe, I worried, I was cracking up from lack of contact with people my own age.

Which is when I rounded a corner, and nearly ran into him.

And realized I hadn't imagined him at all.

He was with two other people. The first thing I noticed about them—the two people who were with him, I mean—was that they were both blond and very attractive, a guy and a girl, around my age. They were on either side of the man from the ravine . . . who, I noted upon closer inspection, wasn't a man at all, really, but a boy, also my age, or maybe a little older. He was tall and dark-haired, like me.

But unlike me, he wasn't covered in sweat or gasping for breath.

Oh, and he was really cute, too.

All three of them looked up, startled, as I came running by. I saw the blond-haired boy say something, and the blond-haired girl looked upset . . . maybe because I almost ran into them, even though I veered in time to avoid a collision.

Only the dark-haired boy smiled at me. He looked right into my face and said something.

Except that I don't know what it was since I had my earphones on and couldn't hear him.

All I know is that for some reason—I don't know why—I smiled back. Not because of Image, or anything. It was weird. It was like he smiled at me, and my lips automatically smiled back—my brain had nothing to do with it. There was no conscious decision on my part to smile back.

I just did. Like it was a habit, or something. Like this was a smile I always smiled back to.

Except that I had never seen this guy before in my life. So how could my mouth even have known this?

Which was why it was kind of a relief to run past them. You know, to get away from that smile that made me smile back, even when I didn't want to. Necessarily.

My relief was short-lived, though. Because I saw them again as I leaned against the hood of our car, panting heavily and polishing off one of the bottles of water my mom had made Dad and me bring with us. They emerged from the woods—the two boys and the girl—and headed toward their own cars. The blond girl and boy were talking rapidly to the dark-haired boy. I wasn't close enough to hear what they were saying, but judging from their expressions, it didn't look like they were too happy with him. One thing I knew for sure: He wasn't smiling anymore.

Finally, he said something that seemed to placate the blond couple, since they stopped looking so upset.

Then the blond boy climbed into a Jeep, while the dark-haired guy slid behind the wheel of a white Land Cruiser . . . and the blond girl slipped into the passenger seat beside him. Which surprised me, since it had looked to me like she and the cute blond guy, not the dark-haired one, were the couple.

But having had little experience in the boyfriend department, I'm not exactly an expert.

I was sitting on the hood of our own car reflecting on what I had just witnessed—a lovers' quarrel? A drug deal of some kind?—when my dad finally came staggering over.

"Water," he croaked, and I gave him the other bottle.

It wasn't until we were inside the car, the air-conditioning blasting on us at full power, that my dad asked, "So. Have a good run?"

"Yeah," I said, kind of surprised by the answer.

"Want to go again tomorrow?" my dad wanted to know.

"Sure," I said, looking at the place where the three people I'd seen—the two blonds and the dark-haired boy—had last stood. They were long gone by then.

"Great," my dad said, in a voice totally lacking any sort of enthusiasm.

You could tell he'd been hoping I'd say no. But I

couldn't do that. Not because I'd finally remembered how much I enjoyed running, or because I'd had a good time with my dad.

But because—fine, I'll admit it—I was hoping I'd see that cute guy—and his smile—again.

CHAPTER THREE

Four gray walls, and four gray towers,
Overlook a space of flowers,
And the silent isle imbowers
The Lady of Shalott.

I didn't. At least, not at the park. Not that next week, anyway. Dad and I went running every day—at around the same time as that first day—but I didn't see anyone in the ravine again.

And I looked. Believe me. I looked hard.

I thought about them—the three people I'd seen—a lot. Because they were the first people my own age I'd seen in Annapolis—outside of those working at Graul's, the local grocery store where we bought trash bags and bread, or waiting tables at Red Hot and Blue.

Was that ravine, I wondered, some kind of local make-out spot?

But the dark-haired guy hadn't been making out with

anybody that I had seen.

Was it where kids went to do drugs?

But the guy hadn't seemed high. And he and his friends hadn't looked like headbangers. They'd been wearing normal clothes, khaki shorts and T-shirts. I hadn't noticed a single tattoo or piercing on any of them.

It didn't appear that I was going to get answers to any of these questions anytime soon. Our days of running in Anne Arundel Park—and my floating in our pool—were coming to an end anyway: School was starting.

It had always been my dream, of course, to start off my junior year as a new student in a high school in a far-away state where I knew no one.

Um, not.

The first day at Avalon High School wasn't a real first day. It was an orientation. Basically you just got assigned classes and lockers and stuff. Nothing cerebral involved, I guess to sort of ease us back into the academic routine.

AHS was smaller than my old school, but had better facilities and more money, so I wasn't exactly complaining. They even had a student guide they handed out on the first official (non-orientation) day, with a small photo and bio on each student. I had to pose for my photo during orientation—me and two hundred giggling freshmen. Yippee—then fill out a form that asked me for my pertinent information: name, e-mail address (if I chose to share it), and interests, so they could put it in the guide. It was so we could all get to know one another . . . sort of Image for the student population.

My parents were super excited on my first day of *real* school. They got up early and made me a big breakfast and a bag lunch. The breakfast was okay—waffles that were only a little freezer burned—but the lunch was really sad: a peanut butter and jelly sandwich with Red Hot and Blue potato salad on the side. I didn't have the heart to tell them that the potato salad would get all warm in my locker before I ever got a chance to eat it. My parents, being medievalists, just don't think about refrigeration that often.

I took the bag they offered me all proudly and just went, "Thanks, Mom and Dad."

They drove me to school the first day because I said I was too emotionally fragile to take the bus. All of us knew this wasn't true, but I really didn't want to deal with the hassle of not having anybody to sit next to, and people possibly not wanting to share their seats with a total stranger, et cetera.

My parents didn't seem to mind. They dropped me off on their way to BWI, the local train station, because they had decided to make a day of it and go into the city to consult with other medievalists on their books—my mom about Elaine of Astolat, and my dad about his sword.

I told them to play nice with the other professors, and they told me to play nice with the other high school kids.

Then I went on into the school.

It was a typical first day—at least the initial half was.

No one spoke to me, and I spoke to no one. A couple of the teachers made a big deal out of my being new, and from the exotic land of Minnesota, and had me tell the class a little about myself and my home state.

I did.

No one listened. Or if they did, they didn't seem to care.

Which was all right, because truthfully, I didn't care very much either.

Lunch is always the scariest part of any kid's first day at a new school. I'm kind of used to it, from previous sabbaticals, though. Like, I knew enough from my experience in Germany that taking my paper bag and going to sit in the library by myself would peg me as a huge loser for the rest of the year.

So instead I took a deep breath and looked around for a table where tall, geeky-looking girls like myself were sitting. After I found some, I went over to introduce myself. Because, basically, that's what you have to do. Feeling like a complete and total dork, I told them I was new and asked if I could sit with them. Thank God they scooted down and made room for me. That is, after all, the accepted code of conduct for tall, geeky-looking girls everywhere.

Granted, they could have told me to get lost. But they didn't. Avalon High, I was starting to think, might not be so bad after all.

I was especially convinced of this right after lunch, which is when I finally saw him. The guy from the ravine, I mean.

I was looking down at my schedule, trying to remember where Room 209 was from my orientation tour, when he came hurtling around the corner, and practically smacked into me. I recognized him at once—not just because he was so tall, and there aren't a lot of guys who are taller than me, but also because he had such a distinctive face. Not handsome, really. But attractive. And nice. And strong-looking.

The weirdest part was, he seemed to recognize me, too, even though he could only have seen me for, like, five seconds that day in the park.

"Hey," he said, smiling, not just with his lips, but with his sky blue eyes, too.

Just *Hey*. That's all. *Hey*.

But it was a *Hey* that made my heart flop over inside my chest.

And, okay, whatever. Maybe it was the eyes, and not the *Hey* so much. Or maybe it was just, you know, a familiar face in this sea of people I'd never seen before.

Except . . . well, I'd seen the girl standing next to him—it was the blond girl, the same one I'd seen him drive away with—before, and my heart hadn't flopped over at the sight of her.

But maybe that's because she was plucking on his sleeve and going, "But I told Lance we'd meet him at the DQ after practice."

To which he replied by putting his arm around her and going, "Sure, that sounds great."

Then the two of them went by me, and were swallowed up in the hordes flooding the hallway.

The whole thing had taken maybe two seconds. Okay, three.

But it left me feeling like someone had kicked me in the chest. Which just—well, it isn't like me. I am *not* that way. You know, the *Oh my God, he* looked *at me, I can barely breathe* type. Nancy's the romantic optimist. I'm the practical one.

Which is why it made no sense at all that the minute I got to my next class, I was whipping out my copy of the student guide and frantically thumbing through it until I found him, paying not the slightest bit of attention to the reading syllabus my new World Lit teacher was trying to go over with us.

He was a year ahead of me, a senior. His name was A. William Wagner, but he was known as just plain Will.

I thought that suited him. He looked like a Will.

Not that I know how a Will should look, really. But whatever.

According to the book, A. William Wagner was quite a star. He was on the school football team, as well as a National Merit Finalist and president of the senior class. His interests included reading and sailing.

It didn't say anything about Will's dating status, but I'd seen him twice now, both times with the same stunningly pretty blonde. And the second time he'd put his arm around her, and she'd talked to him about meeting someone at the Dairy Queen after practice. She had to be his girlfriend.

Guys like A. William Wagner always have girlfriends. You don't have to be the practical type, like I am, to know that.

Since I had nothing better to do—Mr. Morton, my World Lit instructor, was trying to interest us in Gaelic legend, which I probably would have found interesting if I didn't eat, drink, and breathe Gaelic legend whenever I was in the presence of my parents—I looked the girlfriend up in the guide, too. I found her picture—in my class—and saw that her name was Jennifer Gold, and that her interests included shopping and, what a surprise, A. William Wagner.

Her extracurricular was cheerleading.

It so figured.

I flipped through the student guide, looking for the blond boy I'd seen with Will and Jennifer that day in the park. I found him, eventually. Lance Reynolds. He was in Will's class, a senior. He was listed as a guard—whatever that was—on the football team, as well as having an interest in sailing.

As first days of school went, this one hadn't been all that bad. I'd even made some new friends. Some of the girls I'd sat down next to at lunch turned out to be on the track team. One of them—Liz—lived on the same road as me. She said she'd see me on the bus in the morning.

When I came outside after school and saw Mom and

Dad sitting there in our car, I didn't melt with relief or anything. I just got into the car and said, "Home, Jeeves," in a jokey way. On our way back to the house, they asked me about my day, and I told them it had been fine. Then I asked them about theirs. Mom went on about some new text she'd found that actually mentions Elaine—not me, *her* Elaine—in Arthurian legend, unconnected to the famous Tennyson poem about her. Which, you know, is so exciting. Not.

And Dad talked about his sword until my eyes started to cross.

But I listened politely, because that's what you do.

Then, when we got home, I went up to my room, put on my bikini, came back downstairs, and got onto my raft.

My mom came out onto the deck a little while later and looked down at me as I floated.

"You're kidding me with this, right?" she said. "I thought we were through with this, now that school has started."

"Come on, Mom," I said. "Summer'll be over soon, and we'll have to close up the pool. Can't I just enjoy it for the short time I have left?"

My mom went back inside, shaking her head.

I leaned back against my raft and closed my eyes. The sun was still hot, even though it was after three. I had homework—homework, on the first day! I'd been right about that Mr. Morton, the World Lit teacher . . . he was a bad public speaker *and* a tyrant with the essay assignments—but that could wait until after dinner. There were e-mails, too, from my friends back home, that needed to be answered. Nancy was begging to come visit. She'd never been to the East Coast, let alone stayed in a house with its own pool before. But she had to come soon, or it would be too cool to swim.

I had established a very strict floating regimen. I floated on my back, in the center of the pool. If the raft drifted too close to any of the kidney-shaped pool's sides, I shoved off with my foot. The guy who owns the house had put all these big rocks around the edges of the pool, to make it look more like a naturally occurring pond, or something (except you don't see that many ponds with chlorine and filters in them. But whatever).

Anyway, you had to be careful how you shoved off from the rocks, because there was this one really big rock that had a huge—as big as my fist—spider that lived on it. A couple of times when I hadn't looked where I put my foot, I'd almost squashed the spider. I didn't want to upset the delicate ecosystem of the pool, so, like with the snake, I was trying hard not to kill this spider. Also, of course, I didn't exactly want him to bite me and send me to the emergency room.

So I always opened my eyes whenever my raft floated to the edge of the pool, just to make sure I didn't step on the spider when I shoved off again.

That afternoon—on the first official day of school— when my raft bumped into the side of the pool, and I opened my eyes before shoving off, I got the shock of my life.

Because A. William Wagner was standing on top of Spider Rock, looking down at me.

CHAPTER FOUR

His broad clear brow in sunlight glow'd;
On burnish'd hooves his war-horse trode;
From underneath his helmet flow'd
His coal-black curls as on he rode,
As he rode down to Camelot.

I screamed and almost fell off the raft.

"Oh, sorry," Will said. He'd been smiling. After I screamed, he stopped. "I didn't mean to scare you."

"Wh-what are you doing here?" I stammered, staring up at him. I couldn't believe he was just . . . well, standing there. Beside my pool. In my yard. On Spider Rock.

"Uh," Will said, starting to look a little self-conscious. "I knocked. Your dad said you were out here, and let me in. Is this a bad time? I can come back, if it is."

I stared at him, completely dumbfounded. I couldn't believe this was happening. I had lived for sixteen years without any boy ever having paid the slightest bit of attention to me, and then one day, without any warning at all, the cutest guy I had ever seen—and I do mean ever—just shows up at my house. Having come, apparently, to see me.

I mean, why else would he be here?

"How—how do you know where I live?" I asked him. "How do you even know who I am?"

"Student guide," he said. Then, seeming to realize that I was more than a little freaked, he added, "Look, I'm sorry if I startled you. I didn't mean to. I just thought . . . well, never mind. You know what? I was wrong."

"Wrong about what?" I asked. My heart was still thumping really hard inside my bikini. He had startled me much more than that spider that lived on Spider Rock ever had.

But it wasn't just that he'd startled me that was making my heart hammer. I have to admit, a lot of it was because of how good he looked, up there on that rock, with the late-afternoon sun glinting off his dark head.

"Nothing," he said. "I just—I mean, you smiled at me that day in the park like . . ."

"Like what?" I sounded casual, but inwardly, I was freaking out on multiple levels: one, that he remembered me—he really remembered me!—from that day at the park, and two, that it hadn't just been me. The smile thing, I mean. He'd felt it, too!

Or maybe not.

"Look, never mind," Will said. "It's stupid. When I saw you—first in the park, and then again today, it just seemed like . . . I don't know. That we'd met before, or something. But we haven't, obviously. I mean, I can see that now. I'm Will, by the way. Will Wagner."

I didn't let on that I already knew this, from having looked him up the same way he'd looked me up. Because I didn't want him to think that I had a crush on him, or anything. Because how could I have a crush on him? I had only seen him twice before. This made it three times. You can't get a crush on someone you've seen only three times. I mean, if you're Nancy, you can. But not if you're practical, like me.

"I'm Ellie," I said. "Ellie Harrison. But then . . . I guess you knew that."

The blue-eyed gaze was back on mine, but this time, it didn't seem as intense. Plus, Will was grinning.

"Pretty much," he said.

He really was very good-looking. It wasn't often that good-looking guys so much as looked my way, let alone showed up at my house to see me. I'm not ugly, or anything, but I'm no Jennifer Gold. I mean, she's one of those *Oh, I'm so little and helpless, please rescue me, you big strong man* types of girls. You know, the kind all the cute guys in school fall in love with? I'm more the kind of girl little old ladies come up to in grocery stores and ask, *"Can you get that can of cat food down off that really high grocery store shelf for me, dear?"*

Which basically translates to Invisible to Boys.

"I just moved here," I said. "From St. Paul. I've never been to the East Coast before. So I don't know how we could have met before. . . . Unless"—I eyed him uncertainly—"you've been to St. Paul?"

Which was nuts, because if he had, I'd have remembered.

You better believe I'd have remembered.

"No," he said, grinning. "Never been there. Look, really, forget I said anything. Things have been really weird lately, and I guess I just . . ."

His expression darkened, just for a split second, almost as if a shadow had passed across it.

Except that that was impossible, since there was nothing standing between him and the sun.

Then he seemed to shrug off whatever dark thought had occurred to him, and said brightly, "Seriously, don't worry about it. I'll see you in school."

He turned like he was going to jump off Spider Rock and go away. I could almost hear my best friend Nancy's voice screaming in my head, *Don't let him get away, you idiot! He's hot! Make him stay!*

"Wait," I said.

Then, when he turned expectantly, I found myself frantically trying to think of something witty and brilliant to say . . . something that would make him want to stay.

But before I could think of anything, I heard the sliding glass door being thrown back. A second later, my mom called down from the deck, "Ellie, would your friend like to borrow a suit and go for a swim, too? I'm sure one of Geoff's would fit him."

Oh my God. *My friend.* I was sure I was going to die.

Besides which, *go for a swim*? With *me*? She had no idea she was talking to one of the most popular guys at Avalon High, or that he was dating one of the prettiest girls there.

But still. That's no excuse.

"Uh, no, Mom," I called to her, giving Will an apologetic eye roll that he grinned at. "We're okay."

"Actually," Will said, looking up at my mom. *I have to go now.*

That's what I thought he was going to say. *I have to go now*, or *I made a huge mistake*, or even, *Sorry, wrong house.*

Because guys like Will do not hang around girls like me. It just doesn't happen. Clearly, Will had thought I was some other girl—maybe someone he'd met at camp and had a crush on when he was eight, or whatever—and now that he'd realized his error, he'd be leaving.

Because that is how things are supposed to go in an ordered universe.

But I guess the universe had tilted on its axis without anyone mentioning it to me, or something, because Will went on to say, "A swim might be nice."

And not three minutes later, against all laws of probability, Will was emerging from my house in a pair of Geoff's baggy swim trunks, with a towel around his neck. He was also holding glasses of lemonade that my mom had scrounged up from somewhere, one of which he knelt down at the side of the pool to hand to me.

"Free, fast delivery," he said, with a wink, as I took

the plastic glass from him. If he felt, as I did, a jolt of electricity race up his arm as our fingers accidentally brushed, he didn't let on.

"Oh my God," I said, holding the already-sweating glass and staring at him. He had, I was not at all surprised to see, a terrific body. His skin was tanned bronze—from sailing, no doubt—and he was gorgeously well-muscled—but not in a crazy steroid sort of way.

And he was in my pool.

He was in my pool.

"Did she—" I was in too much shock to think of anything else. "Did she *talk* to you?"

"Who?" Will asked, draping himself over Geoff's raft. "Your mom? Yeah. She's nice. What is she, a writer or something?"

"Professor," I said, through lips that had gone numb. But not from the ice cubes in my drink. From the thought of Will Wagner, alone in my house with my parents, while I, too transfixed with horror to move from my raft, had lain in the pool, doing nothing to rescue him. "Both of them."

"Oh, well, that would explain it," Will said lightly.

My blood went as cold as the ice in my drink. What had they done? What had they said to him? It was too early for *Jeopardy!* so it couldn't have been that. "Explain what?"

"Your mom quoted some poem after I introduced myself," Will said, leaning his head back and peering up at the sky through his Ray-Bans. Whatever Mom had said, he clearly wasn't bothered by it. "Something about a broad, clear brow."

My stomach lurched. "'His broad clear brow in sunlight glow'd'?" I asked nervously.

"Yeah," Will said. "That's it. What was that about?"

"Nothing," I said, vowing silently to kill my mom at a later date. "It's a line from a poem she likes—*The Lady of Shalott*. Tennyson. She's taking the year off from teaching to write a book on Elaine of Astolat. It's making her a little crazier than usual."

"That must be cool," Will said, his raft heading perilously close to Spider Rock, though he wasn't, of course, aware of the potential spider-related danger he was in. "To have parents who talk about poetry and books and stuff."

"Oh, you have no idea," I said, in the flattest voice I could.

"How's the rest of it go?" Will wanted to know.

"The rest of what?"

"The poem."

She was so very, very dead. "'His broad clear brow in sunlight glow'd,'" I quoted from memory. It's not as if I hadn't heard it seventy times this week alone. "'On burnish'd hooves his war-horse trode;/From underneath his helmet flow'd/His coal-black curls as on he rode,/As he rode down to Camelot.' It's a very lame poem. She dies at the end, floating in a boat. Weren't you supposed to meet some people at Dairy Queen after practice today?"

Will glanced over at me, as the question had startled

him. I didn't blame him. It had startled me, too. I have no idea where it had come from.

Still. It needed to be asked.

"I guess so," Will said. "How'd you know about that?"

"Because I heard Jennifer ask you about it when I saw you today in the hallway at school," I said. Nancy, I knew, would freak out if she'd heard me say this. She'd be all, *Oh my God! Don't let on that you know about Jennifer! Because then he'll know you went to the trouble to look her up, and then he'll think you like him!*

But not mentioning Jennifer just didn't seem very practical to me.

Nancy wouldn't have liked the next words that came out of my mouth, either.

"She's your girlfriend, right?" I asked, looking at him as he floated past.

He didn't look at me. He lifted his head up to take a sip of his lemonade, then dropped it back down to the air cushion on his raft.

"Yeah," he said. "Going on two years."

I opened my mouth to ask what seemed to me to be the next natural question—the one Nancy *definitely* would have forbidden me from asking. But before I could get a word out, Will lifted up his head, looked right at me, and said, "Don't."

I blinked at him from behind the lenses of my sunglasses. "Don't what?" I asked, because how was I to know—then—that he could read my mind?

"Don't ask me what I'm doing in your pool instead of

hers," he said. "Because I honestly don't know. Let's talk about something else, okay?"

I could hardly believe what was happening. What was this totally great-looking guy doing in my pool? Not to mention, reading my mind?

It didn't make any sense.

But then, I'm not sure it made sense to him, either.

So instead of asking him about it, I asked him something else that had been bothering me: just what, exactly, he'd been doing in the ravine that first day I'd seen him.

"Oh," Will said, sounding surprised I'd even ask. "I don't know. I just end up there sometimes."

Which pretty much answered my question about what he was doing in my pool instead of his girlfriend's: He was clearly mentally unstable.

Except that—the being-in-my-pool-instead-of-Jennifer's thing aside—he seemed totally normal. He was able to make perfectly lucid conversation. He asked me why we'd moved from St. Paul, and when I told him about the sabbatical, he said he knew what that was like—having to move around a lot, I mean. His dad, he said, was in the navy, and had been stationed lots of different places—forcing Will to change schools every other year or so when he was younger—before finally taking a teaching position at the Naval Academy.

He talked about Avalon High, and the teachers he liked, and the ones I should try to stay away from—Mr. Morton he declared, much to my surprise, a good guy. He talked about Lance—he described the month off he and Lance had taken over the summer to sail up and down the coast, just the two of them.

The only thing Will didn't bring up again was Jennifer. Not even once.

Not that I was counting.

I didn't have any trouble figuring out what Nancy would have made of that. Clearly all was not happiness and joy in *that* relationship. Why else was he floating in my pool, and not hers?

Not, of course, that I imagined his interest in me was at all romantic. Because who'd want hamburger when they could have filet mignon? Which isn't—despite what Nancy would say—putting myself down. It's just being realistic. Guys like Will go for girls like Jennifer: perky little blondes who seem to know instinctively what color eyeshadow looks best on them, not girls like me—gangling brunettes who aren't afraid to pull snakes out of the pool filter.

The sun was starting to slide behind the house, and there was more shade than light on the surface of the water when my mom came back out onto the deck and announced that she'd ordered some Thai food, and asked if Will wanted to stay for dinner.

To which Will replied that he'd love to.

Will was the perfect guest, helping me set the table, then clear it afterwards. He finished everything on his plate. And when my parents and I declared that we were stuffed, he ate everything that was left over in the cartons—to my dad's very obvious admiration.

He was nice to Tig, too, when she came over and sniffed the back of one of his shoes. He bent down and put his finger out so she could smell it before she decided whether or not to let him pet her. Only people who've actually spent time around cats know that this is accepted cat etiquette.

He didn't laugh when I told him Tig's name, either. It's kind of embarrassing to have a pet that you named when you were eight. Back then, I'd thought Tigger was the most original, creative name you could give a cat.

But when I mentioned this to Will, he grinned and said Tigger wasn't as bad as the name he'd given his Border collie when he was twelve—Cavalier. Which is a pretty weird name for a dog, if you think about it. Especially a naval family's dog.

During dinner, Will told funny stories about Cavalier and about the pranks the middies down at the academy sometimes played on one another, as well as on their instructors. He didn't look bored when my dad told him all about the sword, or when my mom quoted a few more verses of *The Lady of Shalott*, as she is embarrassingly prone to do after a glass of wine with dinner.

He even laughed at my impressions of the Graul's bag boys, and also at my reenactment of the Great Snake Rescue.

Nancy has always frowned on my joking around with boys. She says boys don't develop romantic feelings for girls who goof around like stand-up comics. How can he fall in love with you, Nancy always wanted to know, if he's too busy laughing?

And while she may have a point—certainly no boys have fallen in love with me, with the exception of Tommy Meadows in the fifth grade, but his family moved to Milwaukee right after he declared his undying devotion . . . a fact which may, now that I think of it, be what spurred the declaration in the first place—my dad says he fell in love at first sight with my mom because at the faculty party where they met, she had written *Demoiselle d'Astolat* on her Hello, My Name Is . . . lapel sticker.

Which they all had got a terrific yuk out of. It's actually a really lame joke, but what do medievalists know?

Not that I was trying to make A. William Wagner fall in love with me, of course. Because I'm perfectly aware that he's taken.

It's just that, remembering the way that shadow had seemed to pass across his face down at the pool, I thought maybe he could use a laugh. That's all.

Will left after dinner. He thanked my parents, calling my mom *ma'am* and my dad *sir*—which made me crack up—and then he said, "See you tomorrow, Elle," to me.

Then he was gone, melting into the twilight exactly the way he'd appeared at the side of my pool. As if from nowhere.

But I actually waited outside until I heard his car door slam, and saw his car's taillights as he headed down our long driveway, proving he wasn't a specter or—what had Mr. Morton been talking about in World Lit today? Oh yeah—a *bocan*, the Gaelic word for "ghost." See, I had been paying attention in class. Sort of.

Elle. He'd called me Elle. As in . . . El. Short for Ellie.

No one's ever called me Elle before. No one. Just Ellie—which, if you ask me, is sort of a babyish name. Or Elaine, which is sort of old-ladyish.

But not Elle. Never Elle. I'm so not the Elle type.

Except, apparently, to A. William Wagner.

"Well," my dad said, when I came back into the house, after watching Will leave, "he seems like a nice guy."

"Will Wagner," my mom said, as she turned on *Jeopardy!* "I like that name. It's a very regal-sounding sort of name."

Oh, God. I could so see where all of this was heading. They thought Will liked me. They thought Will was going to be my new boyfriend, or something. They had no idea—no idea—what was really going on.

But then again, neither did I, really. I mean, the truth is, if somebody had asked me to explain what that all had been about back there—him showing up at the side of my pool, then staying for dinner—I wouldn't have known *what* to say. I had never had a boy do any of those things before . . . let alone laugh at all my jokes.

I was trying not to make a big deal out of the whole thing, though. Will was nice, but he had a girlfriend. A pretty, cheerleader girlfriend.

Who he apparently didn't want to talk about.

Which, when I thought about it, was pretty weird.

But the weirdest part of all was that while it had been

happening—once I'd gotten used to the idea, I mean, of this hot guy hanging out with me—it hadn't actually seemed that weird at all. It was like that smile Will had given me that day in the park, the one I hadn't been able to keep from returning. It had just seemed natural, even right, to smile back, just like it had seemed totally natural—natural and, yes, right—to have Will there, joking around with the silverware as we set the table, laughing at my Graul's bag boy imitation.

That was what was weird. That it hadn't actually *been* weird.

Still, when Nancy called later that evening, and my dad answered first, and said, "Ah, Nancy. She has a lot to tell you," I didn't try to play the whole thing down as much as I should have. Because I knew Nancy would tell everyone back home. About my having had a boy over for dinner my very first day at my new school. I made sure to mention that he was on the football team, sailed, and was president of the senior class, too.

Oh, and that he looked very, very good in a swimsuit.

Nancy practically had kittens right there on the phone.

"Oh my God, is he taller than you?" she wanted to know. This had always been a problem, because for most of my life, I've been taller than the vast majority of boys in our school, with the exception of Tommy Meadows.

"He's six two," I said.

Nancy cooed appreciatively. At five ten, I'd still be able to get away with heels if we went out, she said.

"Wait until I tell Shelley," Nancy said. "Oh my God, Ellie. You did it. You were able to start over at a whole new school and give yourself a total personality makeover. Everything's going to be different for you now. Everything! And all you had to do was move to a totally new state and start going to a completely new school."

Yeah. Things were definitely starting to look up.

That's really what I thought.

Then.

CHAPTER FIVE

A bow-shot from her bower-eaves,
He rode between the barley-sheaves,
The sun came dazzling thro' the leaves,
And flamed upon the brazen greaves
Of bold Sir Lancelot.

I took the bus to school the next day. It wasn't as bad as I thought it would be. Liz, the girl from the track team who lived nearby, was waiting at the stop, so we started talking, then ended up sitting next to each other.

Liz is a high jumper. She let me know right away that she doesn't have a boyfriend or a driver's license yet.

I knew we had solid groundwork for friendship based on the latter two facts alone.

I didn't mention to Liz that A. William Wagner had visited me after school the day before, then stayed for dinner. For one thing, I didn't want to seem like I was bragging. And for another, well, Liz seemed to really like talking about people in school, and I wasn't entirely convinced it was a good thing to have spread around. That Will had come over to my house, I mean.

I got a pretty good idea, in fact, that it was a bad thing when I closed my locker a few periods later and found Jennifer Gold standing on the other side of it, not looking too happy.

"I hear Will came over to your house for dinner last night," Jennifer said, in a distinctly unfriendly voice.

Since I hadn't told anyone that Will had been over, I knew the spillage was courtesy of him. Unless Jennifer had spies in my neighborhood, or something, which seemed unlikely.

So I just said, wondering why tiny girls like Jennifer always get the tallest boyfriends, leaving all the pip-squeaks for giraffes like me, "Yes. He did."

But Jennifer didn't say what I expected her to say. She didn't go, "Well, he's my boyfriend, so hands off," or "If you so much as look at him again, you're a dead woman."

Instead she asked me a question: "Did he say anything about me?"

I looked down at Jennifer wondering if she, like her boyfriend, was also suffering from some kind of mild form of psychosis—only in her case, not on account of liking me.

She looked sane enough in her pale pink cotton sweater set and capris. But it's hard to tell if someone's crazy just by how they dress. The cheerleaders at my old school dressed totally regular, but a couple of them were certifiable.

"Um," I said. "No."

"Or Lance?" Jennifer's perfectly made-up eyes narrowed. "Did he say anything about Lance?"

"Only," I said, "that the two of them sailed up the coast this summer. Why?"

But Jennifer didn't answer my question. She just went, "Good," looking relieved. Then she walked away.

But Jennifer Gold wasn't the only person who asked me about Will that day.

Mr. Morton, my World Lit teacher, announced that for our first nine-week project, he was assigning us each a poem to study and then deliver an oral report about. In front of the whole class. The report would count toward twenty percent of our semester grade, and had to include critical, secondary, and source materials.

As if that weren't bad enough, he was also assigning us partners to work with.

Gee, thanks, Mr. Morton.

He handed out our partners' names first. When I got mine, I raised my eyebrows.

Because my partner's name was Lance Reynolds.

Which didn't seem possible, since I'd been certain yesterday that I didn't have any classes with the guy. I mean, after all, he was a year older than me, like Will.

But sure enough, when I turned around, there he was in the back of the room. He was looking down at the slip of paper Mr. Morton had handed him, his golden brow furrowed as he tried to figure out who Elaine Harrison was. When he glanced up and saw me staring at him, I raised my own slip and mouthed, "Lucky you."

He didn't react the way I'd have expected a jock who'd been assigned to do a project with the too-tall new girl would. Instead of sniggering or even just nodding, he turned a deep, dark shade of umber. It was kind of interesting to watch, really.

Then Mr. Morton gave us each our poem. Ours was *Beowulf.*

My heart sank when I saw it. I hate *Beowulf* almost as much as I hate *Jeopardy!*

"Right, everyone," Mr. Morton said, in his clipped British accent. "Find your partner and discuss how you'd like to approach your topic. I'd like your outlines on my desk by Friday."

I got up and went back to where Lance was sitting, since it didn't seem likely he was going to come up to me. He was pretending that he didn't see me coming, messing around with his books and everything, when I slid into the empty desk in front of his.

"Hi," I said, in a phony voice, like on a commercial. "I'm Ellie, and I'll be your project partner this semester."

He messed up, though. He'd been trying to pretend like he didn't know who I was. But somehow, "I know," slipped from between his lips, and he turned an even darker shade of red.

This was pretty interesting. I couldn't remember ever having made a guy blush before. I wondered what Lance had heard about me, to make him react that way.

"I . . . I saw you that day," he stammered, by way of

explanation. He didn't look like the kind of guy who stammered often. "That day in the park."

"Oh yeah," I said, like I had only just remembered the incident myself. "Right."

"Will had dinner at your house last night," Lance said. Carefully. Too carefully, I thought. Like he was fishing for information.

"Yeah," I said. I wondered if he, like Jennifer, was going to ask if Will had talked about him.

But he didn't.

"So," Lance said. "*Beowulf*, huh?"

"Yeah," I said. "I hate *Beowulf*."

Lance looked kind of surprised. "You've already read it?"

I realized what kind of dweeb I must have sounded like. I mean, it was bad enough I was even taking World Literature. It's an elective, open to anyone in any grade who's interested—or who needs an extra humanities credit, as Lance evidently did. It was even worse that I'd already read most of the books on the syllabus. On my own. Because they're all the same books that have been sitting on my parents' bookshelves forever, and it's not like I ever had much of a social life, so . . .

Not wanting to admit this, however, I just said hastily, "Well, yeah. My parents are professors. Medieval studies. *Beowulf* is kind of their thing."

It was as I was saying this that I noticed a skinny-necked kid in glasses, sitting one desk over, looking at us very intently. When he saw me glance his way, he went,

"Sorry but . . . did I hear you say you guys have *Beowulf*?"

"Yeah," I said, glancing over at Lance, who was staring at the kid with narrowed eyes. I recognized the look. It was the kind of look the popular give to the unpopular—like Lance couldn't believe Skinny Neck had had the nerve to speak to him. "So what?"

Skinny Neck glanced nervously at his partner, an equally nerdy-looking kid.

"We love *Beowulf*," he said, his voice going up a few octaves on the last syllable.

"Yeah," his partner agreed. "Grendel rules."

I supposed Grendel *would* rule to a couple of guys who, back in the Middle Ages, probably wouldn't have made it past the age of five on account of inhalers not having been invented yet, or whatever.

"What'd you get?" I asked Skinny Neck, referring to his assigned poem.

"Tennyson," Skinny Neck said, making no effort to hide his dissatisfaction.

I recoiled.

"Not *The Lady of Shalott*," I said, in horror.

"Yeah," Skinny Neck said. Seeing my expression, he added, "It's way shorter than *Beowulf*."

"Sorry," I said, seeing all too clearly where this was headed. "No can do."

"Wait a minute." Lance butted in. "What's wrong with the shallot lady? If it's short—"

"My mom's writing a book on her," I interrupted, not

mentioning the part about having been named for the main character in the poem.

"Then the paper'll be a cinch," Lance said, brightening. "Just ask your mom what to say!"

I stared at him. I couldn't believe this was happening. And yet, at the same time, I sort of could. Which seemed to be how my life was going at Avalon High. Weird and yet strangely not weird.

"Contrary to how you might do your homework," I said, in a desperate effort to save myself from what I saw barreling down on me, knowing full well there was no escape, "I do my homework myself, without my parents' help."

"This one's shorter," Lance said, taking the piece of paper from Skinny Neck's fingers. "We're doing it."

It was obvious there wasn't going to be any discussion, much less arguing, over the issue. Lance had spoken. And what Lance says—it was perfectly clear, even to the new kid, namely me—goes.

I'll admit it. I was peeved. I'm sick of the Lady of Shalott. Her and her stupid robes of snowy white, loosely flying left and right.

"Fine," I said, snatching the topic paper out of his hands. "I'll write it. But you have to stand up in front of the class and read it."

The smug expression vanished from Lance's face. "But—"

"You're doing it," I said, matching the tone he'd used with me exactly. "Or we can just flunk, for all I care."

He looked stricken. "I can't get an F. Coach won't let me play."

"Then give the report," I said.

Sinking a little deeper beneath his desk, Lance said, "Whatever," which I—and the nerds, who turned in their seats to give each other high fives, triumphant in having secured Grendel—took to mean he agreed.

When the bell rang, I waited until Lance had cleared the room before I followed him, so we wouldn't have to make awkward conversation out into the hallway. I ended up exiting the classroom right behind the nerds. . . .

So I had a front row seat to what happened next.

And that was that some of Lance's friends from the football team met him outside the classroom door. Then one of them—either because he was bored, or mean, or possibly a combination of both—reached out and, as one of the nerds in front of me passed through the doorway, snatched the kid's notebook.

"Rick," Skinny Neck said, in a disgusted voice. "Give it back."

"*Rick*," one of Lance's friends echoed in falsetto. "*Give it back*."

"Get a life," Skinny Neck said, making a grab for the notebook.

But Rick held it high in the air, out of reach of its much shorter owner.

"*Get a life*," one of the other team members said, in the same falsetto. "Christ, look who's talking."

54

The nerdy kid looked like he was about to cry. Until a hand belonging to someone taller than all the other jocks reached out and plucked the notebook from Rick's fingers.

"Here, Ted," Will said to Skinny Neck, giving him back his notebook. Ted took it with trembling fingers, his gaze, as he looked up at Will, worshipful.

"Thanks, Will," he said.

"No problem," Will said to the geek. He had not once cracked a smile, and he didn't do so now, either. To Rick, he said, "Apologize."

"Come on, Will," Lance said, in an Aw-Shucks-We-Were-Just-Joshing manner. "Rick was just messing around with the kid. He—"

Will's voice was cold. "We talked about this," he said. "Apologize to Ted, Rick."

I wasn't a bit surprised when Rick turned to Skinny Neck and said, sounding genuinely regretful, "Sorry."

Because there'd been a steely note in Will's voice that made it clear no one—not even a two-hundred-pound halfback—had better try to mess with him. Or dare to disobey one of his commands.

Maybe it was just a quarterback thing.

Or maybe it was something else.

"'S all right," Ted said. Then he and his friend darted away, disappearing into the throng jamming the hallway.

I followed them, more slowly. Will hadn't noticed me in the crowd, and I was glad. I probably wouldn't have known what to say to him if he'd said hi or whatever.

The sight of him telling that enormous jock what to do—and the jock actually *doing* it—had kind of freaked me out.

If you can call realizing you're head over heels in love with someone being freaked out.

This was bad. *Really* bad. I mean, I did not need to be falling in love with some guy—even a guy who randomly showed up at my house for dinner and was a champion of geeks—who was already taken by one of the prettiest girls in school. This so wasn't going to end happily for me. Not even Nancy, the romantic optimist, would be able to see any possible upside to me falling in love with A. William Wagner.

So I spent the rest of the day resolutely trying not to think about him. Will, I mean.

It wasn't like I didn't have other things to worry about. There was the report for Mr. Morton's class, of course. And I'd found out from Liz during lunch that there were more than a few freshman girls who were running the two hundred meter—my event—at varsity times. Unless I could beat them, there was a chance I might not make the Avalon High track team, should I be considering going out for it.

I didn't want to go to the trouble of trying out for the team, only not to make it because some snot-nosed freshman had spent her summer training and not floating in a pool, like me.

So when I got home from school that day, I changed

into my running clothes. I figured the run would do double duty—it would help get me back into shape for track try-outs, and also keep my mind off a certain quarterback.

But when I went to look for Mom to give me a ride over to the park, she wasn't in her office. I banged on my dad's office door. He grunted, so I went in.

"Oh, Ellie," he said. "Hi. I didn't hear you come home." Then he noticed what I was wearing, and his face kind of fell.

"Oh," he said, in a different voice. "Not today, Ellie. I'm really swamped here. I think I've made a breakthrough. See this filigree, here? That's—"

"You don't have to come with me," I interrupted, not wanting another lecture on my dad's crazy sword. "I just need a ride to the park. Where's Mom?"

"I dropped her off at the train station. She had some research to do in the city today."

"Fine," I said. "Just give me your keys, then, and I'll drive myself over."

He looked appalled.

"No, Ellie," he said. "You only have a learner's permit. You need someone with a valid driver's license with you."

"Dad," I said. "I'm just going to the park. It's only two miles away. There's one four-way stop and a traffic light before I get there. I'll be okay."

My dad didn't go for it. He let me drive, all right. But with him in the passenger seat.

When we got there, a T-ball game and a lacrosse game were going on. The parking lot was crowded with minivans and Volvos. My dad said that's because most of the people in Annapolis are ex-military, and they all want to drive the safest car they can find.

I wondered if Will's dad drove a Volvo. You know, since Will had said he was in the navy.

Oops. I hadn't meant to think about Will.

My dad told me to call him from the pay phone over by the restrooms when I got done with my run—God forbid my parents should get me a cell phone—so he could come back and get me. I said I would, then gathered up my iPod and water and climbed out of the car. There were only a few people on the running path, mostly walking their Jack Russell terriers or Border collies (back home, the most popular dog is the black lab. Here, it's Border collies. My dad says it's because ex-military types want the smartest pet they can find, and that's the Border collie).

Will's dog, Cavalier, is a Border collie. I'm just saying.

It was late afternoon, and still plenty hot. As I broke into a jog, I was instantly covered in a thin sheen of sweat.

But it felt good to work my muscles after a long day of being cramped behind various desks. I sailed past the dog walkers, careful not to make eye contact (my dad would have been appalled), intent on the beat of the music I was listening to. I went around the running path once—dodging a T-ball and nearly running into a kid on a tricycle. It wasn't until my second and final time around that I remembered to glance down into the ravine—out of habit, really, more than that I expected to see anybody in there—and practically tripped over my own feet and fell onto my face.

Because Will was there.

At least, I thought it was Will. My glimpse of him, as I tore by, was fleeting.

Still, after I was done with my second lap, I doubled back, just to make sure. Not because I wanted to go down there and talk to him, or anything. I mean, the guy is clearly taken. I don't go after other people's boyfriends. Not that, you know, if I tried, he'd go for it, or anything. The truth is, I don't go after boys at all. What's the point? I'm not the type of girl they ever think of in that way, anyway.

But what if he was in trouble, or something? What if the reason he was at the bottom of the ravine was because he'd tripped and fallen down it? Hey, it could happen. And maybe he was lying down there, bleeding and unconscious, needing the kiss of life? Administered by me?

Okay, whatever. So I wanted to talk to him some more. So sue me.

I found myself on the part of the running path that overlooks the ravine, and there, down below, was someone who looked a lot like Will. How he'd gotten down there without getting torn up by thorns or tumbling down the steep sides of the ravine, I didn't know.

But I figured I'd give it a try myself. To make sure he was all right, I told myself.

Yeah. That was it. To make sure he was all right.

Whatever.

CHAPTER SIX

All in the blue unclouded weather
Thick-jewell'd shone the saddle-leather,
The helmet and the helmet-feather
Burn'd like one burning flame together,
As he rode down to Camelot.

It actually wasn't that bad, once I got past the initial wall of brambles. It was even cooler in the deep part of the woods than it was on the running path.

And once you were in among the trees and headed down the ravine, you couldn't see the running path at all, much less hear the cars from the highway. It was like a primeval forest, where the trees all grew really close together and practically no sunlight at all reached the forest floor, making it a damp, mulchy mess beneath your feet.

It was the kind of place you'd expect to meet a monster like Grendel.

Or possibly the Unabomber.

It *was* Will, I saw, when the trees thinned out enough to allow me to see to the bottom of the ravine. He wasn't unconscious, though. He was sitting on one of the big boulders that jutted up from the creek bed below. He didn't appear to be doing anything. He was just sitting, staring down at the burbling water in the creek.

Probably someone who'd chosen such an out-of-the-way and hard-to-get-to—I had scratches from the brambles all over my ankles—place to sit and think really wanted to be alone.

Probably I should have just left him there without disturbing him.

Probably I should have turned around and gone back the way I came.

But I didn't. Because I am a total masochist.

I had to pick my way along the stones that stuck out of the burbling little creek to get to the boulder he was sitting on. The water wasn't deep, but I didn't want to get my running shoes wet. I called his name when I was only a few feet away from him and he still didn't seem to notice me.

Then I noticed why. He had headphones on. It wasn't until I jostled one of his feet, dangling above my head, that he started and glanced sharply down at me.

But when he saw it was me, he smiled and turned off his iPod.

"Oh," he said. "Hey, Elle. How was your run?"

Elle. He'd called me Elle. Again.

Was it wrong that my heart did some more flopping

around inside my chest?

I examined the boulder he was sitting on, saw how he'd climbed it, and joined him. I didn't ask if it was okay first, either. I knew it was okay from his smile.

The smile that was making my heart sort of hurt. But in a good way.

"My run was okay," I said, sitting down next to him. But not too close, you know, because I figured I smelled a bit gamy from my run. Not to mention the fact that I'd sprayed myself with about a pound and a half of DEET before I'd left the house, since East Coast mosquitoes seem to love me very much. And DEET isn't exactly the *eau d'amour*, if you know what I mean.

Will didn't appear to notice, though.

"Listen," he said, holding up a single hand as a signal for me not to talk.

I listened. For a minute I thought he wanted me to be quiet so he could say something. Like, you know, how much he loved me. Even though he'd only seen me a few times. And had dinner with me once.

Hey, stranger things have happened. All Tommy Meadows and I had had in common was a deep appreciation for *Spider-Man* comic books.

But it turned out Will didn't want me to be quiet so he could declare his love for me. He actually wanted me to listen.

So I did. All I could hear, besides the babbling of the water, was the chirping of birds and the hum of cicadas in the trees. No cars. No planes. You couldn't even hear the shrieks of encouragement I knew the parents of the lacrosse players and T-ballers had to be letting out. It was like we were in a different world, a sun-dappled oasis away from it all. Though, really, we were only two or three hundred yards away from the Dairy Queen off the highway.

After a minute of this, feeling stupid, I said, "Uh, Will? I don't hear anything."

He glanced my way with the tiniest of smiles.

"I know," he said. "Isn't it great? This is one of the few places around here that people have left alone. You know? No power lines. No Gap. No Starbucks."

He had, I noticed, eyes that were the same color blue as my pool, when I got the chlorine and pH balance exactly right. Except that my pool is only eight feet at the deepest end, and Will's eyes seemed fathomless . . . like if I dove into them, I'd never get to the bottom.

"It's pretty," I said, about the ravine, looking away from him. Because it isn't a good idea to think about how blue some guy's eyes are, if he's already taken, the way Will is.

"You think so?" Will said, looking around the ravine. Clearly, he hadn't ever thought of it that way before. As pretty, I mean. "I suppose. Mostly . . . it's quiet."

Except . . . he hadn't been sitting there enjoying the quiet.

"So what were you listening to?" I asked, picking up the iPod he'd turned off and laid aside as I'd joined him on top of his boulder.

"Uh," he said, looking faintly worried as I clicked it back on. "Nothing, really."

"Come on," I said teasingly. "I've got Eminem in mine. Yours can't be that bad—"

Except that it was. Because it turned out to be a collection of troubadour love ballads. From medieval times.

"Oh my God," I couldn't help blurting out in horror, as I stared down at the words scrolling across the screen. Then immediately wished I could die.

But, instead of being offended, Will just laughed. Really laughed. Like threw back his head and laughed.

"I'm sorry," I said, mortified. "I didn't mean—It's okay. I mean, lots of people like classical . . . stuff."

But when he finally caught his breath, instead of telling me where to get off for being so horrified by his musical taste, he said, shaking his head, "Oh, God. If you could have seen your face. I bet that's exactly how you looked when you opened up that filter basket and found that snake. . . ."

Feeling a little irritated—mainly because his laughter reminded me of Nancy's warning, about being too funny around guys—I said, "Sorry. You just didn't strike me as the type to sit by yourself in the woods listening to"—I looked down at the iPod screen—"*Courtiers, Kings, and Troubadours*."

"Yeah, well," Will said, growing suddenly sober and reaching out to gently tug his iPod from my hands, "I never thought I was, either."

As he said it, I saw the shadow I'd noticed that day at

my pool pass across his face again. And I knew I'd said exactly the wrong thing.

But since I wasn't sure what the right thing to say was—except that I was pretty certain he wouldn't appreciate my speech about how everyone in the Middle Ages had lice and bad teeth—I just kind of sat there.

Besides, I had a good idea that whatever lecturing there was to do on the subject of Will sitting in the woods listening to medieval music, Lance and Jennifer had already covered that day I saw them in the arboretum with him.

Still, I got the feeling that Will's gloomy expression didn't have a lot to do with having been busted listening to lame music. I mean, I have been known upon occasion to crack out my dad's Bee Gees collection when I was feeling completely nihilistic or whatever. But no amount of teasing on the part of my brother Geoff had ever made me look as . . . well, hopeless as Will did just then.

Which made me realize: Will shutting down like that wasn't about my having caught him listening to lame music. It was about something much, much worse.

Wondering what it could be—and hoping it wouldn't be something that might end up making it difficult for him to take me to the prom, if he and Jennifer broke up or whatever—I took a deep breath and plunged. "Look. This isn't any of my business. But are you okay?" I asked him.

The shadow had disappeared from his face by then. He seemed surprised by the question.

"Yeah," he said. "Why?"

"Uh. Let me see." I ticked off the points on my fingers. "Senior class president. Quarterback of the football team. Valedictorian?"

"Probably." He grinned. My heart lurched again.

"Valedictorian," I added to my list. "Going out with the prettiest, most popular girl in school. Likes to sit by himself in the woods listening to medieval love ballads. You see the whole one-of-these-things-is-not-like-the-other part?"

His grin grew broader.

"You don't beat around the bush much, do you?" he asked, his blue eyes twinkling in a manner that I couldn't help feeling was very bad for my well-being. "Is that a Minnesota thing, or just an Elle Harrison thing?"

I don't know how I replied. I know I must have said something, but I don't have any idea what it might have been. What did it matter, anyway? He'd said it again. Elle. *Elle*.

I felt reassured by his flippant response to my question. No, he hadn't really answered it. But if he could joke around, he obviously wasn't thinking about ending it all, or whatever. Maybe that look on his face hadn't meant anything. Maybe he was just a guy who liked sitting alone, listening to medieval music. Maybe he didn't have a pool, and so that's what he had to do to float . . . you know, mentally.

And here I came along, totally busting in where I wasn't needed. Or wanted.

Feeling stupid, I tried to extract myself as quickly as

possible from the situation.

"Okay," I said, starting to get up. "Well, see you around."

But I was stopped by a strong set of fingers that wrapped around my wrist.

"Wait a sec." Will looked up at me curiously. "Where are you going?"

"Um," I said, trying to be casual about the fact that he was touching me. He was touching me. No boy—other than my brother and Tommy Meadows, who asked me to couples-skate during a class trip to Western Skateland—had ever touched me before. "Home."

"What's the rush?" he wanted to know.

"Uh," I said. Maybe I hadn't heard him right. Did he actually want me to stick around? "No rush. I just figured you wanted to be alone. And my dad's expecting me to call. For a ride home."

"I'll give you a ride home," Will said, climbing to his feet, and pulling me up with him . . . so unexpectedly that I sort of started to lose my balance, and wobbled a little on top of the boulder. . . .

Until Will put out his other hand, grabbing me by the waist to steady me.

We stood that way for a heartbeat or two, his hand around my waist, the other holding my wrist, our faces just inches apart.

If someone had seen us, they'd probably thought we were dancing. Two crazy teenagers, dancing on top of a boulder.

I wonder if they'd have suspected that one of the teenagers—namely, me—wanted to stay in this position forever, memorize every line of that face so close to mine, reach out and stroke that soft dark hair, kiss those lips that were hovering just inches above mine. Was Will thinking the same things? I couldn't tell, and I was looking right into those fathomless blue eyes. I thought I felt something—something indescribable—pass between us.

But I must have been wrong, because a second later, Will was saying, "You all right, there, now?" and letting go of my waist and hand.

"Sure," I said, laughing nervously. "Sorry."

Except that I wasn't sorry. Especially since both places he'd touched me were tingling, like they'd been scorched . . . only in a good way.

We started to climb from the ravine, Will leading the way, politely holding back brambles and giving me a hand up the steeper parts, which were hard to climb in my running shoes. If he noticed how, every time his fingers met mine, sparks seemed to shoot up my arm, he didn't let on. Instead, he talked about my parents.

Yeah. My parents.

"You three are funny together," was what Will said.

"We are?"

This was news to me. I mean, I know my dad *looks* funny, with his Dork Strap and all. But he hadn't even been wearing that when Will came over. And my mom's not particularly humorous-looking. She's actually pretty attractive. Until she opens her mouth about broad clear brows and all of that.

"Yeah," Will said. "The way they teased you about keeping the pool filters so clean. And the way you razzed them back about the snake. That was funny. I could never joke around with my dad like that. All he ever wants to talk to me about is where I'm going to go to school next year."

"Oh," I said, relieved we were off the subject of my parents. "That's right. You're graduating in the spring."

"Yeah. And my dad wants me to go to the Academy."

Which was the local shorthand, I'd learned, for the Naval Academy. Only nobody ever calls it by its full name around here. It's just "the Academy."

I wondered what it would be like to have a dad who was in the military, and, you know, organized. I bet Will's dad would never make him a sack lunch that included potato salad.

On the other hand, I bet Will's dad wouldn't have just ignored the air hose warning on the inflatable rafts.

"Well," I said, wondering how Will would look in one of those white uniforms I saw the middies wearing around town. Pretty good, I guessed. Really good, actually. "It's an excellent school. One of the hardest to get into in the country, and all."

"I know," Will said, with a shrug, as he held back a particularly thorny branch for me to pass under. "And I've got the grades and test scores and everything. But I'm not so sure I want to go into the military, you know? Visit new places. Meet new people. And kill them."

"Well," I said, again. "Yeah. I could see how that could suck. Did you, um, mention that? To your dad?"

"Oh yeah."

"And?" I asked, when Will didn't say anything else. "How'd he take it?"

Will gave another shrug. "He pretty much freaked."

"Oh," I said. I thought about my own dad. He and Mom were always telling Geoff and me to become professors because professors get summers off and only have to teach a course or two a semester.

But I would rather eat glass than have to write academic papers all the time like Mom and Dad do. And I tell them so, regularly.

But they don't freak when I say it.

"Well," I said. "What do you want to do instead?"

"I don't know," Will said. "My dad says Wagner men have always been in the military" —he raised his hands and made quotation marks in the air as he added sarcastically—"making a difference in the world." Then he dropped his hands. "And I want to make a difference in the world. I really do. But I don't want to do it by blowing people up."

I thought about the little scene I'd witnessed in the hallway that day at school, and the way Will had handled Rick. It seemed to me like he was already making a difference in the world.

"I can understand that," I said.

"Sorry," Will said with a sudden laugh, running one of his hands through his dark hair. "I shouldn't complain.

My dad wants me to go to one of the best schools in the country, which he's completely willing to pay for and which I shouldn't have any trouble getting into. Everyone should have my problems, right?"

"Well," I said. "It kind of is a problem, if the only school your dad's willing to pay for is the one you don't want to go to. . . . . Especially, you know, if you don't want to be in the military. Because shooting off guns and stuff seems like a big part of being at the Academy. At least judging by all the noise I hear from the gunnery every day."

"Yeah," Will said. We'd reached the footpath by then. A lady walking a Jack Russell terrier hurried past us, clearly freaked by the fact that we had been in the woods, since she refused to look at either of us as she passed by in her pink jogging suit.

I glanced at Will to see if he'd noticed, and saw him grinning.

"Probably thinks we were in there making a sacrifice to Satan," he said, when the lady had power-walked out of hearing distance.

"And her dog's our next victim," I agreed.

Will laughed. We emerged from the woods, and headed toward the parking lot and Will's car. After the darkness of the forest, the last rays of the setting sun seemed especially bright. They seemed to be setting the baseball diamond on fire. There was a hint of smoke in the air, from someone's barbecue. Crickets, just getting started on their evening serenade, trilled.

"Listen," Will said, breaking the companionable silence into which we'd fallen. "What are you doing Saturday night?"

"Saturday?" I blinked at him. It was true those crickets were loud. But I didn't think they were loud enough for me to have mistaken the question.

Because it had sounded . . . well, it certainly sounded to me as if Will were about to ask me out.

"I'm having a party," he went on.

Or maybe not.

"A party?" I asked stupidly.

"Yeah," he said. "Saturday night. After the game." I must have looked blank, since he smiled and added, "The football game? Avalon against Broadneck? You're going, aren't you?"

"Oh," I said. I had never been to a football game in my life. You know that eating glass thing? Yeah, I'd much rather do that than watch a football game.

Unless, of course, A. William Wagner happened to be playing in it.

"Sure, I'm going," I said, wondering frantically what one wears to a football game.

"Great. Anyway, I'm having a party afterwards," he said. "At my house. A back-to-school thing. Can you come?"

I stared at him. I'd never been invited to a party before. Well, not by a boy, anyway. Nancy used to have parties, but no one ever came to them except our other friends, who were all girls. Sometimes at my old school a guy on the men's track team would have a party and invite everyone on the women's team. But we'd all just end up standing around while the boys ignored us and hit on whatever cheerleaders had shown up.

I wondered if Will's party would be that kind of party, and if so, why he'd bothered singling me out for an invitation.

"Um," I said, trying to think up an excuse why I couldn't go. On the one hand, I desperately wanted to see where Will lived. I wanted to know everything about him.

On the other hand, I had a pretty good feeling Jennifer Gold would be there. And did I really want to watch Will with another girl? Not so much.

Will must have sensed my hesitation—sensed it, and misinterpreted it—since he went, "Don't worry, it won't be wild, or anything. My parents'll be there. Come on, you'll like it. It's a pool party. You can bring your raft."

I couldn't help smiling at that.

Or at the friendly fashion in Will elbowed me in the side as he said it.

Oh yes. I was that far gone that even the guy's elbow seemed hot.

"Okay," I heard myself saying. "I'll be there. Um, without my raft, though. It has a curfew. It has to be home by nine."

He grinned. Then, looking past me, said, "Oh, hey. Want some lemonade?"

I glanced in the direction he was pointing, and saw

that some kids—whose small, somewhat rundown house sat on the edge of the park's property—had set up a folding table with a large hand-drawn poster hanging from it that said LEMONAID: 25 CENTS.

"C'mon," Will said. "I'll buy you a lemonade."

"Whoa," I joked. "Big spender."

He was grinning as we approached the table, which someone had gone to great trouble to decorate with a checkered tablecloth and a small, half-blown garden rose in a vase, along with the inevitable plastic pitcher and collection of Dixie cups. The three kids behind the table, the eldest of whom could only have been nine, perked up at the sight of customers.

"Wanna buy some lemonade?" they chorused.

"Is it any good?" Will teased the kids. "I'm not spending a whole quarter on it if it isn't the best lemonade in town."

"It is!" the kids shrieked. "It's the best! We made it ourselves!"

"I don't know," Will said, feigning skepticism. He looked at me. "What do you think?"

I shrugged. "Might as well try it."

"Try it, try it," cried the kids. The oldest one said, assuming authority over the situation, "Look, we'll give you a taste, and if you like it, you can buy a cup."

Will appeared to think about this. Then he said, "Okay, deal."

The oldest kid poured a small amount of lemonade into a cup, then handed it to Will, who made a big deal out of smelling it first, then swishing it around in his mouth the way wine tasters do.

The kids ate it up. They were giggling, loving every minute of the show.

As, I have to admit, was I. Well, how could I not?

"Nice bouquet," Will said, after he'd finally swallowed. "Tangy, and not too sweet. A most excellent year for lemonade, obviously. We'll take two cups."

"Two cups!" the kids cried, scrambling to fill them. "They'll take two cups!"

When the cups were filled, Will took one and presented it to me with a flourish.

"Why, thank you," I said, curtsying back to him.

"My pleasure," he said, and reaching into the back pocket of his jeans, drew out a black leather wallet, from which he pulled a five-dollar bill.

"And you three," he said to the kids, placing the bill on the table, "can keep the change, if you'll give me that rose there."

The kids stared, goggle-eyed, at the five. The oldest one recovered herself most quickly, and plucked the rose from the vase and thrust it at him.

"Here," she said. "Take it."

Will did so, with a polite "Thank you." Then he picked up his cup of lemonade, and turned to go, while behind him, the kids tried to smother their delighted giggles and cries of "Five dollars! That's more'n we've made *all day*!"

Grinning, I fell into step beside Will as we headed

toward his car. "You know they're just going to spend that money on candy that'll rot their teeth," I informed him.

"I know," he said, looking straight ahead, even as he did what he did next. Which was to hand me the rose. "For you."

I looked down at the rose—so tiny and pink and perfect—in astonishment.

"Oh," I said, suddenly consumed with embarrassment. "I couldn't. I mean—"

He turned his head to look at me then, and I saw laughter on his lips.

But not, strangely, in his eyes. His gaze was strong and steady on mine, the way his voice had been earlier that day, when he'd spoken to Rick. It was clear the time for joking around was done.

"Elle," he said. "Just take it."

I took it.

It was the first flower any boy had ever given me.

Which was why, even after he dropped me off at home and drove away, it was hours before my heart started to beat anything like normally again.

CHAPTER SEVEN

She left the web, she left the loom,
She made three paces thro' the room,
She saw the water-lily bloom,
She saw the helmet and the plume,
She look'd down to Camelot.

As I studied up on old Arthur for my World Lit project that evening—which wasn't easy, considering that I'd put Will's rose in a vase by my bed, and my gaze kept straying over to it every two minutes or so—I found out a few surprising things. Such as the stuff from the musical *Camelot*—which my mom loves, and has made me listen to ten thousand times—like how King Arthur performed all of these heroic feats, basically bringing his people out of the Dark Ages and defending them against the Saxons and stuff? And how he had this arranged marriage with this princess named Guinevere, and how she eventually ditched him for his favorite knight, Lancelot (who, in turn, ditched Elaine of Astolat, the Lady of Shalott, for

Guinevere, causing Elaine to become the subject of my mom's new book)?

That stuff probably really happened.

Except that Lancelot didn't end up killing Arthur over Guinevere: Arthur's half brother (or son, according to some translations), Mordred, took care of that. See, Mordred was all jealous of Arthur's accomplishments, and of him being such a beloved king and all, so he plotted to kill him and take over the throne—even marrying Queen Guinevere himself at some point, according to a few sources. . . .

The Pendragons were way dysfunctional as far as families go. Jerry Springer would have *loved* them.

Wild horses wouldn't have gotten me to admit this in front of my parents, but the whole Arthur thing *was* kind of cool. The reason there've been so many movies and books and poems and musicals written about King Arthur—not to mention high schools like Avalon named after the mythical island he eventually went to die on—is that his story is a good illustration of the heroic theory of history: that an individual—not an army; not a god; not a superhero; just a regular Joe—can permanently alter the course of world events.

Which is why, according to another one of my mom's books, there's this whole society—I am not making this up—of people who think that Arthur, whose body was sent to the now nonexistent island of Avalon by the Lady of the Lake, is actually asleep, not dead, and is destined to wake again only when he is most needed.

Seriously. This band of losers calls itself the Order of the Bear, the Bear having been King Arthur's nickname. They think that Arthur's going to wake up one day and lead the modern-day world out of the Dark Ages and into a new age of enlightenment, just like he did fifteen hundred years ago. The only thing keeping him from waking, according to the members of the Order of the Bear, are the forces of darkness.

Um. Okay.

I tried not to let my skepticism about the existence of forces of darkness show in the outline I wrote for our report for Mr. Morton's class, though.

And I definitely didn't mention to my parents that I was doing a project on King Arthur. Because I knew that in their enthusiasm for the subject matter, they'd start chucking source materials at me until I ran screaming from the house. Some things parents are just better off not knowing.

Like the track thing. I never bothered mentioning to them that I was worried about making it onto the Avalon High School women's track team. I was glad I hadn't, too, when it turned out rumors about the speed of certain freshwomen proved to be greatly exaggerated. I made it onto the team at tryouts the next day with ease.

Liz was psyched, and high-fived me when the coach read off my name. Although later, while we were waiting for Stacy, another girl on the team who turned out to live nearby and had promised to give us a ride home, Liz warned me about the initiation.

"It's just this stupid thing Cathy thought up," she said. Cathy was apparently the team captain, whom I'd met only briefly. "They'll come in the middle of the night—well, really about ten—and kidnap you, and take you to Storm Brothers and make you eat a Moose Tracks sundae."

Since this sounded like the kind of initiation I might enjoy—no cat food or raw animal parts involved—I wasn't too alarmed.

But then Liz said they'd probably do it on Saturday.

"That's a problem," I said. "I'm going to Will Wagner's pool party after the Broadneck game."

Liz just stared at me.

"YOU got invited to Will Wagner's pool party?" She sounded completely stunned. Stunned enough that I immediately felt uncomfortable about the whole thing.

"Well," I said, "yeah. I mean, he invited me."

"When?" Liz asked, still sounding stunned.

"Yesterday," I said. "I ran into him running in Anne Arundel Park. Well, I was running. He was sitting—"

"—on that rock?" Liz shook her head. "Oh my God. I'd heard the rumors, of course. But I didn't think they were true."

I glanced at her. "What rumors?"

"You know," Liz said. "About him cracking up."

"Will?" I asked, startled. "Why do people think he's cracking up?"

"Because he's been going and sitting on that rock in that ravine in that stupid park all summer," Liz said.

"He's even skipped football practice twice to do it this week. I heard he says he likes to go there to think. Think! Who even does that?"

I knew right then that Liz would never understand about the floating thing.

"But anyway," she went on. "Some people are saying—"

"What?" I asked more sharply than I meant to.

"Well, some people say he goes there to get away from his dad."

"His dad?" I feigned ignorance, not wanting to let on that Will had already confided in me about this.

"Yeah. On account of what he did."

I stared at Liz, totally confused. "What his dad did?" What was she talking about? Will's dad hadn't done anything. Anything except try to force Will to go to the Naval Academy. But he hadn't succeeded in doing that. Yet. "What did his dad do?"

"Killed his best friend," Liz said matter-of-factly. "Some guy Will's dad has known since basic training, or something. Admiral Wagner transferred him to a combat post overseas a year or so ago, and the guy got killed in a helicopter crash."

"But—" I blinked. The truth was, I didn't know whether to believe Liz or not. She liked to gossip. A lot.

But she didn't strike me as a liar.

"That doesn't mean Will's dad killed him," I said. "He didn't do it on purpose. It was obviously an accident."

"Oh, right," Liz scoffed. "And I suppose it was just an

accident then that six months later, Admiral Wagner married his dead friend's wife."

Whoa.

Apparently, I'd said the word out loud, though I don't remember doing so, since Liz nodded, and went, "Totally. Anyway, now people are saying that Will's dad transferred his friend to a dangerous post on purpose, because he'd been in love with the guy's wife for years and years and was just waiting for a way to get rid of her husband before making his move."

"Geez," I said, shocked. Will hadn't mentioned any of this to me. It wasn't that, after a single dinner and a couple of lemonades, I considered us soulmates, or anything.

But . . . he'd told me so many other things. Like about not wanting to go to the Academy.

And the rose. What about that rose?

"So," Liz went on, "you can see why Will doesn't like to spend a lot of quality time at home. With his new step-mom and a dad who'd do something like that. Not to mention Marco."

"Who's Marco?" I asked, totally confused now.

Stacy, the girl who was offering us a ride, finally showed up, sauntering up behind us as if she had all the time in the world. Well, she was a high jumper. They can be that way. It's not about speed with them, so much as defying gravitational pull.

"Oh my God," she said, having overheard my question. She looked at Liz and laughed. "She hasn't heard of Marco?"

"I know," Liz said, rolling her eyes. "Well, she *is* new."

"What?" I looked from one girl to the other. "Who's Marco?"

"Marco Campbell," Liz said. "Will's new stepbrother. The dead guy's son."

"Town psycho," Stacy said. She pointed her finger at her temple, then twirled her finger around. "Total head case."

I knew I was fully gaping at them both, but I couldn't help it.

"Marco lives with Will and his dad and stepmom?"

"Yeah," Stacy said. "Though I'm sure they'd like to get rid of him."

"Why? What's wrong with him?"

"Stacy already told you," Liz said. "He's a total freak. He got kicked out of Avalon High last year, a month before graduation, for—get this—trying to kill a teacher."

I'd been sitting on the curb in the parking lot next to Liz. Now I got up, and turned to face the two girls.

"This isn't true," I said firmly. "This is part of that— what did you call it? Oh yeah. My initiation. You guys are playing Trick the New Girl, or something."

"Uh," Stacy said, squinting at me, since I was standing with my back to the late-afternoon sun. "You wish. It's true. They tried to hush the whole thing up—and I don't know if there was ever enough evidence to press criminal charges. But the guy got expelled. It was all over school."

"It really is true, Ellie," Liz said, getting up from the curb as well. "Although Marco went around claiming it was self-defense, that the teacher—whoever it was—was trying to kill him, and he was just trying to save himself. Like anyone would believe that. He's supposed to be starting college this year. That is, if he got in anywhere. Which I highly doubt, since his grades sucked. And not because he wasn't smart, either. It was his attitude."

I couldn't believe Will hadn't told me any of this. I mean, the thing with his dad wanting him to go to the Naval Academy, sure. That he'd mentioned. But that his dad had purposefully sent his best friend into a war zone, then snapped up his wife for himself after the guy had been killed? And that he had a stepbrother who'd been kicked out of school for trying to kill a teacher?

Well, maybe that's not the kind of thing you tell a virtual stranger when you run into her in the woods. Even if she did let you have some of her pad thai.

Probably Will didn't want to talk about it. I mean, it was the kind of thing maybe you'd want people to forget.

Still. It definitely explained that look I'd seen cross his face a few times.

My parents are going to be home. That's what Will had said about his party. That his parents were going to be home. Not his dad and new stepmom. His parents.

"What happened to his mom?" I asked Liz, as we began following Stacy toward her Miata. "Will's real mom, I mean?"

Liz shrugged. "She died or something, I think. A long time ago, I guess. I mean, I never heard him talk about her, anyway."

So Will's mom was dead. He hadn't mentioned that, either, I noticed.

Maybe that's why he liked sitting around by himself in the woods, listening to medieval music, so much. Maybe if your dad had killed his best friend, then scooped up the guy's wife for himself, all the while insisting you have to go to military school to make a difference in the world, you'd feel like you had a lot to think about, too.

I was kind of glad right about then that I had been born Elaine Harrison and not A. William Wagner.

"Why are we talking about Will Wagner, anyway?" Stacy wanted to know, as we piled into her car.

"Harrison here scored an invite to his pool party after the Broadneck game Saturday night," Liz crowed.

"Whoa," Stacy said. "Looks like the new girl's doing pretty well for herself. Hanging with the popular crowd already."

"I'm not popular," I said, because the way she'd said it made it sound like it wasn't a good thing. "And it's not like that—"

"Yes, you are," Liz assured me. "If Will Wagner is inviting you to parties at his place, you're part of the In Crowd, big time."

"And I heard you have Lance Reynolds as your partner on Morton's oral assignment," Stacy said.

"It's not like I had a choice," I said. "Mr. Morton assigned us together."

"Listen to her," Stacy said, chuckling. "So outraged!

Don't you know how many girls would die to be in your shoes, Ellie? Lance Reynolds is the school hottie du jour. And he doesn't have a girlfriend. . . ."

"You have got to be kidding me," I said. "That guy is a behemoth!"

"Behemoth," echoed Stacy. "My, that's a bit harsh."

"Yeah," Liz agreed. "For someone going to his best friend's party on Saturday."

"I can't believe people consider Lance hot," I said. I couldn't believe it, either. Compared to Will, Lance was like . . . well, waffles with freezer burn.

"Aw, Lance is all right," Liz said. "Kind of dopey, but nice. Like a teddy bear. The problem is, he's chronically single. He just needs the love of a good woman to mold him into the man he has the potential to be."

"I think that description fits Ellie perfectly, don't you, Liz?" teased Stacy.

"Totally," Liz declared.

Then both girls had a good laugh at my stricken expression.

I knew they were just teasing. And even if they weren't, it was better that they suspected I had the hots for Lance than the truth . . . that the form I was warm for was Will. I had spent all day hoping to see him in the hallway between classes. I'd even rehearsed what I was going to say to him. *I hear Broadneck's 2 and 0. Guess you guys better do some serious playing.*

Yes, geek that I am, I had looked up Broadneck on the Internet the night before, then practiced the line in the mirror a few times that morning. So it would seem like I knew something about football, when, in fact, I knew nothing.

But I'd never seen him. And now I realized it wasn't just football I knew nothing about. I knew nothing about A. William Wagner—the guy I was apparently falling head over heels in love with—either.

But I did know one thing: Anyone who could joke around with a bunch of kids, the way Will had at that lemonade stand, or defend a geek the way he had that day outside Mr. Morton's classroom, would have my good opinion forever, no matter what his dad—or stepbrother—was rumored to have done.

I knew something else, too: that anyone with as dysfunctional a home life as Will's needed a laugh or two now and again. It was no wonder that he'd taken to hanging around me, the Queen of the Yuks.

And no matter what Nancy might think about guys not falling in love with girls who make them laugh, I wasn't changing a thing. Because if that's what Will wanted, that's what I was going to give him.

Even if I broke my heart in a thousand pieces doing so.

CHAPTER EIGHT

There she weaves by night and day
A magic web with colours gay.
She has heard a whisper say,
A curse is on her if she stay
To look down to Camelot.

I've never been a very girly girl. I mean, I've never collected stuffed animals or cared too much about clothes. I've never had a manicure, and my hair is all one length because I'm too lazy to get it cut or styled regularly. I basically just slap it back into a ponytail most days.

But the night of the game and Will's party, I really made an effort to look my best.

I don't know why. I mean, it still wasn't like Will was available. And even if he were, there was no reason to think he'd like me. I mean, sure, I was the girl who'd made him laugh—who'd sat on a rock in the woods and listened as he'd told me about his problems with his dad.

But he hadn't been totally forthcoming with *all* the

details about his dad. It wasn't like I was his big confi-
dante, or anything. I was just a funny girl he'd met. He
obviously liked me: The day after he'd given me the
rose—the day I made the track team—I got home to find
an e-mail from him.

> CAVALIER: Hey! Hope it went well today, and you
> ran like the wind. You're a shoo-in, don't
> worry.

He remembered. I'd only mentioned briefly, as he'd been
dropping me off at my house the day before, that I was
planning to go out for the track team.

And he'd remembered.

Because that's what friends do. They remember
things about each other. It didn't, I told myself sternly,
mean anything. Anything beyond that we were friends, I
mean.

I wrote back at once, of course. Well, it seemed only
fitting to share the good news.

> TIGGERTOO: Hey, back atcha! I made the team.
> Thanks for the well wishes.

> CAVALIER: See? Told you so. Congratulations. With
> you on board, the team's actually got a shot
> at State, for a change.

Which is the kind of thing a friend would say. Because

friends support one another. Just like friends say hi when they pass each other in the hallway (as Will always did). And wave when they see each other in the parking lot (ditto). It's just what friends do.

And Will had a lot of friends. Everyone at Avalon High, it seemed, loved him. He was immensely popular, not just with his fellow jocks, but with the less athletically inclined kids as well. On Friday, when we were summoned to the gym for a massive pep rally prior to the Broadneck game, and Will's name was read and he came running out onto the court, the applause for him was thunderous. Everyone in the entire school—including kids who'd been looking sullen about having to be at a pep rally in the first place, the skateboarders and punk rockers—leapt to their feet to give him a standing ovation.

Will, for his part, had looked embarrassed, and then, when the applause didn't die down, he had to reach for the microphone that Mr. Morton, who was emceeing the event (and generating pep by making us practice the Avalon High rallying cheer, "Excalibur!" which is possibly the lamest cheer in the history of high school), was holding and say, "Thanks, everybody. We're just going to go out there and play our best, and we hope all of you will be there to support us."

The roar this statement provoked was far louder than any of the *Excalibur!*s Mr. Morton had elicited from us.

And when Will was handing the microphone back to Mr. Morton, and his gaze happened to fall on me—me, out of all the people in the bleachers—and he gave me a wink and a smile, I told myself that's just what friends do. Even though both Liz and Stacy, beside me in the stands, glanced at me sharply, and went, "Did he just—?"

"We're just friends," I said quickly.

"Sure," Liz said, just as quickly. "Sure. Because, you know, Will and Jennifer—"

"They're, like, the It Couple," Stacy finished for her.

"Right," I said. "Will and I are . . . just friends."

"Wish I had a friend that hot," Stacy said. "And nice. And smart. And funny."

Liz smacked her in the arm. "What about me? I'm hot, nice, smart, and funny."

"Yeah, but I don't want to stick my tongue in your mouth," Stacy pointed out.

Liz sighed, and gazed down at Will, who was taking a seat with the rest of his team. "True," she said. "If Will Wagner and I were *just friends*, I'd make sure we didn't stay *just friends* for long."

"Oh, right," Stacy said sarcastically. "Good luck competing with *that*."

We looked where she was pointing. Jennifer Gold was doing a series of backflips up and down the gym, in time to the band that was playing a speeded-up version of "What I Like About You." Her deeply tanned legs flashed like scissor blades. Every time she landed, her lustrous blond hair fell effortlessly back into perfect waves.

"I hate her," Liz said, without any real rancor, summing up exactly what I was feeling at that particular moment.

But I knew these kinds of feelings were unfair. Jennifer wasn't a bad person. Everyone liked her. I had no right to hate her. Sure, Will had confided in me, and even given me a rose, and invited me to his party.

But we were *just friends.*

But telling myself that over and over again didn't stop me from fishing out my shortest skirt and using eyeliner and even mousse on the night of the Broadneck game—enough so that when my dad saw me, he went, "All I ask is that you stay away from downtown," on account of the middies.

Then, when I ran out of my house to get into Stacy's car—she was driving Liz and me to the game—both girls let out hoots of mock admiration, and Liz asked me if I would still sit near them, being such a glamour queen, and all.

I didn't mind their teasing me, because I knew it meant I'd been accepted. And that felt way better than if they'd said, all politely, "You look nice, Ellie."

I had never been to a football game before. My brother Geoff had been on the basketball team at my old school, so I'd been to quite a few games to cheer him on . . . not out of any sense of sisterly support, but because Nancy had always had a big crush on Geoff and had insisted on going to his games.

Nancy hadn't had a crush on any of the football players, so she'd never made me go to any of those games.

I honestly can't say I missed out on anything much—at least if the Avalon-Broadneck game was any indication.

Oh, it was fun hanging out in the bleachers, under the vast night sky, eating popcorn.

But the game itself was way boring, and practically incomprehensible. And the players wore so much padding, you could only tell who anybody was by their names on the backs of their jerseys.

Still, I appeared to be the only person in the stands who was of this opinion. Everybody else—including Stacy and Liz—was way into the game, joining Jennifer Gold and the other cheerleaders in their chants, and screaming hysterically every time our team got a point or a down, or whatever they were called.

Liz tried to explain the finer points of the game to me. Will's position, quarterback, was like the brains of the operation. His friend Lance was a guard, whose job it was to keep Will from getting flattened every time he was holding the ball—which was fairly often.

Apparently Avalon High had a good team—so good they had even gone to the state championship the year before. It was widely believed they'd go again this year, if they played as well as they had last year.

But we were not doing as well against the Broadneck Bruins as everyone had hoped we would. At halftime, we were down by fourteen points, and a lot of people in the stands were grumbling about it.

I have to admit, I didn't much care whether or not we won. I hadn't spent a whole lot of time watching the game. Mostly I just watched Will. It was hard not to notice that he looked very cute in his tight white pants while he was out there making up plays and telling everybody else what to do. There's something sort of intoxicating, I guess, about a guy in a position of power . . . at least one with a butt that looked as good as Will's.

I didn't mention my crush on Will to Liz or Stacy, of course. I mean, for one thing, I'd gone to great lengths to convince them that Will and I were *just friends* (which, in his case, anyway, was actually true).

But I knew if I'd confessed to them that in my own case, I longed for more than *just friendship* with him, they'd look at me all pityingly for being stupid enough to fall for such a popular guy—especially one who was dating Jennifer Gold.

Besides, they still seemed to think there was something going on with me and Lance (so not), if the way they elbowed me every time Mr. Morton said his name over the loudspeaker (besides emceeing the pep rallies, Mr. M also announced the game) was any indication.

I didn't tell them to cut it out, or that I didn't like Lance, or anything. It just seemed easier to let them go on thinking that than to let them in on the truth.

Anyway, I was so bored by halftime that I volunteered to get us all hot dogs, and was making my way to the concession stand when I heard someone call my name.

I turned, not having the slightest idea who could be talking to me, since I still barely knew a soul at AHS. I was more than a little surprised to see Mr. Morton, having emerged from the announcing booth, trying to flag me down.

"Hey, Mr. Morton," I said, wondering what he could want. I mean, there were lots of his other students milling around. What was he singling me out for?

"Elaine," he said, in a stern voice. Since he was British, and all, my name sounded even more old-fashioned than if he'd just said it in an ordinary American way. Sort of the way that whenever he said the word "Excalibur" it sounded extra important.

I realized from the sternness in his voice that I was in trouble. What for, I couldn't imagine. I mean, I was only trying to buy a couple of hot dogs, for Pete's sake.

"I read your proposal," Mr. Morton went on.

"Oh," I said. It dawned on me that I probably wasn't in trouble after all. I didn't inherit my dad's bad eyes or his slow-but-steady running habits, but I had inherited his excellent research skills, as well as my mom's talent for mega-organization. Nobody writes a better, more exhaustive term paper than I do. I've never gotten less than an A on one. Ever. Mr. Morton probably wanted to compliment me on the supremely excellent job I'd done on the proposal I'd handed in about *The Lady of Shalott*.

Only that wasn't why he'd stopped me at all, it turned out. He wasn't a bit pleased with what I'd handed in. Not a bit.

"That was not," he said, in the same clipped tone, "the topic I assigned you."

For a second I couldn't figure out what he was talking about. Then I realized what he meant.

"Oh," I said. "Right! I'm sorry. That's my fault, Mr.

Morton. I'd already read *Beowulf*"—I thought it safer to say this than the truth, which is that I hate *Beowulf*. You never know with lit teachers . . . they can be really touchy about that kind of thing—"so we traded topics with someone else. Is that not allowed? I don't remember hearing you say so."

Mr. Morton frowned. Clearly I'd stumped him. Because he'd never said anything about trading topics being a no-no.

Still, that wasn't the only thing he was sore about.

"Did you work with your partner at *all* on that proposal?" he demanded.

My partner?

Then I remembered. Lance. Of course.

"Sure," I said, lying through my teeth. "He helped gather some of the source material—"

"I highly doubt that," Mr. Morton said. He was totally outraged. I could tell by his eyebrows, which were way lowered. An older guy—well past retirement age, if you ask me—Mr. Morton's eyebrows were gray, like his neatly trimmed beard.

"I assigned you to work with a partner for a reason, Elaine," he said severely.

"I'm sorry," I said, truly taken aback. Teachers never yell at me. I'm pretty much a model student—like with my driving. I'm afraid to break the law. Mostly. "I . . . um . . . we . . . uh, we divided the paper up. I wrote the proposal, and he's supposed to do the oral report—"

But Mr. Morton wasn't falling for it. He said, "When

I assign you to work with a partner, you're supposed to WORK WITH THAT PARTNER. You and Lance are to be together. I am not accepting your proposal."

This caused me to make a shocked noise, because no teacher had ever rejected anything I'd ever written before.

But Mr. Morton didn't seem to notice my shock, since he went on with, "And on Monday morning, I want to have a word with both of you. I'll expect to see you and Mr. Reynolds in my classroom, first thing. You can let him know when you see him."

I was stunned. What was this all about?

"All right," I said.

I said "all right," but I wasn't feeling all right. I was definitely freaked. How had he known? How had he known Lance and I hadn't worked together on the proposal?

By the time I got back to my seat in the bleachers, I had calmed down a little . . . but not much.

"Where're the dogs?" Liz wanted to know, when I slumped down into my seat beside her. And that's when I realized I'd been so upset over my conversation with Mr. Morton that I'd forgotten to get the hot dogs.

"Sorry," I said. "Listen to this." And I told them both what Mr. Morton had said to me. "I mean, can you believe it?" I asked, when I was done describing what had happened. "Does he have a reputation for being a stodgy old crank? Mr. Morton, I mean? Or is it just me?"

The question had been rhetorical. I'd fully expected them to say, "Oh, yeah, he's a crank."

But they didn't. Stacy went, "I don't know. Everybody

has always seemed to love Mr. Morton."

"Yeah," Liz said. "He's been voted best teacher every year since he started at Avalon, practically. And everybody gets a real kick out of the way he says 'Excalibur.'"

"Really?" I found this extremely hard to believe.

"I don't get why you're so mad," Stacy said. "I mean, he's practically ordering you to spend more time with your loverboy. Where's the tragedy in that?"

Liz laughingly agreed. "Seriously," she said. "I'd pay cold hard cash to be told to spend more time with Lance Reynolds."

I slumped in my seat. There was no point in telling them that my lack of enthusiasm at having Lance as a research partner stemmed from my being completely in love with his best friend.

So I just shut my mouth and didn't say anything for the rest of the game. . . .

Until, sometime in the fourth quarter, when the teams were tied at twenty-one, something weird happened. At least, I thought it was weird. Not having been to a football game before, maybe it happened every day. Who knew?

But I did see exactly how it happened, because it involved Will, so I'd been watching closely. Will had called out some numbers and someone had snapped him the ball. He'd run with it for a few feet, looking for someone to throw it to.

Then something happened that hadn't happened at any time before during the game: Lance wasn't there to keep Will from getting tackled. Instead, Will got hit, hard, by a member of the opposing team.

Seeing this, I gasped and leapt to my feet, then looked around accusingly for Lance. He came running over from where Jennifer Gold was standing on the sidelines.

Jennifer Gold? What had Lance been doing, chatting up Jennifer Gold while Will was getting the snot knocked out of him?

I wasn't the only one who was appalled. The Avalon coach whacked Lance on the back of his helmet as he went racing to Will's side. A lot of whistles got blown, and the guy who'd tackled Will peeled himself off him. Lance fell to his knees beside Will's crumpled—oh, God! Don't let him be dead!—form, ripped off his own helmet, then leaned over to grab the front of Will's uniform, calling his friend's name.

I watched, my heart in my throat, not realizing I'd been holding my breath until a second later, when Will started, slowly and painfully, to get up.

Then I let out my breath in a whoosh and, my knees too weak to hold me up anymore, sat down. . . .

To find both Stacy and Liz staring at me with their eyebrows raised.

I felt myself blushing, and hoped they wouldn't notice in the darkness.

"I had no idea football was so exciting," I said lamely.

A second later, with Will seeming to have brushed off Lance's apologies with a good-natured laugh, the game started again.

Only this time, no one got close to tackling Will. And the guy from the opposing team who'd knocked him down before? Well, first chance he got, Lance brought him down so hard that the game had to stop again, and the guy had to be removed from the field on a stretcher.

One thing was for sure: Nobody was going to hurt A. William Wagner and get away with it if his best friend Lance had anything to say about it.

Avalon won by seven points. The crowd went nuts.

And then it was time for Will's party.

CHAPTER NINE

She knows not what the curse may be,
And so she weaveth steadily,
And little other care hath she,
The Lady of Shalott.

I made Stacy and Liz come with me. No way was I going to a party by myself, not knowing anyone but the host, who'd doubtless be too busy hosting to talk to me.

Besides, I'd asked Will, when I'd e-mailed him back the other night, if it was okay if I brought a couple of friends, and he'd replied that it was fine.

Stacy had been nonchalant at the invitation, but Liz was excited by the idea of going. She had never, she confessed to me, been to a party at a popular person's house—let alone president of the senior class—and she was dying to see what it was like.

She found out soon enough. What it was like could be described in one word: crowded. Will lived in one of the

really nice houses by the Severn Bridge—on a hill over-
looking the bay, in fact—and we had to park way down
the hill, because there were already so many cars in front
of the house that it made getting close to the driveway
impossible.

"Holy—" was what Liz started to say, when we finally
made it up the hill and into the Wagners' foyer. Because
Will's house was really nice, all marble floors and giant
mirrors in gilt frames. You had to wonder how his dad
afforded it all, on a naval salary.

Liz had apparently been thinking the same thing,
since she whispered to Stacy and me, "Family money," in
a knowing voice.

I met Admiral Wagner almost as soon as we walked
through the door. He was standing in the living room
greeting people as they arrived, a drink in one hand, and
an attractive blonde in the other. This, I assumed, was
the dead friend's widow, and Will's new stepmom.

"Great game, wasn't it?" Will's dad was saying to
anyone who would listen. "Help yourself to a drink.
Great game, didn't you think?"

Will's dad certainly didn't look like an ogre who
would purposefully get his own best friend killed, then
marry his widow and, oh yeah, force his son into a
career he didn't want. He was tall, like Will, with salt-
and-pepper gray hair. He wasn't wearing his uniform, or
anything, although the creases in his khakis looked kind
of sharp for civilian clothes. But that might just be
because I'm not used to seeing a man in ironed pants.

My dad's never worn anything ironed in his life.

I went straight up to him and introduced myself and Liz and Stacy, because it seemed like the polite thing to do. I'll admit that I was also curious to see what Admiral Wagner would be like, after everything I'd heard about him.

But he was totally charming, shaking my hand with energy, seemingly thrilled to pieces that his son had so many friends. He went, "Glad to meet you, girls. Go and get yourselves a drink. Sodas are out by the pool," in a happy, booming voice.

I looked closely at the admiral's new wife, to try to gauge how much she had to do with what Will called "things being weird lately."

But she didn't look mean or anything. She was very beautiful, petite, and blond . . . sort of like Jennifer Gold, actually.

But she also looked kind of sad. Like maybe she missed her dead husband, or something.

Or maybe she just didn't want to be at some dumb high school party. It was hard to tell.

Stacy and Liz and I did as the admiral told us to, and made our way out to the pool. We had had a little trouble finding the house, so Will and Lance and the rest of their teammates—not to mention the Avalon High cheerleading squad—were already there, high-fiving one another and jumping into the heated pool in the glow of about a million paper lanterns.

Stacy and Liz and I went and got ourselves sodas and then stood by the guacamole—which is where tall girls always end up standing at parties—watching everyone. No one paid us the slightest bit of attention. No one, that is, except a Border collie who came over and thrust her nose into my hand.

"Hey, there," I said to the dog. She was gorgeous, her long, silky coat white with just a few black patches. She was well-behaved, too. She didn't jump up and only licked me once.

This, I knew, could only be Will's dog, Cavalier. I found out I was right when Will managed to break away from the adoring throng around him and hurried over, exclaiming, "You came!"

While Liz and Stacy both looked behind them, trying to figure out who he was talking to, I felt myself starting to flush.

Because I knew he was talking to me.

"Yes," I said, as he stopped in front of me. He'd changed into baggy swim trunks and a Hawaiian shirt that was open to the waist. It was hard not to look at his abs, which were extremely six-pack–like. I tried to ignore them as I said, "Thanks for inviting me. These are my friends Stacy and Liz."

While the two girls looked on in total astonishment, Will said hi. Then he said to me, "I see Cavalier found you. She must like you."

It was true. The dog had kind of been leaning on me as I stroked her soft ears. At least until Will came over. Then all of her attention shifted to him.

"She has nice manners," I said lamely, because it was

the only thing I could think of to say. Other than, *I love you! I love you!*

Which wouldn't, you know, have been too socially acceptable.

Will just smiled, then asked us if we were going to swim.

"We didn't bring suits," Liz lied, with a quick glance at Jennifer Gold, who was wandering around, looking perfectly angelic in a snow-white tankini.

"Oh, we have plenty of spares," Will said. "Over in the pool house. Help yourselves."

Stacy and Liz just stared at him, guacamole-laden chips forgotten in their hands. There was about as much chance of the three of us strutting around in our swimsuits in front of the cheerleading squad as there was of a giant meteorite plummeting from the sky and incinerating them.

Not that I was wishing this would happen. Much.

"Have fun," Will said to me, with a grin, completely oblivious to our discomfort, as any guy would be. "I have to go do, you know. The host thing."

"Sure," I said, and watched as he—Cavalier padding close at his side—went to go talk to a tall, good-looking boy who I'd never seen before. Dark-haired, like Will, he seemed vaguely familiar. But I knew he didn't go to Avalon. Liz was only too happy to clear up the mystery of his identity.

"That's Marco," she said, her mouth full of guacamole. "Will's stepbrother."

I stared. Marco was chatting amiably with Will and some of the other team members. He didn't look like he was too upset with the way things had turned out—you know, living in the home of the man who'd sent his father to his death, then married his mother. I mean, that kind of thing could mess a person up.

He also didn't look like the monster I'd been led to believe he was. He certainly didn't look like someone who'd try to kill a teacher. It was true he had a hoop through both ears. And one of those tribal tattoos around one bicep.

But that's pretty much normal, you know, these days.

I watched Marco make his way around the pool, greeting people the way a politician does, with a handshake and a slap on the shoulder if they were guys, and a kiss on the cheek if they were girls. I wondered how I would feel, living under the same roof as the man who was responsible—however indirectly—for my dad's death.

Things were much more interesting in Annapolis than I'd ever suspected they would be, back when my parents had announced that that was where we were moving for the year.

It didn't take Liz long to figure out that she hadn't been missing much, not having been invited to popular kids' parties before. Stacy soon grew bored as well. When they finally announced that they wanted to go— we'd managed to polish off all the guacamole, and it didn't look like more was forthcoming—I nodded, because by then, I wanted to go, too. I'd seen what I'd wanted to see—Will's dad, who, in spite of what I'd been led to believe, seemed very nice; his stepmom, who seemed lovely; and the way Will interacted with Jennifer, which was exactly the way you'd expect a boyfriend and girlfriend to interact . . . not too lovey-dovey, or anything, but they held hands a lot, and I saw him lean down to kiss her once.

Did the sight send a dagger of envy into my heart? Yes. Did I think I'd make a better girlfriend for him than she did? Pretty much.

But the thing was, I wanted him to be happy. It sounds weird, but I really did. And if Jennifer made him happy, well, so be it.

Except . . .

What about that rose? The one that was fully blooming now in its vase on my nightstand, where it was the first thing I saw every morning when I woke up, and the last thing I saw every night before I turned out the light?

It wasn't until we were on our way out that I suddenly remembered I needed to let Lance know about our meeting with Mr. Morton on Monday morning. Telling Liz and Stacy I'd meet them out by the car, I went to find Lance to break the news.

But he wasn't out by the pool where I'd last seen him. And he wasn't anywhere on the first floor of the house, either. Finally, someone hanging out in the line for the bathroom on the second floor said they'd seen him go through the door to a spare bedroom. I thanked them, then went to the door and knocked on it.

But the music floating up from downstairs was too loud for me to hear whether or not Lance had said come in. I knocked a little harder. Still nothing.

Figuring if I couldn't hear him because of the music, he probably couldn't hear my knocking, I opened the door—just a crack—to see if Lance really was in there.

He was in there, all right.

In there making out with Jennifer on the bed. Jennifer, his best friend's girlfriend.

They were so wrapped up in each other, they didn't even notice the door opening. I quickly closed it, then hurried to lean against the wall across from it, my heart feeling as if it were about to leap out of my chest.

But before I even had time to register what I'd just seen—let alone wonder what it meant—I saw something even more horrifying.

And that was Will coming up the stairs, and heading for the very door I'd just closed.

CHAPTER TEN

As often thro' the purple night,
Below the starry clusters bright,
Some bearded meteor, trailing light,
Moves over still Shalott.

"Oh, hey, Elle," Will said, when he saw me.

It was a sign of how freaked I truly was by what I'd just seen that my heartstrings didn't so much as quiver at hearing him call me Elle.

"Hi," I said faintly.

"Have you seen Jen?" Will wanted to know. "Someone said they saw her come up here."

"Jen?" I echoed. My gaze, though I tried not to let it, strayed toward the closed door to the spare bedroom. "Um . . ."

What was I supposed to say? I mean, really? Was I supposed to go, "Sure, I've seen her, she's right in there," and let him walk through that door and find Jennifer and Lance in there, going at it?

Or was I supposed to lie and go, "Jen? Nope. Haven't seen her," and let him continue to live in total ignorance of the fact that his girlfriend and best friend were a couple of lying skanks?

Who could make a decision like that? Why did *I* have to be the one who'd walked in on them? I mean, I wanted Will to break up with Jennifer so he could be free to hook up with me—you know, if hell happened to freeze over, or something, and he asked me out.

But I didn't want to be the person who, however indirectly, caused that breakup by revealing his girlfriend's true nature to him! Because whenever this happens to girls on soap operas or the WB or whatever, they never end up getting the guy. . . .

But before I could decide what to do, Will looked more closely at me and went, "Are you all right, Elle? You look sort of . . . pale."

I *felt* pale. In fact, I felt a little like I might throw up all that guacamole I'd scarfed down earlier.

"I'm fine," I said, though it sounded like a lie even to my own ears.

"You're *not* fine," Will said firmly. "Come on. Fresh air time."

Then something amazing happened. He took my hand—grabbed it like it was the most natural thing to do in the world—and steered me toward a door I hadn't noticed before. Then he pulled me up a narrow, steep stairway that opened out onto this kind of deck all along the roof of the house.

In spite of the party below, which was in full swing, it was quiet out on the narrow little deck. Quiet and dark, with a fantastic view of the stars overhead, and the bay stretched out below us, the moon reflected like a bright ribbon of light across it. A cool breeze lifted my hair from my face, and immediately, I started to feel a little better.

I leaned against the ornately carved railing that ran the length of the deck and gazed out at the bay, at the bridge that arched across it, and the occasional glow of a car's headlights as someone drove over it.

"Better?" Will asked.

I nodded, feeling a little ashamed of myself, and wanting to distract him from looking at me too closely— I sensed that I was still slightly green around the gills—I asked brightly, "So what *is* this thing, anyway?" meaning the narrow parapet Will and I were standing on.

"You really aren't from around here, are you?" Will asked, with a grin. Then he joined me at the railing and said, "They call it a widow's walk. All the old houses around here have them. People like to say they were built for the wives of sailors so they could come out and watch for their husbands' ships to return."

"Nice," I said sarcastically. Because, of course, if the husband didn't return, it meant that his ship had gone down and the wife was now a widow, thus making her pretty little lookout post a widow's walk.

"Well," Will said, with a laugh. "yeah. But that's not

really what they were for. They were built so people could climb up here and put out the flames if their roof caught fire, back when they had to use their chimneys for heat and cooking and everything."

"Nice!" I said again, this time with even more sarcasm.

Will smiled. "Yeah. I guess they should change the name." He shrugged. "The view's the same, no matter what they call it."

I nodded, admiring the shimmering band of light the moon cast across the water. "It's nice," I said. "Soothing." Soothing enough to make a girl forget why she'd had to come out there in the first place. What was I going to do about Lance and Jennifer, anyway?

"Yeah," Will said, totally oblivious to my inner turmoil. "I never get tired of it. It's the one thing that always seems to stay the same. The water, I mean. The color changes. Sometimes it's flat. Sometimes there's chop. But it's always there. You can depend on it."

Not like his girlfriend and best friend.

But I didn't say this out loud, of course.

I couldn't help wondering if the new Mrs. Wagner came out here much, maybe with her morning cup of coffee. Had the irony of his house's widow's walk occurred to Will? You know, her being a widow, and all?

"Do you miss her?" I asked Will suddenly. Too suddenly, I realized, when he looked at me like he had no idea what I was talking about.

"Who?" he asked.

"Your mom, I mean," I said. "Your, um, real mom." I didn't figure there was any point in pretending like I didn't know the story of what had happened with his dad.

"My mom?" He squinted out across the water. "No, not at all. I never knew her. She died when I was born."

"Oh," I said. Because I didn't know what else to say.

"It's okay," Will said with a grin, I guess sensing my sadness for him, and wanting to reassure me. "You can't miss what you never had."

"I guess," I said. "Do you like—" I paused, not sure what I should call his stepmom. "—Marco's mom?" was what I ended up settling for.

"Jean?" Will nodded. "Yeah. I like her a lot."

"Well," I said, "that's good. And Marco?"

"Yeah," Will said. His grin broadened. "How'd you know about Marco and Jean? Have you been asking around about me, or something?"

"Maybe," I said, feeling myself start to flush, and hoping he wouldn't notice in the relative darkness.

If he did, he didn't let on.

"Marco's cool," Will said, with a shrug. "He . . ." He paused, seeming to struggle with how to put what he said next. "He didn't have a lot, growing up. He's been in some trouble. But I think he's starting to chill a little."

"He and your dad get along?" I asked casually, but I was really curious. Would I get along with the man who'd ordered my dad to his death, then married my mom? I was thinking probably not.

Will looked thoughtful. Not sad, or anything. Just like he was thinking hard about what I'd asked.

"You know, I think they do," he said finally. "It's different for Marco. I mean, he's not related to my dad. So there isn't the same . . . pressure between him and Marco as there is between him and me."

"So I guess that's what you meant when you were talking about things being weird," I said. "About Marco and your dad and stepmom and . . . what happened with them, and everything?"

I guess it was wishful thinking. You know, that the thing with Will's parents was really what was bothering him, and not . . . well, the thing with his girlfriend. I mean, did Will suspect? About Lance and Jennifer? He had to. What had happened at tonight's game, with Lance not having been there for him because he was over by the sidelines talking to Jen . . . and now the two of them having disappeared together. . . .

That had to be what he meant about things being weird lately. That had to be the explanation for the dark shadow I sometimes saw fall across his face. Didn't it? I mean . . . didn't it?

"I guess that's part of it," he said, looking out into the water. "But it doesn't explain everything. It doesn't explain. . . ." He tore his gaze from the bay and looked down at me instead.

And I knew—just knew—what was coming. I even closed my eyes, anticipating the blow.

He's going to ask me, I thought. *He's going to ask me*

about Lance and Jennifer. What should I say? I can't be the one to tell him. I just can't. They *should have to tell him. Lance and Jennifer! It's their fault, not mine.* They *should be the ones to have to break the news. It's not fair that it has to be me!*

But then, to my utter astonishment, what Will ended up saying to me instead was, "It doesn't explain what's going on between me and you."

If that meteorite I'd been fantasizing about earlier had suddenly streaked down out of the sky and taken out the Avalon High cheerleading team, I doubt I'd have been as surprised as I was by what Will had just said to me. I was stunned, in fact, into speechlessness and, my eyes flying open, could only stare at him, my mind sluggishly repeating those last three words over and over again. . . . *Me and you. Me and you. Me and you.*

Except that—there was no *me and you.* To me, maybe. But not to Will.

Was there?

But before I could even begin to formulate a reply to his extraordinary statement, he tore his gaze from mine and, looking out across the water again, asked, "Do you ever get the feeling that this can't be it?"

My brain staggered around, trying to figure out what was happening. I'm afraid it was all too much for me, and I ended up going, "Um . . . what?" because it was the only thing I could think of to say.

"You know," Will said, a note of urgency in his deep voice as he looked me in the eye again. "Don't you ever wonder if there's something . . . more? That we're supposed to be doing?"

"Um." Okay. *Okay, apparently this is heading somewhere, hopefully back to what he'd said before, about* me *and you. In the meantime, I'll humor him.* "Sure. Isn't that how we're supposed to feel? Otherwise we'd never move out. We'd all just live with our parents until we died."

He laughed a little at that. I loved the sound of his laugh. It almost made me forget about . . . well, what I'd seen earlier.

"That's not what I meant, exactly," he said. "Do you ever think"—his blue eyes were very bright in the moonlight—"that this isn't the first time you've been alive? Like that you might have done all this—only as someone else—before?"

"Um." I looked up into his face, wondering what he'd do if I reached out and grabbed it, dragged it down to mine, and kissed him. "Not really."

"Never?" He ran a hand through his thick dark hair, a gesture I was starting to realize was habitual for him when he was feeling frustrated. "You've never had a feeling that you've been somewhere before—somewhere you know you've never been? Or read something that you know you'd never seen before that moment, but that felt familiar anyway? Heard a piece of music you could swear you'd heard sometime in the past, but that you know you couldn't have?"

"Well," I said. It would be wrong to kiss him. He

might freak. Guys don't like it when girls make the first move. At least according to Nancy. But how would she even know? It's not like she ever had a boyfriend. "Sure. But there's a name for that. It's called déjà vu. It's a totally common—"

"I'm not talking about déjà vu," he interrupted. "I'm talking about knowing you've met someone before—the way I feel I've met you before—even though there's no possible way we could have met before. That kind of thing. You don't feel it? That there's . . . there's something . . . something between us?"

Oh, I felt there was something between us, all right. It just wasn't, I was pretty sure, what Will was feeling. I mean, I didn't feel like I'd met him before. Because if I had, I for *sure* would have remembered.

Although there *was* that . . . my feelings for him, and the strength of them. The way I wanted him to be mine, but at the same time, I also wanted to protect him from the hurt I knew he was going to feel when he found out— and he *would* find out—about Lance and Jennifer. These weren't the kinds of feelings that stem simply from a guy being nice to you, and buying you a cup of lemonade, and giving you a rose.

These were far, far more than that.

Could there be something to what Will was saying? Could we have met before? If not in this lifetime, then . . . in another?

But before I could admit that I knew where he was coming from, Will sagged a little against the railing of the widow's walk, and shook his head.

"Listen to me. Maybe Lance and Jen are right," he said, in a self-mocking voice, "and I really am going nuts."

Just hearing that Lance and Jennifer had said something like that made me jump to take the opposite stance. Maybe Lance cared about what happened to Will—despite the fact that he was carrying on an illicit love affair with his girlfriend behind his back. I mean, he'd kind of proven that he cared by concussing that guy who'd tackled Will. That showed that he at least felt a little bad about what was going on.

But I had seen no such signs of remorse from Jennifer. In fact, just the opposite, given the way she'd grilled me at my locker about Will's dinner at my house. It was clear that she'd just been pumping me to see if Will suspected anything about her and Lance.

"You're not going nuts," I said emphatically. "Things . . . things have been weird for me, too, lately. But I just thought—I mean, I just figured it's a normal part of being a teenager, or whatever."

"I don't know." Will looked dubious. "I thought teenagers are supposed to think they know everything. And I've never been more sure in my life that I don't know anything at all."

"Oh," I said. "Well, that's probably just a symptom of the massive brain tumor you've got growing inside your head, the one no one's told you about yet."

Then I wanted to kick myself. *What is wrong with me? Why do I have to go and make jokes whenever things look like they're about to get serious? Nancy is right. I'm never going to get a boyfriend at this rate.*

But Will, instead of going—as he probably should have—"Whatever you say, weirdo," just looked at me for a minute. Then he threw back his head and laughed.

And laughed some more.

And really, what choice did I have but to laugh along with him? At least until a sudden breeze sent a strand of my moussed-up hair flying across my eyes. Then, to my surprise, before I had a chance to push it aside, Will reached up and brushed it back for me with his fingers.

And I froze. Because he was touching me. He was touching me. *He was touching me.*

"You're all right, Ellie Harrison," he said softly, his gaze on mine, his voice unsteady. "And, you know, I think I'd like you even if I wasn't sure I'd already met you in a past life, and liked you then."

There's really no telling what might have happened next. Not that I imagined he might have suddenly wrapped his arms around me and kissed me, the way I'd seen Lance kissing Jennifer in the spare room below us.

But you never know. He might have.

If it hadn't been for two things. . . .

CHAPTER ELEVEN

But in her web she still delights
To weave the mirror's magic sights,
For often thro' the silent nights
A funeral, with plumes and lights
And music, went to Camelot:

The first thing that happened was that a cloud went skittering across the moon, blocking out the only light we'd had to see by.

The second was that the door to the widow's walk suddenly burst open, and then Cavalier came rushing up toward us, closely followed by someone else of the human variety. I wouldn't have known who it was if it wasn't for the light from the stairs spilling out behind him from the open doorway.

"There you are," Marco said, when he saw Will. He could not have missed the way Will jerked his hand from my hair and moved it to pat his panting dog, instead. "I've been looking for you everywhere. I wouldn't have found you, if it hadn't been for that damned dog. Didn't you hear her barking?"

Will gave Cavalier a final pat, then straightened up. "No," he said. His voice, which had been unsteady with emotion just seconds before, now sounded totally normal. It was impossible to tell if he, like me, resented his stepbrother's intrusion. "Why? What's up?"

"I need to find Jen," Marco said. "Her car is blocking one of the neighbors' driveways."

Will shook his head the way someone who's just come up from a dive into very deep water does when he breaks the surface. I tried not to think what that meant vis-à-vis . . . well, me.

"What?" Will blinked a few times. "Jen?"

"Yeah." Marco looked at me. Not accusingly. Just speculatively, like he was wondering who I was and what I'd done to make his stepbrother act so dopey all of a sudden.

I could have told him in three words. No one and nothing.

Or is that four words?

"I thought Jen'd be with you," Marco said. *Now* he was starting to sound accusing.

"I haven't seen Jen since she went to go put lipstick on half an hour ago," Will said. But not like it bothered him.

"Well, she's got to move her car," Marco said. "Mrs. Hewlitt's blocked in and is threatening to call the cops."

Will said something under his breath that sounded like a swear word. Then, to me, he said, "Sorry, Elle. I have to go find her."

"That's fine," I said hurriedly, hoping my disappointment over the interruption didn't show. He'd called me Elle again, after all. "I should go, anyway. Liz and Stacy are probably wondering where I went."

Will looked for a second like he didn't know what I was talking about. Then he nodded and said, "Oh, right. Well, come on. I'll walk you out."

He started for the door to the stairs, Cavalier close at his heels. I followed, with Marco tagging along behind me. As we headed back down to the second floor, Marco asked, "Aren't you going to introduce me to your friend?" in a voice I didn't really like all that much . . . though I couldn't say why.

"Oh, sorry," Will said. "Elaine Harrison, my step-brother, Marco Campbell. Marco, this is Ellie."

"Hi," I said to Marco, over my shoulder, as we entered the hallway.

Marco grinned—one of those grins I've sometimes seen described as wolfish in books.

"Pleased to make your acquaintance, Elaine," he said. Then, to Will, he said, "I think someone said they saw Jen go through there." He nodded toward the door behind which I'd found Jennifer and Lance making out.

"Oh, great," Will said.

And he started to place his hand on the doorknob—

"No, wait!" I cried, before I knew what I was saying.

Will looked at me questioningly. So, for that matter, did the dog. Marco's look was the only one that wasn't questioning. His was surprised.

Which was when I knew.

Suddenly I felt like throwing up all over again. Except that I didn't have time to be sick.

"W-wasn't that just her?" I stammered.

Will's hand continued to hover above the doorknob.

"Where?" he asked.

"Wasn't that her just now, calling you?" Practically falling over my own feet, I hurried to the top of the stairs to the first floor. "He'll be right there," I called down. Some people standing at the bottom of the staircase looked up at me like I was insane.

But it didn't matter, because Will couldn't see them.

"She's downstairs," I heard myself say to Will.

And his hand, to my immense relief, fell away from the doorknob.

"Oh," he said. "Great. Well. See you around."

And he started toward the stairs.

That's when it happened. The thing that afterwards, I was never quite sure how to describe, even to myself.

All I know is, Will started toward the staircase, and I glanced at his stepbrother Marco, to see if he'd follow. . . .

Only to find Marco studying me with an amused expression on his face, as if I were a cat that had suddenly started reading the want ads. Out loud.

"Will," he said, not taking his eyes—as dark as his stepbrother's were light—from me. "Why don't you invite Elaine to come sailing with us tomorrow?"

"Oh, hey," Will said, pausing at the top of the stairs, and looking back at me, "that's a great idea. Do you like sailing, Elle?"

Elle. I couldn't help swallowing.

"Uh," I said. What was going on here? I wondered. Thrilled as I was to be included in any plan of Will's, I couldn't help wondering why Marco wanted me to come along. He didn't even *know* me.

And from the way he was looking at me, I wasn't all that sure he even *liked* me. Especially after what we both—Marco and I—knew I'd just done.

"I don't know," I said uncertainly. "I've never been. We don't sail much, back in Minnesota."

"Oh, you'll love it," Marco said. "Won't she, Will?"

"Yeah, you will," Will said enthusiastically. "Meet us by the Alex Haley statue at the city dock tomorrow at noon. You know where that is?" When I nodded, he said, "Great. See you then."

And then he hurried down the stairs to look for Jennifer. Leaving me alone with Marco . . .

. . . with whom I wasn't about to stick around and make small talk.

"Well, see you tomorrow," I said, and started toward the stairs myself. *Get out*, my heart seemed to be saying with every beat.

But I didn't move quickly enough, since Marco's voice

125

snaked out across the landing like an arm, almost physically drawing me back toward him when he asked, in an insinuating tone, "You didn't *really* hear Jen just then, did you, Elaine of Minnesota?"

I froze, one foot on the stairs, and one still on the second floor. For some reason, my blood had run . . . well, cold.

"Sorry," I said. "I . . . I don't know what you mean."

"Oh, I think you do," Marco said, with a wink. Then, as I stood there watching him, he went up to the door Will had come so close to opening, and thumped on it, once, with the side of his fist.

"Jen," he shouted through it. "You in there?"

There was a pause. Then a thin voice called through the door, "Um, yeah, just a sec! I'll be right out."

Marco looked back at me and shook his head.

"Nice try," he said. "But he's gonna find out about them sometime."

So I'd been right. He'd known. He'd known all along. He'd wanted Will to open that door and find the two of them in there.

What kind of sick person *does* something like that?

Will's stepbrother, evidently.

"Um," I said, trying to play dumb. *He'd known.* But that wasn't the weirdest part. I'd *known* he'd known. "I have to go—"

Marco wasn't falling for it, though. Not only did he keep talking, but he crossed the space between us in two long strides and snatched up my arm in fingers that were so cold, they burned. He held me in a grip of iron, so that I couldn't even dart down the stairs the way I'd planned.

"What were you trying to do, anyway?" Marco asked, with a sneer. "Protect him?"

"Let go of my arm," I said in a voice that shook a little. Something about his touch was really creeping me out.

I wasn't the only one it bothered, either. Hearing a low sound coming from somewhere near my feet, I looked down and saw Will's dog, Cavalier—who hadn't, as I'd thought, followed her master downstairs—crouching on the white carpet, growling softly up at Marco.

Really. Growling. At Marco.

He noticed, too, and said, in tones of disgust, "Leave me alone, you stupid mutt," to the dog.

Then Marco thrust me away from him, hard enough to cause me to stumble to my knees and have to grab hold of the banister to keep from falling.

But Cavalier stopped growling. She hurried over to me and licked my arm where he'd touched it.

"Oh, please," Marco said very sarcastically, when he observed this. Then, staring at me—my rapid breathing, my white-knuckled grip on the banister—he shook his head once more and said, "You aren't even supposed to be on his side. You're supposed to like the other one. What kind of lily maid are you, anyway?"

I just blinked at him. Lily maid? Oh, right. The Lily Maid of Astolat, which was another name for the Lady of

Shalott—the one I was named after. Funny.

Not.

And sort of random, for a guy with a tattoo.

"I don't know what you're talking about," I said, in a shaky voice. I felt a little bit braver with Cavalier beside me. "B-but I think you should leave Will alone."

Marco seemed to find this hilarious.

"You think I should leave *Will* alone?" he asked, in a voice dripping with derisive laughter. "Is *that* how it is, then? Christ, did Morton ever have it all wrong."

Morton? *Mr.* Morton? What was he talking about?

"You think what Will's going through *now* is bad?" Marco shook his head, the wolfish grin back, wider than ever. "Are you in for a surprise."

Then the door to the spare room opened, and Jennifer came out, tucking some of her hair back into the clip it had slipped out of.

"Hi, guys," Jennifer said breezily—too breezily. "Sorry, I was just on the phone with my mom. Somebody was looking for me?"

I just stared at her. I couldn't believe anyone could look so great, and be so . . .

Well, cold.

Then, when Marco didn't say anything, and Jennifer looked from him to me questioningly, I stammered, "Y-you need to move your car." I was still feeling sick to my stomach, but I tried not to let it show. "It's blocking their neighbor's driveway."

Jennifer looked blank. "But I parked in the Wagners'

driveway," she said.

I glanced at Marco. He winked.

"Sailing tomorrow's going to be fun," he said. "Don't you think, Elaine?"

CHAPTER TWELVE

And sometimes thro' the mirror blue
The knights come riding two and two:
She hath no loyal knight and true,
The Lady of Shalott.

Stacy and Liz weren't exactly thrilled about how long it took me to join them at the car.

"God, what'd you do?" Stacy said, when I finally staggered down the hill toward them. "Take the long way?"

"Sorry," I said to them. I really meant it, too. I *was* sorry.

Just not for the reason they thought.

I was quiet on the ride home. Maybe too quiet, since Liz asked, "Are you okay, Ellie?"

I said I was. Except I knew it was a lie. How could I be okay after what had happened?

Which was part of the problem. What exactly *had*

happened? I didn't even know, really.

So I had found out Jennifer was cheating on Will. With his best friend. So what? It didn't have anything to do with me.

And so what if I'd met Will's stepbrother and had had a fairly strange conversation with him? Big deal. Guys are weird in general. And guys whose fathers were killed by their mothers' new husbands are probably weirder than anybody. I mean, what did I expect?

But the thing with Marco just seemed—I don't know, *weirder* than anything that had ever happened to me. The way the dog had growled when he'd touched my arm. And the way he'd been talking to me as if we were continuing a conversation we'd had in the past—except that we had only just met! And what had that thing he'd said about the Lady of Shalott been all about? And his reference to Mr. Morton. What did Mr. Morton have to do with anything?

Unless . . .

"Hey," I said, leaning forward in the backseat of Stacy's car. "Who was the teacher Marco Campbell was supposed to have attacked?"

Liz was fiddling with Stacy's CD player, trying to find a track she liked. "I heard it was Mr. Morton."

"God, Liz!" Stacy burst out laughing. "Gossip much?"

"Well," Liz said defensively, "my mom heard it from Chloe Hartwell's mom who heard it from her cousin who's a dispatcher on the Annapolis police force."

"Oh," Stacy said, still laughing. "Then it must be true."

"Why did he do it?" I asked. "Try to kill Mr. Morton, I mean?"

Liz shrugged. "Who knows. Marco's not exactly all there, you know what I mean?"

Did I ever.

Stacy pulled up in front of my house and said, "Don't forget, you still have to let us know when you want to be initiated."

"I will," I said. "And thanks, you guys. For coming with me tonight."

"My first party with the In Crowd," Liz said with a sigh.

"And my last," Stacy said dryly. Then she waved, and they drove away.

When I got inside, my mom and dad were still up, watching the news.

"Hi, honey," my mom said. "How did it go? Did you have a nice time?"

"Great," I said. "I had fun. Avalon won. Tomorrow I'm going sailing with Will."

"That sounds nice," my mom said. "Is Will an experienced sailor?"

"Sure," I said, though technically I had no idea whether or not this was true—just that he and Lance had sailed up the coast over the summer.

"You're not going to wear that skirt on the boat, are you?" my dad called to me, as I ran up the stairs to my room.

"Don't worry, I won't," I called back. "'Night!"

Because after everything that had happened, the last

thing I wanted to do was sit around and chat with Mom and Dad. I needed . . . I needed . . .

I didn't know what I needed.

I showered, changed into my pajamas, and climbed into bed. Then I stared at the rose Will had given me. It was in full bloom now, its petals lustrous in the glow from my bedside lamp.

I was sleepy, and yet I knew if I turned out the light, I wouldn't doze off. I was too wired. All I could think about was Marco. How had he known I'd been named after Elaine, the Lily Maid? This is not a literary character with whom guys his age tended to be familiar.

And was that crack about my liking the wrong guy supposed to mean that it was Lance I should be in love with, not Will? Because Elaine had liked Lancelot?

God, how lame. It wasn't even funny. I love my parents and all, but why did they have to name me after someone so pathetic? The only thing my namesake and I had remotely in common was a mutual love of floating . . . although I preferred to do mine on a raft in a pool, whereas Elaine of Astolat favored floating to her death in a boat. . . .

I suppose, by Marco's reasoning, if I were Elaine, and Lance was Lancelot, that meant Jennifer was Guinevere. Which was kind of funny, actually, since the name Jennifer comes from the name Guinevere . . . just a little something you can't help knowing if you're the daughter of two medieval scholars.

And if you wanted to think along those lines—you

know, Lance being Lancelot, me being Elaine, and Jennifer being Guinevere—then Will could only be King Arthur. Which meant Marco had to be Mordred, the guy who ultimately kills Arthur and brings down Camelot, after the whole Guinevere thing.

Except from everything I'd read, Mordred was Arthur's half brother, not his stepbrother.

Still, all that, coupled with the fact that the school we all go to is Avalon High, home of the Excaliburs?

Freaky.

Maybe Marco hadn't meant it to be funny. Maybe he'd meant it *literally*.

Yeah. And maybe tomorrow, my dad would let me borrow the car and drive it by myself, without a licensed driver in the passenger seat.

Well, what did I care, anyway, if Will's stepbrother wanted to compare me to some chick who'd killed herself over a mythical knight from Camelot? As insults went, it wasn't even that cutting. He couldn't have known, of course, about my great antipathy toward all things medieval.

Which just made the whole thing even lamer.

Except . . .

Except that none of this explained the coldness of his fingers. Or the way Cavalier had reacted when Marco had touched me. Or what he'd meant about Mr. Morton. Or why Marco had wanted Will to find out about Lance and Jennifer in that horrible way. . . .

Still feeling a little sick, I rolled over and turned off

my bedside lamp. As I lay there in the semidarkness, I heard a thump. A second later, Tig joined me for her nightly snuggle.

Only tonight, for some reason, she couldn't seem to settle down. She kept sniffing where Cavalier had licked me—and Marco had touched me—even though I'd washed all those parts when I showered. When I peered at Tig in the moonlight that spilled in from behind my blinds, I could see she was wearing an expression Geoff called Cat Face—her mouth partly open, like she'd smelled something bad.

Then, giving my arm a last and final sniff, she threw me a look that clearly indicated I'd betrayed her somehow, then stalked off the bed and left to sleep elsewhere.

Which meant she was *really* peeved.

I lay there thinking to myself that things were really going great if my own cat didn't like me anymore. What had *happened* at that party, anyway? And what was I going to do about it?

What *could* I do, anyway? I mean, I supposed I could talk to Lance—I was going to have to talk to him, anyway, about the whole World Lit thing. Maybe while I was doing that, I could convince Lance to come clean with his friend. It had to be better for Will to find out that way than the way Marco had planned on having him find out. . . .

I wished I hadn't agreed to go sailing with Will and the rest of them the next day. I had no desire whatsoever to watch Will and Jennifer holding hands, however sweetly they did it, knowing that the whole thing—well, as far as Jennifer was concerned, anyway—was just a scam.

And I was fairly certain Marco was going to do something to upset everyone—or Will, at least—because he hadn't managed to do so successfully tonight.

But . . . but part of me wanted to go sailing with Will. The part of me that wanted to do anything with Will, just to be around him. The part of me that was in love with him, despite his having a girlfriend already. The part of me that, every time I saw a rose now, started thinking about Will. . . .

God, I had it bad.

Sadly, that part of me seemed to be stronger than the rest of me, since, when I woke up the next day, I knew without a doubt that I was going sailing with A. William Wagner and Company.

And not just so I could hang around with Will, either. I woke up feeling like it was my duty to go. Because—or so I told myself—that way I could keep an eye on Marco myself. He was definitely out to stir up trouble for his stepbrother.

Only . . . why? Why would he want to hurt Will in that way? I couldn't imagine that Will had done anything that hurtful to him. Was it just because of what had happened between their fathers? Was Marco really that resentful of Will's dad marrying his mom? I could sort of see why he would be, if the part about Admiral Wagner assigning Marco's dad to a post where he was sure to be killed or whatever was true. But why take it out on Will? It was Admiral Wagner he should be worried about punishing, if you ask me.

Just as he said he'd be, Will was waiting for me by the statue of Alex Haley that sits at the end of what the locals call Ego Alley, the city dock at the end of Main Street in downtown Annapolis. I could see as my parents and I pulled up why they call it Ego Alley . . . there are all these yachts there. And to get them out to sea, you have to sail them past all these outdoor cafés and bars where people sit along the water all day, watching the boats. It's like a fashion show at the mall or something, only with boats.

Alex Haley, who wrote the book *Roots*, must have lived in Annapolis, because the whole dock was devoted to him. There was a big statue of him, with these smaller statues of kids lying around on the ground beneath him, like he was reading them a story. Will was leaning against one of these kid statues, waiting for me.

The minute I saw him, my heart did that somersaulting thing inside my chest. That's because, for a second, I thought he was there alone . . . that, by some miracle, it would be just the two of us out on his boat. But then I saw Jennifer's golden head bob up. She and Lance and Marco were waiting in a rubber dinghy in the water just below the dock, the dinghy that would take us out to Will's boat, anchored a short distance offshore. My heart, instead of doing more gymnastics, fell.

It fell more when my parents decided to actually get

out of the car and go over and chat with Will, whom I guess they considered their big friend now, since they'd let Will chow down on all of our pad thai and wear my brother's bathing suit, and all.

"Hey," my dad said, leaning an elbow on Alex Haley's shoulder. "Nice day for a sail."

"Yes, sir," Will said, straightening up and smiling at us. He had on a pair of Ray-Bans to keep out the glare of the sun. The warm breeze tugged at his dark, curly hair and the open collar of his blue shirt. To me, he said, "Glad you could make it."

But before I had a chance to reply, my mom started asking Will all these worried questions, like how long he'd been sailing, and whether or not he had enough life preservers . . . that kind of thing. You know, the kinds of things you always wished your mom would ask the guy you have a major crush on when he's invited you to go sailing with him.

Not.

Will's answers must have satisfied my mom, since she finally grinned at me and said, "Well, have a nice time, Ellie." And my dad went, "See you later, kiddo." Then the two of them climbed back into the car and went to have brunch at Chick & Ruth's Delly.

I looked at Will and said, "Sorry."

"No problem," Will said, with a grin. "They care about you, is all. It's cute."

"Please just shoot me now," I begged him, and he laughed.

"Can we go?" Jennifer called from the dinghy. "We're losing prime tanning time."

"And God forbid the homecoming queen should be pasty," Marco said, causing Jennifer to take a playful whack at him. Lance, holding the rudder, just sat there grinning at the two of them, looking godlike in a throwback that showed off his grapefruit-sized biceps.

"I'm with Jen," he said—an unfortunate choice of words to those of us in the know. "I'm sick of these tourists staring at us."

It was true that some people wearing T-shirts that screamed DON'T HASSLE ME, I'M LOCAL had come up and were asking Will and me if we knew where the line to the *Woodwind*, the tour boat that went around the bay, was. Will showed them where they needed to go, then handed something to me that he took from the floor of the dinghy. It was a life preserver—not, thankfully, one of those big orange puffy ones that make the people who wear them look like the Pillsbury Doughboy, but a slim and stylish navy blue one.

I was busy fastening it when a group of kids about our own age showed up by the Haley statue and started piling into a small motorboat a few slips down from ours. They had one of those big inner tubes with them, and as they swung it into the boat, it bumped into the boat beside it—a much fancier one than ours, with an older man and woman in it, just getting ready to set out toward their yacht.

"Sorry," I heard one of the kids say, and he pulled the

inner tube back into his own boat.

"You're sorry?" The older man looked disgusted. And angry. "I'm sorry. Sorry they ever started letting people like you have the run of the place."

I stopped fastening my life preserver and just stood there, totally shocked. Nobody ever says things like that back in Minnesota.

"Hey, man," one of the other kids in the motorboat said. "He didn't mean anything—"

"Why don't you people go back where you came from?" the older man wanted to know, while his wife looked on, tight-lipped, her knees pressed firmly together.

"Why don't *you* go back where you came from?"

But this didn't come from any of the boys in the motorboat. It came, I was startled to realize, from Will.

The old man looked just as startled as I was. He flung Will a surprised look from beneath his little captain's hat, then said, in a disapproving voice, "I beg your pardon, young man, but I was born in this country—and so were my parents."

"Yeah, but were *their* parents?" Will asked him. "Because unless you're Native American, I don't think you can go around telling other people to go back to their country."

The wife's mouth dropped open at this. Then she elbowed her husband, and he furiously started his outboard motor.

"This used to be a *nice* place to live," the man said

pointedly, as he chugged away.

We watched as he and his wife made their way down Ego Alley . . . then exchanged glances.

"Some people," Will said to me mildly, "have more money than sense."

I sighed. "You can say that again."

Then Will handed me down into the boat. . . .

CHAPTER THIRTEEN

There the river eddy whirls,
And there the surly village-churls,
And the red cloaks of market girls,
Pass onward from Shalott.

Which wasn't easy, seeing as how there wasn't a whole lot of room in there. I sat down and found myself squashed between Marco and Lance, while Jennifer found herself in the uncomfortable—or enviable, depending how you looked at it—position of being crammed between Lance and Will.

Not that it appeared to bother her.

"What was that all about?" she wanted to know.

"Oh, that was just Will," Marco said, in a bored voice. "Playing the White Knight again."

"Ready?" Will asked, ignoring his stepbrother's jibe. "This is your last chance if you need something from shore. We won't be seeing land again for a while."

When no one protested, Will started the motor, and the motorboat began putt-putting toward the spot where Will's sailboat, the *Pride Winn*, was anchored in the harbor.

I knew right then that, in spite of that unpleasant scene in Ego Alley, I'd made the right decision in coming. Oh, not that it was such a pleasure to see Will and Jennifer sitting so close together that their shoulders touched (with Lance's shoulders brushing hers on her other side). Or that it was so fun to watch Marco make rude gestures at the people sitting in deck chairs outside the bars, watching us as we motored by (clearly no one had ever talked to Marco about Image).

It was just so nice to have the salt spray in my hair, and the cool bay breeze on my face. It felt good to feel the water rushing beneath us, and see the ducks, with their little lines of ducklings, hurrying out of the dinghy's path.

And then, when we finally got to Will's boat, seeing it sitting there, so long and gleaming, all glossy white with wood trim and a tall, slender mast, made even the unpleasantness back at the pier seem worth it.

There's lots you have to do on a sailboat, it turns out, before you can take it out to sea. So we scrambled around doing what Will, and sometimes Lance, told us to do. At least, Jennifer and I did. Marco seemed to do what he pleased, although a few of the things he did appeared to have something to do with getting the *Pride Winn* sea-ready.

Mostly, though, he just grinned at me whenever Jennifer, scrambling over the deck, would find Lance in her way, and have to say, "Excuse me," in a polite voice that I highly doubted she used when it was just the two of them together.

By the time we'd finally set sail, I was pretty sick of Marco's secret smiles at me. I'd been hoping to have a moment for a word alone with Lance before we set sail— a chance to tell him about Mr. Morton, and then casually slip in the fact that I was on to him and Jennifer . . . but even worse, so was Marco. And ask him if he could do something about it. Such as come clean to Will.

But it's not easy to find any privacy on even a fair-sized boat like the *Pride Winn*, and there was never a moment when I could speak to Lance without fear of someone overhearing.

And then when the sail suddenly billowed out and we were moving, gliding fast over the water, not even feeling the hot sun because of the cool ocean breeze, it was hard to feel worried about any of the stuff that had happened back on shore. Everyone seemed to feel the exhilaration of it, even the ever-sardonic Marco, who caught my eye and said, with a grin, "This is the life, eh?"

"Really," I said, meaning it, and thinking maybe I'd been wrong about him. Maybe he wasn't so bad after all. "You're so lucky."

"Lucky?" He looked at me curiously. "Why?"

"Well, because you've got a boat," I said. "All we've got is a station wagon."

He gave me a smile that actually looked sincere and said, "I'm not the lucky one. Will is. It's his boat. Until my mom married his dad . . . Well, we didn't even have a station wagon, let's put it that way."

And then the moment of warmth between us fizzled like sea spray when Marco suddenly shot Will a look I could only describe as . . . well, not nice. No, not a nice look at all.

But then Will, who hadn't noticed the look, asked, "What do you think, Elle? We gonna make a sailor out of you?"

And I forgot all about what Marco had said, because Will looked so handsome standing there at the wheel, with the wind pushing back his hair, calling me Elle.

"Absolutely," I said, meaning it. I was going to have to talk my parents into buying a boat. It would be hard, since they knew as much about the sea as they did about swimming pools. But this was really too good not to do on a regular basis. It even beat floating by a significant percentage. Because you can't have a picnic lunch while you're floating. Well, you can, but it's messy.

Marco's mom had packed all sorts of delicious stuff in this hamper, including crab rolls and a homemade potato salad that was even better than Red Hot and Blue's. There's something about being surrounded by blue water that makes you ravenous. As we ate, everybody talked about the party the night before and who had hooked up with whom (I noticed Jennifer talked about this the most—maybe in an attempt to ward off any discussion about where she had disappeared to for the majority of the party?) and who had been wearing what.

I made a mental note to tell Liz that this is what the In Crowd—the female members, anyway—does after parties . . . talk bad about everyone who showed up behind their backs.

It was only as lunch was winding down that I got a chance to ask Will something that had been bothering me. And that was what was up with the name of his boat.

Marco, hearing the question, laughed out loud.

"Yeah, man," he said to Will. "Tell her what *Pride Winn* means."

Will shot Marco a mock dirty look, then said, looking embarrassed, "It doesn't mean anything, actually. It's just a name that popped into my head when my dad and I first started talking about buying a boat. And it sort of stuck."

"Sounds like a grocery store," Lance said, his mouth full of crab roll.

Jennifer kicked him playfully in the foot. "That's Winn-Dixie," she said.

"Still a lame name for a boat," Lance said.

It wasn't until the conversation eventually drifted from fellow students at Avalon High to teachers that I remembered Mr. Morton, and, abandoning all hopes for a private word about it—and other things—with Lance, I said, "Oh, Lance, I almost forgot. Mr. Morton stopped me at the game and says he wants to see us in his classroom first thing tomorrow morning."

Lance looked up from the bag of barbecue chips he was polishing off.

"Are you serious?" he asked, with a pained expression on his face. "What for?"

"Um," I said, suddenly aware that everyone was listening to us, and feeling embarrassed. "I think something to do with our research paper proposal."

"Didn't you hand it in?" Lance asked, looking dismayed.

"Of course I did," I said. "It's just that . . . I don't know. He seemed to be able to tell somehow that you didn't have any part in writing it."

"Because it wasn't riddled with grammatical errors and run-on sentences like everything else Lance hands in?" Will teased.

"You know I'm not good with that stuff," Lance said, with a groan. "Aw, man. That blows."

"Sorry," I said. "He's all hot to trot on the whole working-with-your-partner thing."

"I wonder why," Marco said, in a tone that suggested he, for whatever reason, knew perfectly well why.

But when I looked his way to ask what he meant—not that I was so sure I wanted to know—I saw that Marco wasn't even paying attention anymore. Instead he was gazing out across the water at an ancient and very small motorboat that came chugging slowly by. After a second or two, I recognized it. It was one belonging to the same bunch of guys we'd seen down at the dock—the ones with the inner tube. The boat was so crowded that a couple of the pudgier guys—and none of them were actually all that slender—were sitting so far over the back of the boat, their backs were getting wet from its wake.

"Oh, hey," Marco said, observing this delightedly. "Check out the lardasses."

No one laughed. In fact, Will said, sounding tired, as if it were something he had to say a lot, "Marco. Cut it out."

But Marco ignored him.

"Watch this," he said.

And he reached for the wheel that Will had let go of in order to eat his lunch.

"Marco," Will said, as Marco started to swing our boat around. "Leave 'em alone."

But Marco only laughed and set the *Pride Winn* on what appeared—to me, anyway—to be a collision course with the tiny boat.

"That craft does not appear to be seaworthy, Will," Marco said. "I just want to make sure they realize the error of their ways."

But it looked to me like he was going to do a lot more than that . . . especially as the motorboat's driver, realizing Marco had no intention of turning, suddenly jammed his wheel to the right, causing the boat to lurch abruptly to one side. . . .

. . . and causing one of the guys on the back of the boat—the chubbiest one—to fall overboard.

"Did you see that?" Marco cried, laughing. "Oh my

God, that was hilarious!"

"Real funny, Marco," Will said, as we watched the kid flounder in the frothy white wake.

"Hey," Jennifer said. "He doesn't have on a life preserver."

And then, as the other guys on the motorboat clustered around the side of the craft, trying to pull the chubby kid back up, we saw his spiky crew-cut bob once . . . then twice . . . then finally disappear altogether beneath the waves.

"Great," Will said angrily, pulling off his deck shoes. "Thanks a lot, Marco."

And then, before any of us could say anything, Will had dived from the side of the *Pride Winn*, his long, lean body vanishing as the dark water closed over it.

CHAPTER FOURTEEN

And moving thro' a mirror clear
That hangs before her all the year,
Shadows of the world appear.
There she sees the highway near
Winding down to Camelot:

This wasn't the clear, still water of my pool back home.

This was deep, opaque seawater, choppy with waves. There were probably sharks down there. And riptides. As Will's head disappeared beneath the dark surface, I sucked in my breath, wondering if he'd ever resurface.

I wasn't the only one, apparently, with this concern. Lance, scanning the waves for some sign of Will, growled at Marco, as menacingly as Cavalier had the night before.

"If anything happens to him," Lance snarled, "you're a dead man."

"If anything happens to him, your life'll get a whole lot easier," Marco said evenly. "Won't it?"

I saw Lance's face flush darkly, then noticed him exchange glances with Jennifer. On her pretty face was an expression of naked fear—but was it fear for Will? Or fear for herself, over what Marco had said?

A second later, Will's dark head popped up from the waves. Then he began swimming, with long, hard strokes, toward the spot where Crew-cut Kid had disappeared.

"Turn us around," Jennifer commanded Marco, in a sharp voice I couldn't help but admire. She, at least, wasn't taking any guff from this guy.

"Fine," Marco said, his jaw tightening, twisting the *Pride Winn*'s wheel. Then, noticing that I was staring at him, he grinned. "I don't get what the big deal is. They're just a bunch of tourists."

Then, when I just glared at him, he said, "Joke! I'm joking. God, nobody around here can take a joke. Remember that, new girl."

"Maybe it's just *your* jokes," I said. "They aren't really very funny."

The motorboat's driver had cut his engines, and now he, as well as most of his passengers, were clinging to the side of the craft, scanning the water for some sign of the missing boy. Will, reaching the spot where Crew-cut Kid had gone under, disappeared once more beneath the waves.

"Where are they?" Jennifer, standing beside me, reached out and took my arm and squeezed, staring tensely at the water. "Where *is* he?"

And I felt a surge of guilt for every mean thought I'd ever had about her. Because her anxiety was real. No one is that good of an actress. Yeah, she was in love with Lance. But I got the feeling that a part of her—a big part—still loved Will as well . . . and would probably always love Will, no matter what ended up happening between them. . . .

. . . or what ended up happening now.

I'd been looking at Jennifer—at her pretty face transfixed with anxiety, her blue-eyed gaze scanning the water. Suddenly, I saw her expression change. She smiled and flushed with relief.

I glanced back at the water to see that Will was towing Crew-cut Kid—sputtering seawater—back toward the motorboat.

"Thank God," Jennifer said, and seemed to sag against me. Lance had gone visibly pale beneath his dark tan. Marco, for his part, yawned and went to open a new can of Coke for himself.

We sat in tense silence until Will returned. At least, Jennifer and I did. Lance kept up a running commentary on what was going on over on the other boat: "Okay, they got the kid back on board. He's heaving up a lot of saltwater, but he'll probably be fine. Looks like Will's gonna swim on back. Okay, here he comes. . . ."

Marco just ate another crab roll and fiddled around with the radio, trying to find a station that wasn't playing oldies. When Jennifer looked at him in annoyance, he went, "What?" all innocently, like he couldn't imagine what was wrong with her.

When Will finally got back to the *Pride Winn*, his face was tensely drawn.

"They're not going to call the harbor police," Will said, after Lance had helped him back onto the deck.

Marco made a derisive sound. "Why should they?" he wanted to know. "Then the cops would know they were flagrantly flaunting shipboard safety regulations, cramming that many people onto such a small boat. Besides, it was that stupid kid's own fault. He shouldn't have been sitting so—"

"That 'stupid kid' nearly drowned," Will interrupted, his blue eyes crackling. "Come on, Marco. What were you thinking?"

"Gee, I don't know." Marco lifted a single brow. "Maybe I just couldn't take the tension anymore."

"What tension?" Will asked exasperatedly.

"The sexual tension," Marco replied.

And I saw his dark-eyed gaze flick toward Jennifer, who stood near the bow. She had been getting a towel for Will, but now she froze, the towel limp in her hands, watching Marco warily.

"Oh, don't tell me you haven't felt it," Marco said, glancing from Will to me to Lance and then to Jennifer, and then back again. "My God, it was making me nuts!"

"I think," I said loudly, certain I knew what was coming next, and wanting to avoid it at all costs, "that we should go back now. Don't you, Jennifer?"

Jennifer hadn't taken her eyes off Marco. It was like

she was watching . . . well, a snake, wondering if it was the nice kind, like the one I'd fished from the pool, or the deadly kind that was going to send her into a coma.

"Yeah," she said, at last. "I agree with Ellie. I think we should go."

Lance started to say something, but happened to glance at Jennifer. She must have sent him a warning look—although I didn't see it—because he fell silent. Will, who'd crossed to take the towel from Jennifer and now stood with it around his neck, said, sublimely ignorant of what was *really* going on, "The girls want to go, we'll go. Lance, let's take down the sail. I think we should power back—"

"Oh, right," Marco burst out, as Lance began untying the knots that held the sail in place. "Better take down the sail, Lance. Better not think for yourself, Lance."

Lance suggested that Marco do something I'm not entirely sure was anatomically possible.

Will glared at Marco with dangerously narrowed eyes.

"What is your *problem*?" he asked his stepbrother, in the same voice I'd heard him use with the jock, that day outside Mr. Morton's classroom. It was so cold, it seemed to come from the very depths Will had just snatched that kid out of. It scared me a little.

"What's *my* problem?" Marco let out a bitter laugh. "Why don't you ask Lance what *his* problem is?"

"Because I don't *have* a problem, Campbell," Lance said. "Except for the one I've got with you."

But Marco just laughed some more at that.

"Oh, right," he said. "I forgot. You like being Will's lapdog, doing everything he tells you to."

Lance was beginning to flush. "I don't—"

"Oh yes, you do, man," Marco said. His voice dropped into a somewhat uncanny imitation of Will's: *"Take the sail down, Lance. Tackle that lineman, Lance. Gotta protect the QB, Lance."* Then, in his own voice, he said, "God, it's no wonder you couldn't take it anymore. I don't blame you, man. I really don't."

My heart starting to pound, I looked at Lance, silently begging him not to respond—

But it was too late.

"I don't know what you're talking about," Lance began, the muscles in his neck bunching menacingly. "But—"

"Just ignore him, Lance," Jennifer said quickly. "He's just trying to cause trouble."

"I'm causing trouble?" Marco flung a disbelieving look in Jennifer's direction. "You think *I'm* the one causing trouble? What about you?" he demanded. "Why don't you ask your precious friend Lance here where he was during most of your party last night, Will? Huh? Go ahead. Ask him."

Jennifer blanched, while Lance's flush, on the other hand, increased. But he managed to choke out, "You don't know what you're talking about, Campbell."

"Really, Marco," Jennifer said, her voice sounding uncomfortably shrill. "Just because you don't have any friends of your own—"

"Yeah, well, then I'm a lot better off than old Will here, aren't I?" Marco's smile was snide. "I mean, with friends like you guys, who needs—"

"Marco," I said, taking a step toward him, my heart in my throat. "Don't."

"You really do have it bad, don't you, Lily Maid?" Marco's gaze on me was almost pitying. "But you still don't seem to realize you've fallen for the wrong one. . . ." Then he raised his eyebrows. "Or is Lance the one you're trying to protect, and not Will?"

Lance went for him then. I doubt he even knew what Marco was talking about. But to Lance, it clearly didn't matter. The QB was under attack, and it was Lance's job to protect him—even if, as in this case, the fault was all his own. Lance lunged—all two hundred pounds of hard muscled guard, aimed at Marco's gut.

Who knows what would have happened if the two of them had connected? Surely at the velocity Lance was moving, they'd have both plunged over the side of the deck and into the cold water of the bay.

But they didn't connect. Because at the last possible moment, Will reached out to seize Lance, pinning both his arms behind his back.

Meanwhile, a slim, tanned shadow slipped in front of Marco, crying, "Stop it! All of you! Just stop it!" Jennifer's voice broke off with a sob.

"Campbell started it." Lance hurled the words at the world in general, breathing hard as Will struggled to hold him back.

"Oh, I think we all know who started it," Marco said insinuatingly.

"Have you both gone insane?" Will wanted to know.

"Don't listen to him, Will," Jennifer cried urgently. "Everything he says is a lie, and always has been."

"Oh, that's rich coming from you, Jen," Marco sneered. "Why don't you just tell him where you were last night when he looked all over the house but couldn't find you? Why don't you tell him?"

Will had let go of Lance now. Not because Lance had stopped struggling to be set free. But because it was like suddenly Will forgot to hold on.

"What's he talking about?" Will asked, looking from Jennifer to Lance with a stunned expression on his face. Then, when neither of them replied right away, he said, "Wait. Why do you guys look so—"

"Because they're in love," Marco said, with obvious relish. "They've been seeing each other behind your back for months now, while you just—"

CHAPTER FIFTEEN

Or when the moon was overhead,
Came two young lovers lately wed;
"I am half sick of shadows," said
The Lady of Shalott.

Marco never got to finish his sentence. Because Lance, without Will to hold him back, flung himself at Marco with all his might. The two of them crashed to the deck of the *Pride Winn* with enough force to cause the boat to lurch. I had to grab on to some rigging to keep from falling overboard at the impact of their bodies.

By the time I righted myself, Lance had managed to subdue Marco. All it took, apparently, was a single blow to the face. Marco lay in a ball, moaning.

I can't say I felt too sorry for him.

But Will. Will, on the other hand, my heart went out to at once. Because he had fallen back onto one of the boat's padded benches as if his legs had simply given out beneath him, his face as white as the sail snapping above us, despite his tan.

"It's not true," Jennifer was saying to him. She had hold of both his shoulders, and was crying. Really crying. And not prettily, either, the way the cheerleaders at my old school had cried after losing a game or whatever. There was actual snot involved.

"He's lying," Jennifer was saying, in an impassioned voice. "We would never do that to you. Would we, Lance?"

When Lance didn't answer right away, Jennifer flung a nervous glance at him.

"Would we, Lance?" she repeated. "Lance?"

But Lance still didn't answer. That's because he was standing in the middle of the boat deck, his fists at his side, staring at a point just between Will's feet. As I stood there watching, Lance slowly lifted his head, as if he were straining beneath a great weight, until, finally, his gaze met Will's.

And then Lance said the words that were to change everything forever after:

"It's true."

One of Jennifer's hands flew to her mouth. She swung her stricken gaze from Lance to Will—both of whom were completely immobile—and then back again.

No one spoke. No one breathed. The ocean breeze snapped at the sail above our heads, but that was the only sound on the *Pride Winn* . . . except for the tinny noise from the radio Marco had been playing with earlier.

Finally Jennifer took her hand away from her mouth and said in a voice I will never forget, it was so filled with genuine sorrow and remorse: "Will. Will. I'm so sorry."

Will didn't even look her way. He was still staring at Lance.

"We couldn't help it," Lance said, with a shrug of his heavy bare shoulders. "We tried not to. Honest, Will."

Jennifer, tears running freely down her face, said, "We did. Really. We were going to tell you. But with everything—well, with your dad, and . . . Well, there just never seemed to be a right time—"

"Is there ever a right time?" Marco inquired nasally from where he lay with his hands over his face. "To tell a guy you're scamming on his girl, I mean?"

"Shut up, Marco," I said.

Marco took his hands from his face and looked at me with a lopsided smile. One side of his mouth was rapidly swelling.

But I had no interest in whatever he was about to say. I had eyes only for the scene unfolding in front of me.

"Will." Lance still stood where he was, his gaze never having strayed from his friend's face. "Say something, man. Anything. Or hit me. I don't care. I deserve it. Just . . . do something."

Will was the one who lowered his gaze first. He looked down at his bare feet. He hadn't yet had a chance to put on the shoes he'd shed to dive overboard and save the Crew-cut Kid's life.

When he spoke, his voice was devoid of any emotion

at all. It was still as cold as the sea.

"Let's go back," he said.

And he got up to start undoing the main sail.

The ride home was terrible. Terrible and silent. Well, except for Marco, who complained bitterly about his split lip, until I fished out one of the cooler packs and handed it to him, just to shut him up.

There's as much to do, it turns out, when you're coming back from a sailing trip as when you're heading out on one. So we wrapped and tied and cleaned and put things away, all in utter silence—except for when Will asked one of us to do something . . . and Marco, of course, who continued to whine about his lip and how everyone shoots the messenger—until finally, when the *Pride Winn* was safely anchored in the harbor, Will said, "Let's head to shore."

So we climbed into the motorboat and headed for shore. We were probably the soberest group ever to head down Ego Alley. As the afternoon had worn on, more and more people had gathered in the deck chairs belonging to the bars around the dock. I could feel the tourists' envious gazes on us as we motored by. They all sat there in their white slacks and loafers, clutching beers and diet sodas, with no idea that in our boat—the one going by them right at that very moment, the one they were so jealous of—three hearts were breaking.

I wasn't counting my own heart, even though it seemed to hurt a little more every time I looked at Will's drawn face. As Marco put it, when he turned to help me from the dinghy once we reached shore, "Don't look so stricken, Lily Maid. This doesn't have anything to do with you and me."

"Which is exactly why," I said to him, "you should have stayed out of it."

"Hey, you had your chance at Lancelot," he said. "It's not my fault you blew it."

How was I even supposed to reply to that?

Behind us, Will was lashing the boat to a nearby mooring post. Jennifer reached out and tried to touch his shoulder.

"Will," she said, in a voice that—in my opinion, anyway—could have melted the hardest heart.

But Will just turned away and started walking toward his car.

He and Marco had apparently come in the same vehicle together, since the latter gave me a courtly bow and said, "It was a pleasure, Lady Elaine," before trailing after Will's departing figure.

Which left me alone with Jennifer and Lance, neither of whom seemed to be able to look at me . . . or at each other.

"Um," I said. Since it seemed like someone needed to say something. "Well. I better go. So. Bye."

They didn't even acknowledge me. I left them standing there together by the statue of Alex Haley. I don't think I'd be exaggerating, either, if I said it looked to me as if the bottom had just fallen out of both their worlds.

I called my parents from a pay phone on the corner and asked them to come pick me up. They seemed surprised to hear from me so soon . . . it was only a few hours since I'd left, and I'd led them to believe I'd be gone through dinner.

But when they asked me what had happened as I climbed into the car, I just shook my head. I didn't want to talk about it. I *couldn't* talk about it.

They didn't press me . . . even when, five minutes after getting home, I came down the stairs from my bedroom and walked past them in my bikini, headed for my raft.

To give them credit, they didn't say anything like, "Not again," or "I thought we'd finally moved on from the floating thing."

Instead, Mom just went, "Pizza for dinner okay, Ellie?"

And I nodded my assent.

Then I went outside.

The sun had disappeared beneath a towering column of gray clouds, but I didn't care. I climbed onto my raft and lay there, staring up at the leaves above my head.

I couldn't believe what I'd just witnessed. I really couldn't.

The thing is, stuff like that just doesn't happen to me. I mean, not that any of it had anything to do with me—Marco was right about that, anyway.

But the fact that I'd *been* there . . . that I'd seen it all happen. That was what I couldn't believe.

I knew why Marco had done it. And I couldn't say I blamed him, really.

But to have done it like that—in front of Lance and Jennifer . . . in front of me. Well, that hadn't really been necessary.

But then, Marco probably felt that way about the death of his dad.

I hoped Will was going to be all right. But really, what could I do to help him? Nothing, I guess. Except be his friend. Except be there for him. Except—

—go to the ravine, where I was sure he'd have gone after what had happened, and ask him if there was anything I could do.

Yeah, that was it. I needed to go to the arboretum. Now. Right now . . .

But no sooner had this thought occurred to me than I'd opened my eyes, and saw Will sitting on top of Spider Rock, looking down at me.

CHAPTER SIXTEEN

A red-cross knight for ever kneel'd
To a lady in his shield,
That sparkled on the yellow field,
Beside remote Shalott.

I didn't scream this time. I can't even say I was all that surprised to see him. It seemed almost natural, in a way I couldn't explain, that he'd be there.

He'd changed out of the wet clothes he'd worn on the boat. Now he was in jeans and a different T-shirt.

But he was wearing the exact same expression he'd had the last time I'd seen him . . . an expression completely devoid of any emotion whatsoever. I couldn't see his eyes, because he still wore his sunglasses, even though the sun was hidden behind the clouds.

But I suspected that even if I could have seen his eyes, they'd have been as unreadable as the rest of his face. Even his voice, when he finally spoke, seeing that

I'd opened my eyes at last, was totally neutral.

"Did you know?" he asked me tonelessly.

No "Hi." No "How are you, Elle?"

Not that I supposed I deserved one, since I had known and hadn't told him. Still. I wasn't going to lie to him. He'd been lied to enough. So I said simply, "Yes."

No reaction. At least, not any that I could see.

"That's why you were acting so weird last night?" he asked me. "At the party. Outside the spare room. You knew they were in there?"

"Yes," I said, though it felt as if the word had been wrenched from me.

But what else could I say? It was the truth.

I leaned up on my elbows, expecting recriminations . . . prepared for them, even. I deserved them. If nothing else, Will and I were friends, and friends don't let friends . . . well, not know that their girlfriend is cheating on them with their best friend.

But to my surprise, he didn't say any of the things I expected him to. There was no demanding *How could you not have told me?* or *What kind of person are you?*

I should have known there wouldn't be, of course. Will wasn't like everybody else. Will wasn't like *anybody* else I'd ever met before.

Instead, he said, in that same neutral voice, "It's weird. I feel like I already knew, in a way."

I blinked at him. This was not what I'd expected him to say. "Wait," I said, thrown. "What? Really?"

"Really," he said. "While it was happening, I was kind

of like . . . *Oh, yeah. Sure. Of course.* To tell you the truth—I kind of felt . . . relieved." He took off his sunglasses then, and looked at me. *Really* looked at me.

And I could see that he didn't look hurt, or devastated, or even sad. He just looked sort of . . . thoughtful.

"That sounds screwed up, doesn't it?" he asked. "That I felt relieved. That my girlfriend and my best friend are sneaking around together behind my back. Who would feel relieved about finding out something like that?"

I didn't know what to say. Because I knew exactly what he was talking about.

What I didn't know was . . . well, *how* I knew this.

"Maybe . . ." I said slowly, feeling my way. "Maybe you felt that way because you know, deep down, that they're meant for each other. That it's . . . right? Lance and Jen, I mean. Don't get me wrong—she really does love you, Will. Lance, too. More than anything. You can tell. But that also might be . . . well, why they belong together."

I glanced at him to see whether or not he agreed with this—or if he even understood it, because I wasn't sure I did.

"Not that you and Jen didn't make a good couple," I added, because he still hadn't said anything. I was probably babbling, but what else was I supposed to do? I mean, he had come to *me*. Of all the people in the world he knew, he'd come to *me* in his hour of need. I had to say *something*. "I mean, Jen's totally nice, and stuff. But—"

"I could never really talk to her," Will interrupted.

167

"Not about stuff that mattered. It was like she didn't want to hear it. Gossip and clothes and stuff. That was fine. But when it came to talking about how I felt about things—things like . . . well, that stuff you and I talked about, my dad, and the woods, and the widow's walk . . . things outside of football and school and the mall, or whatever—she just . . . she just didn't understand."

He didn't add, *the way you do, Elle.*

But that was okay. He'd come to me, hadn't he? He was sitting here with me. In my backyard. Next to my pool. On Spider Rock.

And okay, maybe he was only here because I'm a virtual stranger, and it's easier sometimes to talk about stuff with strangers than it is with people you know.

And yeah, probably he only thinks of me as a friend— a friend who makes him laugh—and not the way I think of him—as the man with whom I want to spend the rest of my life someday.

But that's okay. That's totally okay. Because with Will, I was willing to take what I could get. And if friendship was all he had to offer, well, it was more than enough.

So when he asked what he did next—which was, "So what are you doing for dinner tonight?"—in a voice that was completely devoid of self-pity or anything, really, I said, "I don't know. I think my mom's ordering pizza," in a kind of stunned way.

To which he replied, "Do you think your parents would mind if I took you out? I know a place that makes a mean crab dip."

"Um," I said. "No, I don't think they'd mind." Not that I'd have cared if they did.

They didn't. Which was how I found myself dining with A. William Wagner once again. How I made him laugh over the plate of steaming hot crab dip we shared at Riordan's downtown, by doing what I considered a brilliant imitation of Ms. Schuler, the track coach. How I almost made him choke on his Moose Tracks ice cream at Storm Brothers while I told him the story of the time I stuck the red hot up my nose when I was four, just to hear him laugh again, and then about the time I decided to cut my own hair and ended up looking just like Russell Crowe in *Gladiator*.

Then, because I had trig homework, and he said he had physics, we went back to my house and sat down at the dining room table to work together, since he showed no signs of being ready to leave for home.

Not that I blamed him, really. I mean, what did he have to go home to, really? A father who wanted something for him that Will didn't want for himself, and a stepbrother who'd taken absolute glee in revealing something that, yeah, maybe had needed to be revealed . . . but not the way he'd done it.

My dad came in at one point while we were working and asked me if I could pull a staple out of his thumb, because Mom was in the shower. It was only one of those mini staples little kids use, because those are the only ones we keep around since everyone in my family is so accident prone, so there wasn't a lot of blood. I pulled the staple out, and my dad went away again. I started to go back to my homework, then realized Will had stopped writing. I looked up, and caught him staring at me.

"What?" I asked, lifting a hand to my nose. "Do I have something on my face?"

"No," Will said, with a smile. "It's just . . . the way you are with your parents. I've never had that with anyone, let alone my dad."

"Because your dad is probably capable of stapling something without getting his thumb in the way," I pointed out dryly.

"No," Will said. "It's not that. It's the way you talk to each other. Like you—I don't know. Actually care about what happens to the other person."

"Your dad cares what happens to you," I assured him, secretly feeling that I'd like to grab Admiral Wagner and shake him a few times. "Maybe not in the way you want him to. But, I mean, that's the whole reason behind his wanting you to go into the military. Because he cares about you and thinks that's what would be best for you."

"But he wouldn't think that," Will insisted, "if he'd ever bothered to get to know me. If he knew me at all— if he had ever bothered to stop and talk to me on the way out to one of his millions of meetings—he'd know that I think that . . . well, that bending an enemy's will through military force is the absolute *last* way a nation ought to go about solving their problems."

I couldn't help feeling a stronger rush of admiration than usual for Will at that moment. I mean, bending an enemy's will by force? Problem solving? The guy was discussing stuff I'd never heard anyone close to my own age talking about before. Geoff and his friends had always talked almost exclusively about Xbox and whatever girl in school was wearing the shortest skirt at the moment.

"Have you ever told your dad that?" I asked him. "I mean, that you feel that way? Because he might surprise you, you know."

Will just shook his head. "You don't know him," he said flatly.

"What about your stepmom?" I asked. "Do you two get along?"

"Jean?" Will shrugged. "Yeah."

"Well, why don't you tell her," I suggested, "what you told me? Then maybe, if you can get her on your side, she can work on softening up your dad. He may not want to listen to you, but he'd probably listen to his wife, right?"

Will's eyes seemed to glint an even stronger blue than ever as he gazed at me.

"That's a good idea," he said . . . and don't think I didn't blush at his praise, although I ducked my head, hoping my hair would hide my cheeks. "I can't believe I never thought of that."

"Well, you aren't used to having two parents," I said. "When you've grown up with both a mom and a dad, you learn how to play one against the other. It's something of an art."

"I can't imagine," Will said, with a grin, "your dad

ever saying no to you about anything."

"He doesn't, really," I agreed. "But my mom . . . she's a lot tougher."

Then I felt something warm and heavy fall across my fingers. When I looked up, I was surprised to see that Will had laid one of his hands over mine.

"Like you," he said.

"I'm not tough," I said, thinking that if he knew how his mere touch had made my heartbeat stagger, he'd realize how not tough I really am.

Will's fingers didn't loosen their hold.

"It's not a bad thing," he said. "It's one of the things I like best about you, in fact. I wouldn't want to get on your bad side, though."

As if you ever could, was what I wanted to say. Only I couldn't, because I was too stunned. Not just by what he'd said about liking me—he said he likes me!—but by what I'd felt, the moment his fingers touched mine, which was the exact opposite of the coldness I'd felt at Marco's touch—a sudden jolt of white-hot electricity that had raced up and down my arm. . . .

I didn't know what kind of connection the two of us had, if any—why he'd thought he'd known me, when we'd never met before, and why he felt he could tell me things he couldn't tell anyone else . . . or why I loved him so fiercely, I was ready to protect him from anything, even himself.

But I wasn't about to question it. Especially not now that he was free. True, I'm no cheerleader. I'm not blond or perky, and the only reason I turn heads when I walk into a room is because I'm generally the tallest girl there.

But out of everyone he knew, Will had come to me. Whether he'd felt the jolt when he touched my hand or not—whether he thought of me as just a friend or maybe something more—nothing would ever change the fact that *I* was the one he'd come to when he'd needed someone most.

He let go of my hand after that, and said, holding his pencil like it was a cigar, and doing a very, very bad imitation of Humphrey Bogart from *Casablanca*, "Elle, I think this is the beginning of a beautiful thing."

"Friendship," I corrected him, trying not to let him see how deeply his words had thrilled me. "The line is—"

"Whatever," Will said, in the same bad Humphrey Bogart imitation. "Get to work." And he tapped my homework with his pencil/cigar.

Grinning, I bent over my logarithms. I don't think I'd ever been happier in my life.

What I didn't know then was that what he'd said about this being the beginning of a beautiful thing? Yeah. Not true.

It was actually the *middle* of something that had been going on for a long time . . . something that most definitely wasn't beautiful. Something that was about as ugly as can be.

And something that was about to snowball beyond anyone's control.

CHAPTER SEVENTEEN

Out flew the web and floated wide;
The mirror crack'd from side to side;
"The curse is come upon me!" cried
The Lady of Shalott.

I was the first one into Mr. Morton's classroom the next morning. Not even Mr. Morton himself was there yet. I sat down in a seat in the front row, glancing at the clock on the wall. It was seven forty. First period started in twenty minutes.

So where was Lance?

When Mr. Morton rolled in, at seven forty-five, Lance still hadn't shown up. Mr. Morton, neat in his bow tie and herringbone jacket—too warm, I thought, for Annapolis, this time of year—put down his steaming mug of coffee, his newspaper, and his briefcase, and pulled the chair out from behind his desk.

He sat, but didn't open the paper or sip his coffee.

Instead, like me, he stared at the clock.

Though I doubt Mr. Morton was thinking the same thoughts I was. I was having a not unpleasant time remembering the evening before . . . the way Will, done with his own homework, had leaned over and swiped mine and started doing logarithms for me. The way he'd smiled when my dad had finally come downstairs and said, "Kid. It's eleven o'clock. Go home already, will ya?" The way Will had said, "See you tomorrow, sir," to my dad . . . which could only have meant he was planning on coming over again.

Seven fifty.

"You told him, didn't you?" Mr. Morton wanted to know. "Mr. Reynolds?"

"Of course I did," I said. "He'll be here."

Except that I was beginning to think that maybe he wouldn't. Maybe he'd forgotten. So much had happened since the day before . . . not just to me, but to Lance, as well. After all, he may have gained a girlfriend, but he'd also lost his best friend . . . or so he probably thought, anyway, since I assumed Will hadn't called him up and said, *No hard feelings, buddy*.

At least, as of eleven o'clock last night, he hadn't.

Not that Will wasn't going to. He'd talked about it the night before, between logarithms. He didn't feel he could exactly hold a grudge against Lance and Jennifer if all he'd felt, upon hearing that the two of them were involved, was relief. I'd commented that this would be a grave disappointment to the rumor-mongers of the school—Liz, in particular, though I didn't mention her by name—who would be expecting some dramatic snubbing in the cafeteria.

Will had just laughed and said that he would never do anything that might deprive the student population of Avalon High of their right to be entertained, so maybe he'd wait a day or two before publicly forgiving the pair.

But Lance, of course, didn't know this. I knew he cared about Will, and that the guilt over what he'd done to him had to be eating him up inside.

Considering what had to be going on inside his head at the moment, it wasn't likely Lance was going to remember a meeting with a teacher.

"Maybe I should have called to remind him," I said apologetically to Mr. Morton. "He's, um, got a lot on his mind right now."

"What he's going to have," Mr. Morton said severely, "is another flunking grade in this class, to match the one he got in it last year."

"Oh, don't do that," I couldn't help crying out. "He's having a really hard time right now."

"I'm not interested in hearing about the trials and tribulations of Avalon High's star guard," Mr. Morton said, in a tired voice. "I'm sure he's very sorry for what he let happen to Mr. Wagner during Saturday night's game, but that isn't any of my affair."

"I'm not talking about that," I said. "I mean, there was this whole blowup with his best friend and his girlfriend, and—"

"I would imagine any blowup between Mr. Reynolds's best friend and his girlfriend would hardly be any of Mr. Reynolds's concern." Mr. Morton raised one gray eyebrow. "And certainly would not excuse his absence here."

"That's just it." I felt stupid telling a teacher stuff that really wasn't any of his business. On the other hand, I really did feel Lance had a legitimate reason to have forgotten our meeting. "He *caused* the blowup. Lance did. I mean, it's not really his fault—well, I guess it sort of is. But I don't think he could help it any more than Jen could." Then, seeing that Mr. Morton was staring at me sort of incredulously, I realized I was babbling, and said, "Look, the whole thing's this huge mess, and he probably just forgot. Is there any chance we could reschedule for tomorrow? I swear I'll—"

I broke off, because Mr. Morton's face had suddenly gone as gray as his beard.

He looked like he was going to be sick.

"Mr. Morton?" I rose from my desk in some alarm. "Are you all right? Do you want me to get you some water or something?"

Mr. Morton had risen from his chair. Now he stood clutching the edge of his desk like it was the only thing keeping him upright, murmuring something. When I hurried up to him and leaned closer to hear what it was—I thought maybe he was whispering for me to call nine-one-one—I was surprised to hear him saying, "Too late. Started . . . so soon. I had no idea. We're too late. Entirely too late."

I glanced at the clock.

"We're not too late, Mr. Morton," I said confusedly. "There are still five more minutes until the bell—"

Then he looked up.

And I stumbled back a step. Because I had never seen as much despair—coupled with a strong dose of fear—in anyone's eyes as I saw in Mr. Morton's at that moment.

"It's happened already, hasn't it?" he rasped. "She's with him? With Reynolds?"

I swallowed. I'd expected there to be some gossiping about what had happened between Will and Jennifer and Lance. When I'd climbed onto the bus that morning, I'd heard a few people murmuring that Avalon High's It Couple had broken up, although no one—at least if Liz's very direct questioning of me was any indication—appeared to know why.

But for a teacher to take such an interest in his students' love lives? It seemed a little bizarre. Mr. Morton looked positively suicidal. His pale gray eyes, peering out from beneath slightly craggy brows, had a beaten look to them, as if they'd seen something almost too heartbreaking to bear.

"Um," I said. "Do you mean Jennifer Gold? Because she and Lance are . . . well, they're together now." And then, because it was what I'd told Will he should say to everyone, if he wanted to prove he really was relieved, like he'd said, about the two of them being together, I added, "And Will is really happy for them."

But this didn't seem to have the desired effect, since

Mr. Morton blanched even more.

"He knows, then? About them?"

"Well," I said. I couldn't, for the life of me, figure out what was going on here. Since when did a teacher care so much about whether or not a high school's It Couple had broken up? Then again, this was Mr. Morton, the most beloved teacher in the school—to some people, anyway. The ones who didn't want to kill him, the way Marco had.

"Um," I said. "Yeah. I mean, yes. Will knows. He found out yesterday. But"—I added hastily, when Mr. Morton's face crumpled—"he's fine with it. Really."

Mr. Morton sank slowly back into his desk chair. He sagged there, a look of hopeless desolation on his face.

"We're doomed," he whispered, to the wall.

Which was when I decided that this? Yeah, this was probably not normal. Even for Mr. Morton.

I didn't know what to do. Mr. Morton appeared to be having some kind of breakdown right in front of me.

But why? Why should Mr. Morton care so much about who Jennifer Gold was dating?

Then I remembered where I'd last seen Mr. Morton. At the game.

And suddenly, it all made sense. Well, sort of.

"Really, Mr. Morton," I said. "I think you're overreacting. Lance and Will are good friends. They'll probably only emerge stronger because of this. And, you know, you really shouldn't worry so much about it."

Mr. Morton lifted his head to look at me. His lips, I

saw, were moving, but no sound was coming out. Then, slowly, he seemed to find his voice.

"I tried," he wheezed, his face as white as the chalk marks on the board behind him. "They can't say I didn't try. I did my best to bring the two of you together. But we were simply too late . . . too late. . . ."

His expression was one of the bleakest I had ever seen.

"They've won," he continued. "They've won again."

"Mr. Morton," I said, in what I hoped was a soothing voice, "I really think you're making too big a deal out of this. Avalon's still got a very good chance at making the district football finals. Will and Lance'll work it, out. You'll see."

I smiled at him brightly . . .

. . . but my smile faded as he stared at me coldly.

"Um," I said. "You *are* talking about football, aren't you, Mr. Morton?"

"*Football?*" Mr. Morton looked as if he were about to choke. "*Football?* No, this isn't about football, you stupid girl. This is about the never-ending battle of good versus evil. It's about one man, born with the capability of saving this planet from ultimately destroying itself, and the forces of darkness that are keeping him from doing so."

I had no idea whatsoever how to respond that. Mr. Morton had leaned forward. His gray-eyed gaze seemed to hold me transfixed. I couldn't move. I couldn't speak.

I couldn't even breathe.

"It's about all of us being plunged once again into the Dark Ages," Mr. Morton went on, in that same raspy voice, "and this time having no light to lead us out again. It's about us being forced to stay there until another can be born, grow, and rise to take his place . . . if we can get to him before they do next time, that is. It's about *failure*, Miss Harrison. *My* failure. For which everybody else on this planet will suffer for the rest of their lives. That is what it's about, Miss Harrison. *Not football*."

I blinked.

"Oh," I said.

Well, what else *could* I say to all of that?

Mr. Morton sagged back in his seat and dragged his hands over his face.

"Get out, Miss Harrison," he said through his fingers. "Please. Just go away."

I picked up my backpack. I didn't know what else to do. He obviously didn't want me there. Whatever he was going through—whatever he was talking about—it didn't have anything to do with me. It was likely it didn't have anything to do with anyone . . . anyone but Mr. Morton and whatever he was keeping in a bottle in his bottom desk drawer. . . .

Because he was clearly unhinged, poor man. Nobody in his right mind talks about the forces of darkness taking over the planet. Nobody.

Except that . . .

Well, he'd seemed so sane up till then.

Then, just as I reached the doorway, something that he'd said struck me—reminded me, in a strange way, of the words of another. . . .

I turned to look back at him.

"Mr. Morton," I said.

When he glanced at me—his face still a mask of utter despair—I went on. "Does this have anything to do with . . . with the Lily Maid of Astolat?"

I'll never forget the look that came over his face then. Never for as long as I live.

"How—how did you know about that?" he breathed—so raspily, it was clearly an enormous effort for him to speak at all. "Who told you?"

"Um," I said. "I'm doing a report on her. Remember?"

Mr. Morton looked visibly less tense. At least until I added, "And, uh, Will's stepbrother, Marco, mentioned something, too. . . ."

And there went the color from Mr. Morton's face.

"The stepbrother." He shook his head, looking bleaker than ever. "Of course. If only . . . if only—"

And then, I could have sworn he said, "If only I had stopped him when I had the chance. . . ."

"Stopped who, Mr. Morton?" Except that I knew. Or thought I did, anyway. Marco. He could only be talking about Marco.

Except that I thought he *had* stopped Marco. Stopped Marco from trying to kill him. Isn't that how the rumor went? That Marco had been trying to kill Mr. Morton, and Mr. Morton had stopped him?

"Mr. Morton." I stood irresolute in the doorway. What was happening? What was going on? It was true I had fantasized the other night that Jennifer was Guinevere and Lance was Lancelot, and that Will was Arthur, and Marco was Mordred. . . .

But that was only because . . . well, of what Marco had said about me being Elaine of Astolat. Not to mention the fact that we all go to Avalon High, home of the Excaliburs. I hadn't thought—I hadn't even dreamed—it could be remotely *real*.

Because it couldn't be. All of that had happened—if it had really happened at all—hundreds of years ago. As the daughter of two historians, I know better than anyone that history can—and often does—repeat itself.

But not like *this*.

And no one—no one in his right mind, anyway—would believe it could.

Except . . .

Except for a member of the Order of the Bear, the group I read about who believe King Arthur is destined to be reincarnated one day, to lead the world from the dark ages. . . .

But Mr. Morton couldn't be part of something so ridiculous. He's a *teacher*. A good one, from everything I'd heard. Teachers don't believe in silly things like that a medieval king is going to be reborn and save the world.

I was letting my imagination run away with me while Mr. Morton, over by his desk, was still suffering. There had to be something I could do for him. The poor man was clearly in need of . . . something.

"Mr. Morton," I said. "Won't you . . . won't you let me get the nurse? You don't look well. I think . . . I think you might be sick."

Mr. Morton did something strange then. He lifted his head and smiled at me. It was a sad smile. It didn't come easily, either.

But he smiled, just the same.

"I'm not sick, Elaine," he said. "Except at heart."

I fingered the strap to my backpack. "Won't you tell me why? I might be able to help, you know." I had no idea how, of course. But I had to ask.

Mr. Morton seemed to understand, since he spoke more kindly than he'd ever spoken to me before.

"It's too late, Elaine," he said, in the same defeated voice. "Thank you all the same. But it's far too late. And better for you, in the end, not to know. After all, your part in it was over before it could even begin this time."

"What do you mean 'this time'?" I shook my head. "What do you mean by my part in it?"

But just then the bell rang.

And Mr. Morton sighed tiredly and said, "You'd better get along to class, Elaine."

"But what about Lance? Don't you want to reschedule?"

"No." Mr. Morton took the newspaper from his desk

and dropped it, unread, into the trash can. His tone, when he spoke again, had a knell of finality to it. "It doesn't matter now, you see."

And with that, I knew I was dismissed.

CHAPTER EIGHTEEN

And down the river's dim expanse—
Like some bold seer in a trance,
Seeing all his own mischance—
With a glassy countenance
Did she look to Camelot.

I told myself I was being crazy. I told myself I was being ridiculous.

I told myself lots of things.

But I did it, anyway. Instead of joining Liz and Stacy—who'd informed me my "initiation" had been scheduled for the upcoming weekend—for lunch, I did what I always did when I didn't know what else to do: I called my mother.

I didn't want to. But after my strange meeting with Mr. Morton, I'd moved through my morning classes in a sort of daze, feeling more and more uneasy with every passing minute.

Your part in it was over before it could even begin this

time. Mr. Morton's voice rang inside my head. *My* part? *This* time?

If only I had stopped him when I had the chance. . . . Stopped who? Marco? Stopped Marco from doing what?

None of it made any sense. It was like the ravings of a lunatic.

But I'd looked into Mr. Morton's eyes, and I hadn't seen a hint of insanity. The only thing I'd seen in them was despair.

And fear.

It was stupid. It was impossible.

But when the lunch bell rang, I was on the nearest pay phone anyway.

"The Order of the Bear?" my mother echoed wonderingly. "What on earth—"

"Come on, Mom," I said. "I know you know it. It was in one of your books."

"Well, of course I know it." Mom sounded amused. "I'm just surprised to hear you've actually *read* one of my books. You've always been so adamantly against all things medieval."

"I know," I said, straining to hear her over the din in the hallway. It would die down when everyone finally got into the caf. "I told you. I need to know for this report I'm writing. Just a couple things—"

"Well, Ellie, honey," Mom said. "I hardly think it's fair for you to get help from an Arthurian scholar for your little report. What about all the other students who don't have an Arthurian scholar at home to consult?"

"Mom," I nearly shouted. "Just answer the question."

"About the Order of the Bear? Well, it's a group of people who believe King Arthur will rise again someday and—"

"—bring us out of the Dark Ages," I finished for her. "I know. But I mean . . . isn't that kind of like believing in aliens, or something? I mean, they seem like a bunch of kooks—"

"The Order of the Bear is not made up of kooks, Ellie. It's a highly respected and well-educated group of men and women," she said. "It's a very elite organization, and extremely difficult to get into. Besides, there's proof Arthur actually existed, and there's no convincing proof— to me, anyway—that we've ever been visited by creatures from another planet. Whereas we can actually trace Arthur's lineage. His father was Uther Pendragon, his mother Igraine, the wife of the Duke of Cornwall. Which, as you can imagine, was a bit of a difficulty, seeing as how she was married to a man who was not the father of her child with Uther. But Uther took care of that by slaying the duke in battle, and was able to marry Igraine and eventually make Arthur his legitimate heir—"

I sucked in my breath because this—slaying a guy in battle, then marrying his wife—sounded so familiar. Except, of course, Jean was just Will's stepmom, not his real mom.

"But what about the parts like—like Mordred?" I asked. "And about Arthur having been surrounded by mystical beings like Merlin and the Lady of the Lake? I mean, that stuff can't be true."

"Well," my mom said, "most likely some of it was. Mordred did kill Arthur, in the end, in a battle over the throne. And Merlin was probably a religious mystic or sage, not a wizard, of course. And as for the Lady of the Lake, well, now, she's a character who has always been shrouded in mystery—"

"But Lancelot," I interrupted. "And Guinevere? They were real, too?"

"Of course, sweetie, though references to them appear much later than, say, references to other Arthurian characters, such as, oh, his dog, Cavall, for instance—"

I nearly dropped the phone.

"His . . . dog?"

"Yes, the legendary hunting dog of King Arthur, Cavall." My mother, warming to the subject—which was, after all, her favorite—began to lecture, something professors can't help doing. "Cavall supposedly possessed a humanlike ability to read situations and people—"

Cavall. Cavalier.

No. No, it just wasn't possible. It just wasn't.

My throat had gone dry. But I managed to croak, "Did Arthur have a boat?"

"Well, of course, all great heroes had a boat. Arthur's was the *Prydwyn.* He had many adventures at sea—" She seemed to remember she was speaking to her daughter and not one of her grad students, since she suddenly broke off and asked, "Ellie, are you all right? You've never been interested in this kind of thing. Are you coming down with something? Do you need me to come to school to pick you up? You know Daddy and I are going into D.C. tonight for that dinner with Dr. Montrose and his wife, right? I hope you'll be all right alone. It says on the Weather Channel there's supposed to be some kind of storm. You know where the flashlights are, don't you, if the power goes out?"

Prydwyn. Pride Winn.

I remembered the way Will had chuckled the day before when he'd been explaining to me how he'd come up with such an odd name for his boat.

It had just popped into his head. And stuck there.

Like the name Cavalier for his dog.

And the fact that he liked listening to medieval music.

And thought he knew me.

From another life.

"I gotta go, Mom," I said, and hung up, even as she was asking, "What kind of report is this, anyway, Elaine? It sounds awfully detailed for a high school paper. . . ."

Because I'd noticed that, hanging from the booth I was standing in, was a tattered Anne Arundel County phone book. I lifted it.

I didn't do it because I expected to find anything. I did it to prove to myself that what I was thinking was completely insane. I did it because I *knew* it couldn't be true. I just wanted proof of that fact. I did it to wipe from my memory the look on Mr. Morton's face—that expression of dread I'd seen written across his craggy features when I'd told him about Lance and Jennifer.

I did it to dry up the sweat on my hands.

I turned to the W section.

Because the *A* in A. William Wagner's name had to stand for something. It had never occurred to me to ask before, but now I wanted to know.

Generally, when a guy goes by his middle name, it's because his first name is the same as his father's. Will's father's name was probably Anthony. Or Andrew. Will probably didn't like being called Andrew because having two Andrews or whatever in the family was too confusing—

I found it almost at once. *Wagner, Arthur, ADM*, lived at Will's address.

I stared disbelievingly down at the page.

Arthur. Will's real name was Arthur.

And he had a dog named Cavalier, and a boat named *Pride Winn*.

And his best friend's name was Lance.

And his girlfriend—now ex—was called Jennifer, which was English for Guinevere.

And his dad had married another man's wife after her first husband had died, some said at Admiral Wagner's own hand. . . .

I dropped the phone book. I needed to get a grip. I was being ridiculous. It was all just a coincidence, the similarities between Will's life and the life of the king I'd just heard about from my mom. Because Jean—that was what Will had said his stepmother's name was—wasn't

Will's mom, the way Igraine had been Arthur's. Will's mom had died when he was born, years ago. Will and Marco were stepbrothers, not blood relations. Not blood relations in any way.

See? What Mr. Morton was thinking wasn't true. It couldn't be. And it wasn't.

I picked up my backpack and headed for the ladies' room. Once there, I ran cold water in the sink and splashed my face with it, then looked at my dripping face in the mirror above the line of sinks.

What on earth was I thinking? Did I really believe that Arthur—ancient king of England, founder of the Round Table—had been reborn at last and was living in *Annapolis*?

And did I really think that I, Elaine Harrison, was the Lady of Shalott, a woman who had killed herself over a guy like *Lance*?

That thought acted like a splash of cold water to my mind. First of all, okay, *no way* am I the reincarnation of a dope like Elaine.

And second of all, people—even legendary kings of England—don't come back. These kinds of things do not happen. I mean, we live in an orderly world, and in an enlightened and educated age. We don't have to make up myths and stories to explain things we don't understand like they did in the old days, because we know now that there are scientific explanations for them.

Will Wagner was *not* a modern-day Arthur reborn.

And yet . . .

What if it *were* true?

I gripped the sides of the sink, staring at my reflection. What was happening to me? Was I really starting to believe something so completely unbelievable? How could I? I was the practical one. Nancy was the romantic, not me. I'm the daughter of educators. I can't let myself believe in this kind of stuff.

And yet . . .

And yet seconds later I'd grabbed my backpack again and was hurrying back to the classroom I'd been sitting in a few hours before. I needed, I knew, to speak to Mr. Morton, to find out if he really believed what I suspected he did, and whether that meant that he—or I—or the both of us—was crazy.

I didn't know what I was going to say to him. That I knew? But *what* did I know? I didn't know anything . . .

. . . except that I still couldn't seem to get this buzzing sound out of my head.

But when I got to his classroom, it wasn't Mr. Morton who was at the chalkboard. It was Ms. Pavarti, the school vice principal.

"Yes?" she said, when she saw me. Every head in the room—people who had fifth period lunch, not fourth like me—had swiveled toward me, eyes raking me as I stood in the hallway, clutching my backpack and looking, I'm sure, like a giant freak, with water stains still down my shirtfront, my ponytail half falling down, and my eyes all huge.

"May I help you?" Ms. Pavarti asked politely.

"I—I'm looking for Mr. Morton," I stammered.

"Mr. Morton has gone home for the day," Ms. Pavarti said. "He wasn't feeling well. Shouldn't you be in class? Or the lunchroom? Where's your hall pass?"

I turned from her numbly.

Mr. Morton had gone home. Mr. Morton had gone home for the day.

Nice try, buddy. You aren't getting out of this *that* easily.

"Excuse me." Ms. Pavarti had followed me out into the hall. "Young lady. I asked you a question. Where is your hall pass? What class are you supposed to be in right now?"

I didn't even glance back at her. I headed for the doors to the school.

"Stop!" Ms. Pavarti's voice was loud in the empty hallway. I saw people in the administrative offices glance our way, curious about what was going on. "What is your name? Young lady! Don't you walk away from me!"

Except that by that time, I wasn't walking anymore. I was running.

And I didn't stop running until I was off school property. Not that Ms. Pavarti had ever had a hope of catching me. I just couldn't bring myself to slow down. It was almost like if I ran fast enough, it would turn out not to be true. My head would clear, and I'd realize what an idiot I was being, and it would all go back to normal.

Except that when I finally slowed down, I didn't feel that way at all. That things were back to normal. If anything, they were worse. Because now, for the first time in my life, I was skipping school. I had left school grounds without permission.

I was truant.

I was a delinquent.

And the worst part of all?

I didn't even care.

CHAPTER NINETEEN

Down she came and found a boat
Beneath a willow left afloat,
And round about the prow she wrote
The Lady of Shalott.

Half an hour later, when the cab pulled up in front of the apartment complex, and I handed the driver almost half the money I'd had with me—eight dollars, leaving me with only that much to get back to school later—I still didn't care.

I didn't care about the fact that I was in a part of Annapolis I'd never been to before. I didn't care that I had no idea how to get home, or money enough left to get me there anyway. I didn't care about anything except that I'd found him—with the help of Information and another pay phone—and now I was going to get some answers that made sense.

I hoped.

I knew he was home. I could hear the TV blaring from behind the door I'd pounded on. Maybe he couldn't hear me because the volume was turned up so loud. Maybe that's why he took so long to answer.

But when he finally did pull the door open, I saw that it wasn't that he hadn't heard me. That's not why it had taken him so long to answer the door at all. He hadn't answered right away because he'd been looking through the peephole to see who was there.

And had grabbed an extremely large frying pan to hit me with, in case I turned out to be someone dangerous.

At least that's what I assumed, since he lowered the frying pan as soon as he saw I was alone.

"Oh," Mr. Morton said. "It's you."

He didn't seem surprised. Resigned, is more like it.

"Go away," he said. "I'm busy." And he started to close the door.

But I was too fast for him. Before he could close the door all the way, I thrust my foot inside the doorway, the thick rubber on my Nike sole keeping the door from slamming shut in my face.

I don't know what came over me. I had never done anything like this in my life—skipped class, left school property without permission, gone to a teacher's apartment, stuck my foot in his door to keep him from shutting me out—that wasn't me. *None* of this was me. My heart was pounding, my palms slick with nervous sweat. I thought I might even be sick.

But I hadn't come all this way just to get sent home.

This was something I had to do. I didn't know why.

Except maybe that I'd grown up in a house full of people who knew all the answers to the questions on *Jeopardy!* And now, finally, I wanted some answers of my own.

Mr. Morton looked down at my foot. He did seem surprised then. Surprised by my resourcefulness.

But he didn't try to fight me. He shrugged and said, "Suit yourself."

And turned away to continue what he'd been doing when I'd knocked. Which was packing.

He had his clothes spread out everywhere. But that wasn't what he was putting into the suitcases that lay scattered about the floor. He was filling those with books. Thick books, like the kind my dad is always bringing home from the university library. Most of them looked extremely old. I had no idea how Mr. Morton thought he was going to lift a single one of those suitcases once he'd finally managed to get them closed.

I looked at the suitcases. Then I looked at Mr. Morton, who was sorting through a pile of books he held in his arms. Some went into a suitcase. The others he just threw on the floor. It was clear he simply didn't care what happened to the things he was leaving behind.

"Well, what do you want?" Mr. Morton asked, still sorting. "I haven't got all day. I have a plane to catch."

"I can see that," I said. I lifted the book nearest me. Its title wasn't even in English, but I recognized it, because my dad had it on his shelf back home in St. Paul. *Le Morte d'Arthur*. The Death of Arthur. Great. "Kind of a sudden trip, isn't it?"

"It isn't a trip," Mr. Morton said shortly. "I'm leaving town. For good."

"You are?" I glanced around at the room's furnishings, which were sparse and fairly new, though not very expensive-looking. "Why?"

Mr. Morton flicked a single appraising glance at me. Then he went back to his sorting.

"If it's about your grade," he said, ignoring my question, "You shouldn't worry. Whoever they get to replace me will certainly give you an A. That proposal you handed in was actually very well written. You can clearly string two sentences together, which is a lot more than most of the little cretins at that school can do. You'll do just fine. Now please go. I've got a lot of things to do, and a very short time to get them done."

"Where are you going?" I asked.

"Tahiti," he said, studying the spine of a book before tossing it into the suitcase in front of him.

"Tahiti?" I echoed. "That's kind of far."

He ignored the question, moving behind me to close the door I'd left open.

"I told you," he said, when the door was safely closed. He spoke in so terse and quiet a tone that I could barely hear him above the sound of the television, still blaring from the next room. "Your part in this is over. There's nothing more you can do . . . nothing more you're *expected* to do. Now be a good girl, Elaine, and go back to school."

"No." I moved a pile of books, then sat down in the space I'd created on his sofa.

Mr. Morton blinked down at me as if he couldn't quite believe what he'd heard.

"Pardon me?" he said.

"No," I said. I sounded so adamant, I surprised even myself. Inwardly, of course, I was quaking. I had never disobeyed a direct order from a teacher—or any adult, really—before. I had no idea where these hidden reserves of courage were coming from, but I was very glad to find them so unexpectedly. "No, I'm not leaving. Not until you tell me what's going on. Why do you keep saying 'your part in this is over'? My part in *what*, exactly? And why are you trying to get out of here so fast? What are you afraid is going to happen, anyway?"

Mr. Morton sighed and said in a tired voice, "Please. Miss Harrison. Elaine. I haven't time for this. I have a plane to catch." He reached for the books I'd moved from the couch. I noticed for the first time that his hands were shaking.

I stared up at him, truly taken aback.

"Mr. Morton," I said, "what is it? What are you so afraid of? What are you running away from?"

"Miss Harrison." He sighed heavily. Then, as if he'd given the matter some thought, he said, "Your parents are here on a sabbatical, aren't they? They can take some time off from their research. Why don't you ask them if the three of you could take a trip? Somewhere far from the eastern seaboard. It would be best if you could leave at once." His gaze flicked toward the window, through which I could see clouds had obscured the bright afternoon sunlight. "The sooner the better."

Then he turned and added more books to the suitcase he was packing.

"Mr. Morton," I said carefully, "I'm sorry, but I think you need help. From a mental health professional."

He glanced at me over the rims of his glasses. "That's what you think, is it?" was all he said, and this with a note of indignation in his voice.

I didn't blame him for being offended. It wasn't really my place to say all this. Still, *someone* had to. The poor guy was completely bonkers. Not that he didn't have good reason to feel a little off-kilter about the whole thing. But still.

"I know all this stuff with Will and Lance and Jennifer seems kind of . . . coincidental," I went on. "But you're a teacher . . . an educator. You're supposed to use reason and intelligence. Surely you can't really believe in something as ridiculous as King Arthur being reincarnated."

"And that's why you came all the way here," Mr. Morton said. "To tell me what I believe in is ridiculous. You're worried about me, I suppose? Afraid I might be mad?"

"Well," I said, feeling bad about it, but knowing I had to be truthful. "Yes. I mean, I can see how someone—even someone who doesn't belong, you know, to this cult you belong to—"

He looked only mildly surprised to hear I knew about his little group. His tone was mild, too, as he rebuked me. "The Order of the Bear, Miss Harrison," he said, "is a fraternal order, not a cult."

"Whatever," I said. "I realize how someone like me, for instance, could look at all these coincidences—Will's parents; his name; the thing with Lance and Jennifer; Will's names for his dog and his boat. Stuff like that— and think to themselves, 'Hey, yeah. That's King Arthur, reincarnated.' But you know, there are important differences, too. Will's real mom isn't Jean—his real mom is dead. Marco is his stepbrother, not his half brother. And I am most certainly not the Lily Maid of Astolat. I couldn't fall in love with Lance if I tried. You're a *teacher*, Mr. Morton. You're supposed to be a rational thinker. How can a man like you believe in something so completely ridiculous as King Arthur rising from the dead—unless, of course, you really are nuts?"

He blinked. Just once.

Then he said, "Not 'believe,' Miss Harrison. *Know*. It's a fact. Arthur *will be* back. *Is* back. Only—" His expression darkened.

Then he seemed to shut down again.

"No. It's no good. You're better off not knowing," he said, shaking his head. "Knowledge . . . it can be danger- ous. I sometimes . . . well, I wish *I* didn't know, most of the time."

"Try me," I said, folding my arms across my chest.

He stared at me for a minute.

Then he said, "Very well. You're an intelligent girl—at least you seemed to be, up until now. What if I were to tell you that my order—the Order of the Bear—is a secret society whose only function is to attempt to thwart the forces of evil that are keeping King Arthur from rising once again to power?"

"Um," I said. "I'd probably tell you that I already knew that. Also that there are medications you can take to prevent these kinds of paranoid delusions."

His expression grew sour. "We don't expect the man to just come popping up from his final resting place, Excalibur in hand. We are not simpletons, Miss Harrison. Like the monks in Tibet who search the world over for the next Dalai Lama, the members of the Order of the Bear look for potential Arthurs in each and every generation." He removed his glasses and began polishing the lenses with a handkerchief he'd taken from his back pocket. "When we find one we think might have a serious chance, we send a member of the Order to the boy's town, to observe him, generally in the guise of a teacher, like myself. Most of the time, these boys disappoint us. But every once in a while— such as in Will's case—the order is given reason to hope. . . ."

He put his glasses back on and peered at me through the now shining lenses.

"And then it's just a matter of keeping the dark

forces from destroying the boy's chances of reaching his potential."

"That's where you lose me," I said. "Dark forces? Mr. Morton, come on. What are you talking about? Darth Vader? Voldemort? Give me a break."

"Do you think what happened with Lancelot and the queen, all those years ago, was merely an affair?" Mr. Morton asked, sounding shocked by my naïveté. "Because it was something far more insidious, and caused, not just by weakness of character on the part of those two, but by the strength of the forces against Arthur, who were looking to destroy him—not just his faith in himself, but his people's faith in him, as well. That was when Mordred—who is, and always will be, an agent of evil—moved in for the kill."

"Uh," I said, staring at him. I was having a little trouble digesting some of what he'd been telling me. Well, okay. *All* of what he'd been telling me. "Okay."

I must have sounded convincingly interested, since, encouraged, Mr. Morton went on.

"You know he was actually too late that first time. Mordred was, I mean. The Dark Ages died in spite of his—and evil's—best efforts, because Arthur had been on the throne long enough to lead his people out of them. And in the end, it wasn't Mordred who lived on through the annals of time as a good and just king, but his brother Arthur.

"But Mordred learned from that mistake," Mr. Morton continued. "And since that time, whenever

Arthur has tried to rise again, Mordred has been there to stop him, earlier and earlier in the life cycle, so that the Light might never have any success at all. And so it will go, you see, Elaine, until the end of time . . . or until good finally triumphs over the darkness, once and for all, and Mordred is put to rest."

I cleared my throat.

The thing was, Mr. Morton *seemed* lucid enough. He seemed as sane as—well, my own father.

But what he was saying—what he and his "order" believed. . . . It was just *nuts*. No rational person could think that Will Wagner was the reincarnation of King Arthur. The thing with our names—and Cavall—aside. . . . Well, it just didn't make any sense.

And that wasn't all that didn't make sense.

"I don't understand," I said flatly. "If you really think Will is Arthur—and that's a pretty big if, mind you—why are you running away? Shouldn't you stay here to help him? Correct me if I'm wrong, but weren't you the guy your order put here to protect him?"

Mr. Morton looked genuinely pained.

"There's no point now," he explained. "Once Guinevere leaves him, Arthur is vulnerable to whatever Mordred has in store for him. We've seen it happen time and time again, no matter what we've done to try to stop it. Mordred—with the help of the dark side, of course—will rise to power, as he has in so many different incarnations in the past. Think of the most diabolical political leaders in history, and you'll have a good idea what I'm talking about. All of them Mordred. And Arthur will . . . well."

"He'll what?" I asked him curiously.

"Well," Mr. Morton said, looking uncomfortable, "he'll die."

CHAPTER TWENTY

And at the closing of the day
She loosed the chain, and down she lay;
The broad stream bore her far away,
The Lady of Shalott.

"Die?" I stared at him in disbelief.

"Well," he said, having the grace, at last, to look faintly embarrassed, "yes."

"But . . ." I could only seem to sit there and parrot what he'd just told me. *"Die?"*

"Yes, of course." Mr. Morton sounded a bit exasperated. "What did you think was going to happen, Elaine? Why do you think I'm leaving? You can hardly think I want to stay and watch it happen."

"But . . ." I just stared at him some more. I had heard some crazy stuff today. But this, by far, took the cake. "You mean *Will*? You think *Will* is going to die?"

"He has to," Mr. Morton said apologetically. "For

Mordred—or in this case, Marco—to achieve his supremacy—"

"You think Marco's going to do something to Will?"

"I don't *think* so, Miss Harrison," Mr. Morton said calmly. "I *know*. Marco told me so himself in my classroom last year, when I foolishly attempted—against orders, I might add—to reason with the boy. In the same way that you evidently do, I once had a difficult time believing any person could be entirely evil. I thought if I could only reach out to the young man, he might come around. I was proven wrong—quite painfully, I might add."

"When Marco attacked you," I said, putting two and two together and coming up with—well, more craziness. "And got kicked out of school."

"Precisely," Mr. Morton said. "I see now it was a fatal error on my part. Letting Marco know of the existence of the Order, and his preordained role in the next life cycle of Arthur, did not serve, as I thought it would, as a warning to him to guard against evil, but rather as an excuse for him to embrace it. Something along the lines of, 'Well, it's my destiny, anyway, so why fight it?'"

I could only blink at him. "So you told Marco that he's the reincarnation of Mordred?" I could only imagine how Marco must have taken the news. Derisive laughter would have been involved.

But also, apparently, violence. Against the messenger. And perhaps not undeserved.

"I am ashamed to admit that I did," Mr. Morton said.

"Though I can't say that at the time, I was altogether certain he believed me. The fact that he recognized, however, that you are Elaine of Astolat seems to indicate that he's come around to the idea."

"I am *not*," I said slowly and angrily, "Elaine of Astolat."

Mr. Morton smiled sadly. "Funny. That's exactly what Marco said. Only in his case, he insisted he wasn't Mordred."

"He *isn't* Mordred," I said. I was outraged. Really. This had all gone way too far. "And you should have your teacher's license revoked for going around telling impressionable young students that they are reincarnations of mythical characters!"

Mr. Morton shook a finger at me. "Now, Elaine," he said. "You know perfectly well they aren't mythical."

I wanted to throw something. I couldn't believe I was even having this conversation.

"Fine," I said. "So they were real. Once. And yeah, Arthur really did exist. And let's just say, for the sake of argument, this whole reincarnation thing really could be possible. You warned Marco about it. Have you said anything about it to Will?"

"It won't do any good, Elaine," Mr. Morton said sadly. "As I said before, it's too late now, anyway. And members of the Order have tried in the past to warn the Bear of what was to befall him—just as I tried, unsuccessfully, to turn Marco to the Light—and it never did any good, in all his various incarnations. Most of the time, he didn't even believe us. And inevitably, the Dark rose up and defeated us . . . and him."

I blinked at him. "So if all this stuff is true, and what you and your order believe really is happening—Marco is going to kill Will, and you don't think it would do any good to maybe give Will a call and let him know?"

"It's too late, Elaine," Mr. Morton said, shaking his head. "He's already lost Guinevere. He hasn't the will to live anymore—"

"But that's what I was trying to tell you this morning," I all but shouted, fighting for patience. Not that, even for a minute, I believed in any of this hogwash. But just for the sake of argument. . . . "Will is fine with Jen leaving him for Lance! Really. He told me he was *relieved* when he found out."

Mr. Morton smiled down at me sadly.

"And if we did tell him, Elaine, do you think he would believe us—much less take the necessary steps to protect himself, which would, in any case, be a fruitless effort? Do you think it would make the slightest difference? You have no idea what we're up against. The battle for Arthur between the Light and the Dark has gone on for centuries. Evil won't stand for any interference from the Light. It will throw insurmountable obstacles in our path—deadly obstacles. Mordred, with the help of the dark side, will find a way to kill his brother no matter what we—"

"Marco doesn't want to kill Will," I cried, still not believing I was even having this conversation. "Why would Marco possibly want to kill Will?"

"Besides the fact that, through his own greed and selfish disregard for others, he's fallen into the embrace of the powers of darkness?" Mr. Morton frowned. "Think about it, Elaine."

I thought about Marco, his earrings and snide manner. Sure, he was mean, and with that ice-cold skin of his, more than a little creepy.

But a murderer? Sure, he'd tried to kill Mr. Morton—but the guy had been telling him he was the reincarnation of one of the most detested historical figures of all time. Why would he want to kill *Will*? I mean, he had even admitted himself that since he'd come to live with Will and Admiral Wagner, his life had improved dramatically. He'd even gotten a boat. Or at least, the use of one. What was it he'd said that day?

I'm not the lucky one. Will is.

Could *that* be it?

"You think Marco's going to try to kill Will," I said to Mr. Morton, "because he's jealous of Will? And angry about what Will's father did to his? Is that it?"

"This time?" Mr. Morton nodded. "There's a great deal more to it than you can possibly imagine, but I would think that might be part of it."

"It's different every time?" This was the part that was making it so hard to believe it really was paranoid delusions, as I'd first tried to insist. The fact that, taken as a whole, the story was so well thought-out, it actually sort of made sense.

"Variations," Mr. Morton said, "on several themes. Mordred hated Arthur, you see, because he wanted the throne. He turned his back on his own people, not caring an iota for their concerns, seeking only to cater to his own self-gratification. That's when the Dark took him completely, and made him one of their own—"

"Stop it!" I threw my hands up over my ears, beginning to feel overwhelmed. "I don't want to hear any more about the dark side, okay? What I want to know is how—if you're so sure this is what's going to happen—you think you can just run away and let Will get murdered. I understand that you're afraid of . . . of the darkness." Now I sounded as insane as he did, but I didn't care. "But for Pete's sake, won't you even go to the *police*?"

"And say what, Elaine?" Mr. Morton's smile was rueful. "That according to an ancient prophecy that has been fulfilled time and time again, this young man is going to kill his stepbrother some day, and then wreak havoc upon the world? I can't do that. You know they wouldn't listen."

No. They wouldn't listen. *I* didn't even want to listen. Because it was all completely psycho.

"And even if they did," Mr. Morton went on, "there's nothing the police could do about it. Revolvers and nightsticks are useless against the wrath of the dark side. And I would be guilty of risking innocent souls in a war they can never hope to win. The commonly held belief—though it's yet to be proven—is that only those in Arthur's closest circle can put an end to the dark side's reign, in any case."

"So . . . " I pushed some of my hair away from my eyes. "Who, then? Lance? Jennifer?"

"Certainly," he said. "Either of them. Just not . . . well. You."

I gave him a dirty look. "Because Elaine of Astolat never even met King Arthur historically, is that it?"

"I told you that you were better off not knowing," Mr. Morton reminded me in a sad voice.

"I'd be bummed," I assured him, "if I actually believed any of this."

Mr. Morton looked at me, concern softening his craggy features.

"Elaine," he said gently. "Go home. Get your parents to take you somewhere far away from here. Back to Minnesota, perhaps. It might be better for you if you . . . well, if you simply went back home."

Something about the way he said the word *home* caused me to snap.

Simply put, I lost it. I'd tolerated all the rest. Talk of the powers of darkness and the dangers of attempting to thwart it. Jennifer as Will's reason for living. Even Tahiti.

But this I simply could not take.

"*Home?*" I echoed. "What do you know about *home*? Home isn't just a place, you know. It's *people* who make a home . . . people you care about, and who care about you . . . or who would, if you didn't turn around and abandon them for Tahiti because you believe in some dumb prophecy. I don't know if this Light and Dark thing is for real, Mr. Morton, but I do know one thing: if you and this so-called Order really were on Will's side, you wouldn't just leave him without even trying to help. He would never do that to you. He would never say, 'Oh, well, this is the way it's always happened, so I guess I better not even try to change things, because I tried that once and it didn't work, and the dark side always wins.'"

My voice broke, but I didn't care. I just kept right on yelling.

"Because isn't that what made your precious Arthur so popular in the first place? He was supposed to be this great innovative thinker who wouldn't do things the way people told him they had to be done, because that's the way they'd always been done. If Will really is Arthur—and I'm not saying he is, because I think this whole thing is wack—would he really just sit back and say, 'Oh, well, I can't change this, because no one's ever done it before,' and just leave you to die? No, he wouldn't. And you know what, Mr. Morton? I'm not going to, either."

And without another word, I turned around and walked out of Mr. Morton's apartment with my head held high and my shoulders thrown back as if I, and not Jennifer Gold, had been a queen in a past life.

CHAPTER TWENTY-ONE

Lying, robed in snowy white
That loosely flew to left and right—
The leaves upon her falling light—
Thro' the noises of the night
She floated down to Camelot:

I knew from my brother Geoff, who'd been a practiced class-ditcher, that it generally took the administration a full workday to catch up with delinquents. So I knew I was safe from any summonses to Vice Principal Pavarti's office to explain my absence from fifth through sixth periods for at least a day.

Still, I thought it safer to hide in the ladies' room until the next period bell rang, rather than risk being discovered roaming through the halls.

So I ducked into the nearest restroom.

The first thing I was going to need to do, I realized, was find Will. I had no idea what classes he had for seventh and eighth periods, but I was going to have to find out somehow, then catch him and let him know that at least one member of the Avalon High faculty suspected that he was the reincarnation of an ancient medieval king, and that he was in grave and mortal danger from his stepbrother.

Mr. Morton had been right about one thing: Will wouldn't believe it, of course. Who in his right mind would?

But that didn't mean he didn't have a right to know.

I was busy redoing my ponytail in the mirror above the sinks when I realized I wasn't alone in the restroom. I heard sniffling from behind the last stall door, which was closed. Ducking down to look beneath the partition between the stall door and the floor, I saw a pair of white aerobics shoes, onto which were tied a pair of Avalon High's distinctive blue and gold pom-poms.

There was a cheerleader weeping in the ladies' room with me.

And, just given how my day had gone so far, I had a pretty good idea which cheerleader it was.

"Jennifer?" I said, tapping on the stall door. "It's me, Ellie. Are you okay?"

I heard a particularly slurpy sniffle. Then Jennifer's throaty voice said, "Go away."

"Come on, Jennifer," I said. "Open up and talk to me. It can't be that bad."

There was a pause. And then I heard the lock slide back, and Jennifer—still exquisitely lovely, even with red-rimmed eyes—stepped out of the stall, wiping her eyes on the long sleeves of her cheerleading sweater.

"D-don't tell anyone," she said, looking up at me with huge, worried blue eyes, "that you caught me in here crying. Like those gossipy girls from the track team you hang out with? Okay? Because they hate me enough, and that'll just make things worse."

"I won't mention it," I said, grabbing a handful of paper towels from the dispenser on the wall and wetting them a little from the sink before handing them to her. "But they don't hate you."

"Are you kidding?" Jennifer dabbed at her red eyes with the paper towels. "Everybody hates me. On account of what I did to Will."

"Not everybody hates you," I said. "*I* don't hate you. And Will doesn't hate you, either."

To my dismay, this only made Jennifer start crying again, just when I thought she'd stopped.

"I *know!*" she burst out tearfully. "That's the worst part! Will came up to me this morning and was so totally sweet! He said he knew Lance and I hadn't meant to hurt him, and that he was completely fine with us b-being together. He even said he th-thought we made a good couple. Lance and me! Oh my God. I wanted to die!"

"Why?" I asked, patting her on the arm—to comfort her, I guess. "Don't you believe him?"

"Of course I believe him!" Jennifer said, with an incredulous laugh. "I mean, that's the one thing about Will—he never lies. Not even to make someone feel better. Well, maybe, you know, if you were sick he'd say you looked great or whatever. But not about—not about big stuff. So I know he was telling the truth. That's the thing. He really doesn't mind about me and Lance. He's just so . . . nice."

Something cold gripped my heart, but I told myself I was being silly. And selfish.

"So you want to get back together with him?" I asked her, way more lightly than I felt. Because of course I suddenly realized how much I'd been hoping that now that Will was free, he might possibly stop thinking of us as *just friends*, and more of . . . well, whatever.

But if he and Jennifer got back together, that would never, ever happen.

"I don't know," she said miserably. "A part of me will always love him. But the rest of me. . . . Do you think it's possible to love two boys at the same time?"

I shrugged helplessly. "I don't know," I said. "I mean, I've only ever loved one—"

"Will, right?" Jennifer asked, as she wiped her eyes.

I stared at her in total shock. "Wh-what? No! Of course not! I meant this other guy. Um, this guy named Tommy—"

"It's okay," Jennifer said. She'd stopped crying, and now whipped her makeup bag from her purse, and was trying to make repairs. "I mean, I don't blame you. And you two would look cute together. You're both so dark. And so tall."

I felt as if I were choking. "I don't—I don't feel that way about him."

"No?" She pursed her lips, then dotted lip gloss onto them. "Well, he likes you. I mean, from the first moment he saw you, that day at the park, remember? It's like he knew you from another life, or something."

I smiled ruefully. Because, of course, if what Mr. Morton believed about me was true—which it wasn't—*I* wasn't the one Will had known in his past life. That honor was entirely Jennifer's.

"He just likes me as a friend," I said, for what seemed like the millionth time that day.

"I wouldn't be so sure," Jennifer said a little darkly. "I mean, he invited you to go sailing with us. He doesn't invite just anybody onto that boat of his. And he says that stupid dog of his likes you. Plus, he says he can *talk* to you. Will's gotten very into talking lately. He's . . . changed, you know." She glanced at me meaningfully.

But I was clueless.

"Changed how?"

"Since we started dating," she said, with a shrug. "It used to be, all he cared about was sailing and football. Then he got into student council. Sometimes"—she threw me a horrified look—"he even wants to talk about politics. Politics! Over the summer, he was talking about not going out for the football team, so he'd have more time for the debate team, or something. Can you imagine? Lance talked him out of that one, thank God. But the truth was, I felt like he was turning into somebody I didn't even know. . . .

"That's the one thing I like best about Lance," she

went on, snapping her makeup bag closed. "He's not into *talking* all the time, the way Will's been, lately. I swear, sometimes it was like he'd rather talk than—well, you know."

I *did* know. And the thought made me blush.

"It would be so cool if you and Will started going out," Jennifer said, her eyes lighting up. "Because then people would get off my back about the whole Lance thing. Because, you know, even though Will's turning into a bit of a weirdo, with this quitting-football-and-going-and-sitting-in-the-woods thing, he's still as popular as ever. Think about it, will you?"

She gave her bouncy blond curls a toss, then turned to face me instead of the mirror. "Well, what do you think? Can you tell I was bawling my brains out a minute ago?"

I looked at her. And my heart sank.

Because she was gorgeous. Even after, as she put it, bawling her brains out. I could never in a million years compete with that, no matter what she said.

And it wasn't just that she was so pretty. If it had just been that, I'd have been able to hate her, and without guilt.

But it was impossible to hate her, because it wasn't as if she were a phony. She cheerfully volunteered that she thought that the boy she was still partly in love with was actually more interested in me . . . and then—again without the slightest twinge of conscience—urged me to date him, because it would make things easier for her socially.

How could you not like someone like that?

"You look great," I said, meaning it.

"Thanks." Jennifer tilted her chin to look up at me.

"You really won't tell anyone, will you?" she asked.

"No," I said. "I really won't."

"It's so weird," she said, moving to the ladies' room door. "But I totally believe you. And I hardly know you. You must just be one of those people. You know, the kind you feel like you've met before, even if you haven't. Kind of," she added brightly, as we moved out into the hall-way, "like Will."

"Well," I was going to say. "Not exactly."

But my voice died in my throat. Because I could have sworn, at that moment, that I heard Mr. Morton, of all people, behind us.

CHAPTER TWENTY-TWO

Heard a carol, mournful, holy,
Chanted loudly, chanted lowly,
Till her blood was frozen slowly,
And her eyes were darken'd wholly,
Turn'd to tower'd Camelot.

I spun around just in time to see Mr. Morton turning the corner toward the guidance counselor's office, one hand protectively hovering over the center of a slender woman's back. It was hard to tell from behind, but it looked just like Will's mom.

When I heard Mr. Morton's clipped, British tones saying, "This way, Mrs. Wagner," I knew it *was* Will's stepmom.

What on earth was Mr. Morton doing back at school? Shouldn't he have been on a plane to Tahiti?

And why was he with Mrs. Wagner, of all people?

This, I knew, could only mean trouble.

"I'll see you later," I said to Jennifer, who'd continued

222

down the hallway, oblivious to what was going on behind us.

"Oh," she said, glancing back at me over her shoulder. "Uh, sure."

I whirled around and ran after Mr. Morton, who was holding open the clear glass door to the counseling office for Mrs. Wagner.

"This way," he was saying. "I'll just see if the conference room is free—"

"Mr. Morton," I said, barging in behind them.

Mrs. Wagner turned and blinked at me. "Oh," she said. Amazingly, in spite of the dozens of people she had to have met the night of Will's party, she seemed to recognize me. "Hello, again. I'm afraid I forgot your name."

"Ellie Harrison," I said quickly. "Mr. Morton, can I just have a quick word with you out in the hallway here?"

"No, Miss Harrison," Mr. Morton said firmly. "I'm afraid you may not. As you can see, I am quite busy with Mrs. Wagner, here. Mrs. Wagner, if you'll just come in here and have a seat, I'm sure Mrs. Klopper"—the guidance office receptionist rose from behind her desk obediently—"will find you some coffee while we wait for your stepson to arrive."

"Wait." I stared at Mr. Morton, who was making not very subtle *go-away* gestures at me behind Mrs. Wagner's back. "You're meeting with Will *and* Mrs. Wagner?"

"Yes, I am, Miss Harrison, if that's quite all right with you. We have some important things to make clear to

Will. Don't you have a class you need to be getting to right now?"

Important things to make clear to Will? No way was I going to miss this. I sank down onto one of the blue couches in the outer office, picked up a copy of *National Geographic*, and said, "Actually, I have a meeting right now with my counselor."

Mrs. Klopper, returning from the coffeemaker with two cups, looked at me curiously. "I don't have you on the schedule," she said. "And Ms. Enright stepped out."

"I need some guidance," I said, trying to look upset. "About something personal. It's an emergency."

Mrs. Klopper's expression turned into one of concern. "Well, I'll see if I can find someone to speak with you, dear." She handed Mr. Morton the cups of coffee and hurried back to her desk to see if there was a counselor on duty who could speak to me.

While she was on the phone, Mr. Morton whispered to me, "I wouldn't be doing this at all if you hadn't guilted me into it. The least you could do is not make it harder for everyone."

"How am I making it harder for everyone?" I started to whisper back.

But at that moment, Will himself appeared in the doorway, holding an office pass and looking quizzical.

"Someone wanted to see me?" he asked, his voice trailing off as he noticed his stepmother through the glass walls of the conference room. "Jean? Mr. Morton? What's this all about?"

"Nothing to be overly concerned about, young man," Mr. Morton said, in what had to be the biggest understatement of the year. "Come in here, will you? I just wanted to clear a few things up between you and your, um, Mrs. Wagner."

Will moved slowly past my couch, toward the open conference room door. The eyebrow he lifted at me as he walked by said it all: *What is going on?*

I don't know, I mouthed at him, from behind the pages of the magazine I held up to shield my face from Mr. Morton's view. Because I really didn't know. At least, not what Will's stepmom could have to do with any of it.

Will grinned, a little lopsidedly, at me, then went into the conference room. Mr. Morton, with a final warning glance in my direction, shut the door. He didn't bother lowering the blinds in the room, so I saw him pull out a chair for Will to sit in, and then take a seat himself. Then, his hands folded on the tabletop, Mr. Morton began to speak.

I couldn't hear a word. I could only see the look on Mrs. Wagner's face (I couldn't see Will's, since he was sitting with his back to me). She went from looking politely alert to genuinely puzzled to defensive in the space of two minutes.

What on earth could he be saying to her?

"Um," Mrs. Klopper said, dragging my attention away from the scene unfolding behind the glass. "Ellie, is it? I'm afraid no one can see you at the moment, but Ms. Enright is on her way back and should be here in fifteen minutes. You can wait that long, can't you?"

"Sure," I said, holding up the magazine and pretending to be engrossed in it. But really I was trying to read Mr. Morton's lips. Why had I taken all those useless classes like bio and German when I should have been taking lipreading?

I didn't need to have taken lipreading to interpret what I saw next. And that was Mrs. Wagner suddenly throw a hand up to her mouth in shock over something Mr. Morton said. Then she promptly burst into tears. The next thing I knew, she was nodding and stretching out a hand toward Will.

Will, for his part, had leaped away from his stepmother's hand, getting up from his chair and backing away from the table. I still couldn't see his face, but I could see that he was shaking his head.

What was happening? Had Mr. Morton just told Will he was the reincarnation of King Arthur? But that shouldn't have made Will jump up, shaking his head. It should have made him laugh, because it was so ridiculous. What had Mr. Morton told him that could have made Will so upset and his stepmother cry?

"You're not supposed to be here!"

Mrs. Klopper's panicked tone was the only thing that caused me to drag my gaze away from the scene unfolding behind the glass walls. And only because I thought she was talking to me.

She wasn't. She was talking to the guy who, without my having heard him, had entered the guidance office,

226

and was standing there staring at the trio in the conference room, as if no one else in the building existed.

"Marco," I said, jumping up from the couch.

But he didn't hear me. He was breathing hard, his car keys dangling from one hand, as he stared at his mother and stepbrother, his dark eyes filled with something I didn't like. I didn't know what it was, exactly. But I knew it wasn't good.

"You know you're not supposed to set foot on school grounds, Marco," Mrs. Klopper was saying, in a voice that shook with fear as she lifted the receiver on her office phone and started punching buttons. "Not after what happened last time. I'm calling the police. You had better leave now."

But Marco didn't leave. Instead, he started toward the door to the conference room.

I don't know what made me do it. I am not, ordinarily, a very brave sort of person . . . except maybe with snakes. There was nothing remotely snakelike about Marco at that particular moment. Or rather, he was like a snake, but not the half-drowned kind you find curled up in the pool filter; more like the very much alive kind you find coiled at your feet, ready to strike, with poisonous fangs.

But that didn't stop me from insinuating myself between Marco and the conference room door . . . just as Mr. Morton looked up and noticed Marco's presence for the first time.

"Marco," I said, finding that, oddly, I was breathing

as hard as he was. "Hey. How's it going?"

He didn't even look down at me. His gaze was riveted on Will. "Ellie. Get out of my way."

"I don't think you're supposed to be here," I said, throwing an anxious glance over my shoulder. Mrs. Wagner, noticing Marco through her tears, was attempting to dry them. Will just looked stunned. "Mrs. Klopper called the police. You better go."

"Not," he said, his gaze still on his mother, "until I know what they're talking about."

"I think whatever they're talking about is private," I said. "Between Will and your mom."

"And Morton?" Now Marco finally looked at me. And when he did, one side of his mouth twisted in a sarcastic grin. "What's *he* got to say to my mother?"

"Whatever it is," I said, fervently hoping it wasn't what I was pretty sure we were both thinking it might be—Mr. Morton's belief that Will was the reincarnation of King Arthur, "it's clearly none of our business, so—"

"Wrong," Marco said. "Move. Now. Or I'll move you."

"If you lay one hand on that girl, Marco Campbell," Mrs. Klopper said shrilly, "you'll regret it. You know you're not even supposed to be here—"

Which was when Marco, obviously tired of hearing this, reached out and flung me aside, as if I were a shower curtain that had been in his way.

I fell to the sofa. I wasn't hurt.

But that didn't stop Mrs. Klopper from screaming and rushing to my side. Nor did it stop Will, who'd

"No," I said. The wind was beginning to gust, tossing the branches of the trees. "They went into D.C. for dinner."

"Want me to walk you inside?" Officer Jenkins asked.

"No," I said. "Really. It's okay. I'm all right."

It seemed like I'd been assuring everyone of this all afternoon—from the time the cops had arrived, to the time they'd finally finished taking my statement and agreed to let me go . . . right up until I realized I had no way home, and was forced to beg for a ride. With Mrs. Wagner having completely lost it, forcing a chivalrous Mr. Morton to offer to drive her home, and Will having taken off after Marco via the very same window he'd escaped through, Mrs. Klopper and I had been the only ones left to describe what had happened. . . .

And we could barely believe it ourselves.

"Well, I don't like to gossip about students," Mrs. Klopper had said to Officer Jenkins, after Mrs. Wagner had been carefully led away by Mr. Morton, and the two of us were asked to make statements concerning the incident. "But since you ask, it appears—unless I'm mistaken—that Will Wagner's stepmother is actually his real mother . . . and neither he nor his—well, I guess he's his half brother, Marco—knew it until today."

When the police officer had looked questioningly at me, I had just shrugged and said, "Yeah. I mean . . . that's what I gathered, as well."

What I couldn't understand, of course, was why Mr. Morton had done it. Why had he come back? Had it

apparently seen the whole thing, from tearing open the conference room door, and shouting, "Marco! What do you think you're doing?"

"Funny," Marco said coldly, "I was about to ask you the same question."

Then he strode into the conference room, slamming the glass door behind him with enough force to cause the entire room to shudder.

"Oh, my dear," Mrs. Klopper cried, as she tried to pull me up from the couch. "Did he hurt you?"

"I'm fine," I said quickly. I couldn't hear—let alone see—what was happening in the conference room with her hovering over me. Leaning over so I could look past Mrs. Klopper's broad shoulder, I could see Mr. Morton trying to speak calmly to a very agitated Marco. Mrs. Wagner had stopped crying, and she, too, was saying something to Marco—something Marco didn't look too happy to hear. He kept glancing at Will, who appeared to be experiencing a number of conflicting emotions, if his expression was any indication—rage; disbelief; and, finally, impatience, apparently for something Marco said.

Something Mrs. Klopper and I heard only too clearly, because Marco shouted it loudly enough to be heard even through the thick glass walls: "I don't believe it!"

It was right then that the cops came bursting into the guidance office, and Mrs. Klopper, still hovering over me protectively, cried, pointing a shaking finger at Marco, "There he is! He attacked this poor girl! He's violating the terms of his probation by even being on school grounds!"

One of the cops, to my horror, reached for his nightstick. He said to his partner, "I know this kid. Call for backup."

The partner reached for his walkie-talkie, while the first cop laid a hand on the conference room door and pulled it open.

And when he did, Marco's voice—his back to us, he was oblivious to the entry of the cops—could be heard, loud and clear, shouting, "You're not his mother! Tell him! Tell him it's a lie!"

To which Mrs. Wagner, her hands clenched to her chest, murmured, "I can't, sweetheart, because it's true. I'm so sorry. But it really is true."

Which is when the cop said, "I hate to break things up here, people, but we got a complaint—"

He never got to finish. Because Marco, wheeling around and realizing, at last, that he was in trouble, made a lunge that would have caused high-jumper Stacy to turn green with envy, propelling himself over the conference room table until he stood in front of the room's single window . . .

. . . through which he hefted one of the conference room chairs, shattering the glass into a million pieces.

Then he leaped.

CHAPTER TWENTY-THREE

For ere she reach'd upon the tide
The first house by the water-side,
Singing in her song she died,
The Lady of Shalott.

"Turn here," I said to the police officer who was driving me home.

He made the turn down the long driveway to the house we were renting, the headlights from his squad car startling a deer that had been grazing at the edge of the road. Although it was still late afternoon, massive gray clouds had rolled in from the bay, blocking out the sun, moving as fast as smoke caught in a breeze. What I'd mistaken for the rumble of rifle fire turned out to be thunder, not practice down at the gunnery.

There was a storm brewing.

"The lights are all out," Officer Jenkins observed, as the house loomed into view. "Your parents aren't home?"

really been because of what he'd said—my "guilting" him into it with my speech about how Will would never have left him in *his* hour of need?

But how on earth was Mr. Morton's getting Mrs. Wagner to admit that she was, in truth, Will's real mother, and not just his stepmother as he'd been led to believe, supposed to have helped?

"Well, grab a flashlight as soon as you get inside," Officer Jenkins said, "so you don't have to look for one in the dark if we lose power. The electricity goes out a lot this side of the Severn during big storms."

"Thanks," I said to the police officer.

"And don't worry about Campbell," he said, in his big, reassuring voice. "I doubt he'll show up here."

I thanked him again, not mentioning that Marco Campbell showing up at my house was the *last* thing I was worried about.

Then I got out of the squad car and ran to the front porch, fumbling in my bag for my key. Officer Jenkins waited until I'd found it and opened the door before he pulled away, leaving me alone with the big dark house and the approaching storm and the forces of good and evil battling it out over the fate of a long-dead king.

Right.

I let myself into the house, flicking on lights as I made my way to the laundry room, where the professor who owned the house had left a plastic bin marked EMER-GENCY. I pulled back the lid and grabbed the flashlight and handful of candles I found there. Then I brought them all into the kitchen and turned on the television.

The local news was issuing a thunderstorm warning for all of Anne Arundel County. They'd already had reports of dangerous lightning and high winds, coupled with torrential rain and some hail.

Great.

There was a note on the refrigerator. It said, *Hi, honey. Leftover ribs in the fridge. Just heat them up in the microwave. We'll be home by eleven. Call if you need anything. Mom.*

I opened the fridge and looked at the ribs. But I wasn't really seeing them. Instead, I was seeing the rage on Marco's face when his mother had made her gut-wrenching confession. I was seeing Will, as he'd followed Marco out that window, causing my heart to leap into my throat.

And, okay, it had turned out to have been a first-floor window. And when we'd all rushed to it, we'd seen both boys sprinting for the student parking lot, Marco first, with Will in hot pursuit, clearly none the worse for the stunt.

But I'd happened to glance at Mr. Morton at that moment, and I'd seen the fear on his face. Crazy or not, Mr. Morton was afraid for Will.

And his fear was catching.

I closed the refrigerator door. This was stupid. I couldn't just stay here and do nothing while I knew Will was out there somewhere, trying to deal with a guy who was clearly off his rocker with fury over his mother's unfaithfulness to his father.

I took a deep breath and picked up the phone.

"Here goes nothing," I said to Tig, who was sitting in the middle of the kitchen floor, washing herself.

And I dialed Will's cell number.

A recorded voice told me all circuits were busy.

I flinched and hung up. Well, so much for that.

I opened the refrigerator and took out the ribs. I wasn't hungry, but I had to do something, or I was sure I'd lose my mind. I popped them into the microwave—then jumped, as outside the window over the kitchen sink, a brilliant flash of lightning lit the yard.

The power flickered off, then back on again. Tig, startled, quit washing herself.

I counted, like the kid in *Poltergeist*. One one thousand. Two one thousand. Three one thousand.

Thunder crashed, sounding nothing like distant gunfire now . . . more like a sonic boom from a fighter jet as it broke the sound barrier. Tig streaked from the room like a stone from a slingshot, headed for parts of the house unknown.

The storm was three miles away.

I tried Will's cell again. All circuits still busy.

I put the phone down, thinking maybe our lines were crossed. He might, for all I knew, be trying to call me, right at that very moment. After what had happened today, you'd think he'd want to talk to somebody—somebody to whom he wasn't related. I was kind of surprised, in fact, that he hadn't called already.

But there were no messages on the answering machine.

Then again, maybe he'd turned to Lance or Jennifer

instead of me. After all, they'd known him a lot longer than I had. It made sense he'd call one of them before me. . . .

A part of me will always love him, Jennifer had said in the ladies' room. Maybe he was on the phone with her right now, and they'd had a chance to talk things out, and now they were back together. Maybe they—

I shook my head, wondering what was wrong with me. I was losing it. I really was.

I sat down in front of the TV with the leftover ribs and a tub of potato salad, and ate—without tasting anything—as the newscasters read off all the events that were being canceled or closed in light of the approaching storm: high school football games; various lacrosse tournaments; the county fairgrounds; a regatta.

A reporter in Baltimore, where the storm—which had apparently appeared from nowhere—had already hit, stood beside a car that had been flattened by a tree felled by lightning and warned about the dangers of driving during inclement weather.

Another reporter came on to say that the Beltway— where my parents would be driving home later that night—had been shut down due to a severed power line that had electrified the guardrail.

Another reporter started talking about how this unexpected squall was the storm of the decade, then showed footage of raging floodwaters that washed an SUV right off the road and into a ditch, trapping a family of four inside. . . .

Suddenly, I wasn't blaming Mr. Morton so much anymore for wanting to go to Tahiti.

Which was just silly, of course. It wasn't the powers of darkness causing this storm. The meteorologist came on and talked about nor'easters and cold fronts meeting warm fronts and storm surge and riptides.

Then, just as he was about to advise us what to do in the event of a power failure, a brighter bolt of lightning than any of the ones before lit up the sky outside.

But it didn't turn the sky white, the way lightning usually does. Instead, just for an instant—so briefly that afterwards, I'd thought I'd dreamed it—the sky turned a deep bloodred before turning dark gray again.

Then all the lights went off.

The TV died. The air-conditioning churned to a halt. The digital clocks on the stove and microwave went black. The refrigerator stopped humming. There was complete total silence. . . .

Until a terrific blast of thunder ripped through the sky, causing the glasses in the china cabinet to rattle.

Then the phone rang.

And I screamed.

I was being ridiculous, of course. It was just the phone. Of course the phone would still work in a power failure—the ones that weren't cordless, anyway.

Still, my heart seemed to be rattling as loudly as the glasses had, and my fingers shook as I reached out to grab the receiver.

"H-hello?" I said.

"Ellie?" It was my mom's voice, as comforting as a favorite blanket. Just hearing it slowed down my pulse. "We just heard Anne Arundel's supposed to get the worst of this storm. Are you all right, honey?"

"The lights went out," I said, trying not to sound as scared as I felt.

"Yes," my mom said. "I guess that happens a lot. Look in the phone book and call the power company, just to make sure it's the whole district, and not only us. Then sit tight. Daddy and I canceled our dinner, and we're on our way home."

"No, you're not," I said, in a tight voice. "They've shut down the Beltway. A downed power line has electrified the guardrails."

I heard my mother convey this information to my dad. I heard my dad swear. Then Mom said to me, "Well, listen, honey . . . you got a flashlight?"

I reached for the one on the counter. I didn't quite need it yet—there was still enough light from outside to see by. But I said, "Yes."

"Good. Find a good book to read, and we'll be there as soon as we can."

"Will do," I said. "Bye, Mom."

Outside, lightning flashed again. I hung up and ran toward the window, craning my neck to see whether or not the sky was going to turn the same bloodred again.

It didn't. It did turn a really pretty purple, though.

I picked up the phone. This time I dialed Will's house. Busy.

Then I remembered I was supposed to call the power company, so I hauled out the phone book and found the number.

Then I entertained myself for a good five minutes listening to my options—press one to report lights that were flickering; two, if I smelled anything burning; three, if I was experiencing partial loss of power; and finally four, which I hit, to report a total loss of power.

The recorded voice told me they were aware of the problem and that crews had already been dispatched. I was glad I didn't work for the power company. I would have hated being "dispatched" in this weather.

Then, just as I was contemplating turning on the flashlight and starting my trig homework, the phone rang again. This time when I answered it, I didn't recognize the voice on the other end.

"Hello?" It was a woman speaking. "Is, er, Ellie Harrison there?"

"This is she," I said, using the polite phone manners my mother had drilled into me.

"Oh, Ellie, hello," the woman said, sounding relieved. "This is Jean Wagner. Will's, er, stepmom."

Suddenly I was clutching the phone very hard.

Still, I tried to remain calm. "Hello, Mrs. Wagner. I . . . I'm sorry. About what happened today at school."

"So am I," Mrs. Wagner said. "You can't imagine how much. That's why I'm calling, actually. I was wondering if by any chance Will was with you?"

By now I was clutching the receiver so hard, I thought I might break it in half with the force of my grip.

"No," I said, feeling as if my heart might suddenly leap from my chest, it was drumming so hard. "I was hoping you might have heard from him."

"Not since"—Mrs. Wagner coughed—"what happened at the school. I was hoping—I don't know where either of them has disappeared to, and I wouldn't have bothered you except that I know Will's been spending time at your house lately, and I was hoping he might be there—"

As Mrs. Wagner had been speaking, I'd crossed the room to the sliding glass door that led to the deck. I hadn't looked out at the pool since I'd gotten home, I'd been so wrapped up in the approaching storm.

Now I twitched the curtain back, telling myself that it was all going to be all right. I'd see Will down there, sitting on Spider Rock. I'd pull back the sliding glass door and yell, *"Hey, you big goof. Don't just sit there. Can't you see it's going to rain? Come inside."*

Only he wasn't there, of course. As I watched, my favorite raft was actually lifted up out of the water and thrown into the bushes by a powerful blast of wind. The water churned even though the filter wasn't working, thanks to the power outage. It looked like a giant witch's cauldron, set to boil.

I quickly moved the curtain back into place.

"—or that you might have some idea where he could be," Mrs. Wagner was saying. "We checked the marina already, and he's not there . . . not that he would take the boat out in this kind of weather. I've talked to his friend Lance and to little Jenny Gold, and neither of them have heard from him." I heard barking through the phone line, then Mrs. Wagner's voice saying, "Cavalier! Cavalier, be quiet!"

A second later, she said to me, "I'm sorry. Will's dog . . . I don't know what's gotten into her. She's normally so well-mannered. The storm seems to be upsetting her. The thing is, Marco . . . Well, I'm afraid Will might be in some . . . well, some danger."

"Danger?" The hand clutching the phone had started to sweat now. I could barely hang on to the receiver, it was so wet. "What kind of danger, Mrs. Wagner?"

Not the powers of darkness, I prayed. Please don't say powers of darkness. Had Mr. Morton gotten to her, too?

Her voice broke.

"Oh," she said. "Oh, dear, I'm sorry. I don't mean to— I swore I wouldn't cry. It's Marco, you see." She was weeping openly now, while Cavalier barked steadily in the background. "Arthur—my husband—says not to worry, but I don't see how I can't. . . . His gun case was broken into, you see. Arthur's gun case. And one of his pistols is missing. I think Marco might have taken it. I think Marco might be planning on doing something—"

But I never got to hear what Mrs. Wagner thought

Marco might be planning. That's because there was another bright white flash of lightning, and the receiver let out a staticky shriek and seemed to spark in my ear. I dropped it with a yelp, and when I stooped to pick it up again, the line was dead.

CHAPTER TWENTY-FOUR

In the stormy east-wind straining,
The pale yellow woods were waning,
The broad stream in his banks complaining,
Heavily the low sky raining
Over tower'd Camelot

Not that it mattered. About the phone dying in the middle of Mrs. Wagner's sentence. I didn't need to hear the rest. I knew what she was going to say.

Just like I knew what I had to do.

Because I knew where Will had gone. If he wasn't home or on his boat, and he wasn't with Lance or Jennifer or me. . . .

Well, there was only one place he could be.

The trouble was, I had no car to get me there. The rain hadn't started yet, but the sky was getting darker every second. In seconds, not minutes, the clouds would burst.

And the lightning hadn't quit. If anything, the bolts

243

were growing more frequent. Thunder was an almost constant rumble now.

Flash. One one thousand. Boom.

The storm was only a mile away.

But so what? I thought to myself, as I threw on my running shoes. You're not sugar, Harrison. You won't melt.

Admiral Wagner's gun case had been broken into.

The park was two miles away. I run two miles every day—more, most days. Okay, not along open road, after a meal, and in the middle of a record-breaking thunderstorm.

But what else was I supposed to do?

I reached for the first coat by the door—a waterproof windbreaker of my dad's. It even had a hood. Perfect.

A gun. He's got a gun.

I was halfway out the door when it happened again. This time I saw the bolt streaking across the sky like a crack in a giant celestial plate. It was so close, I thought it hit our neighbor's house.

And then, just like before, the sky turned a deep bloodred. Only for as long as it took me to blink at the sudden change of light.

Then the sky was a leaden gray once more.

"It's just lightning," I told myself. "Not the forces of evil conspiring against you."

Still, my voice shook as I said it. What were the chances of Marco going after Will in weather like this? Surely he, too, would think twice about going out in the middle of a raging nor'easter.

Then I remembered the gun. If Marco was crazy enough to steal one of his stepfather's guns, he wasn't going to let a little thing like the storm of the decade bother him.

Great.

Well, there was nothing I could do about the weather. But the gun. Marco's gun . . .

Revolvers and nightsticks are useless against the wrath of the dark side, Mr. Morton had said.

And suddenly I'd turned away from the front door and was pounding up the stairs to the second floor.

"Don't let him have taken it with him," I breathed, hurrying down the hall toward my dad's office. "Don't let him have taken it with him—"

He hadn't. It was lying there where he'd left it, tossed as casually across his desk as a pen. I wrapped my hand around the hilt and lifted it. It was much heavier than I remembered.

But there was nothing I could do about that now.

I wrapped it in my dad's windbreaker. I vaguely remembered reading somewhere that you aren't supposed to get swords wet. Although that might have been the string of a bow—the kind you shoot arrows with. But I couldn't run down the street holding a sword, anyway. What would the neighbors say? Our Image would be totally blown.

Cradling the windbreaker-swaddled sword in my arms, I hurried back down the stairs. I couldn't even say what I planned on doing with my dad's sword. I mean, was I really going to use it to threaten Marco? A sword—especially a rusty, useless one from the Middle Ages—against a gun? Yeah. That'll work. He'll probably surrender the minute he sees it.

Not.

But I had to do something.

And I guess—if you wanted to believe that the nor'easter tearing through Annapolis at that moment was the work of the dark side, and not, as the meteorologist had said, a collision of two weather fronts—my bringing the sword along was upsetting somebody upstairs, since no sooner had I stepped through the door with it than the sky was torn in two by the closest lightning strike yet. . . .

It was so close, in fact, that for a second I thought it had hit me, because the hair on the back of my neck had risen. I shrieked, not daring to look to see what color the sky was turning above me. I couldn't look. I was too busy running. I ran straight down our driveway, then onto our street, my legs seeming to propel me forward without my even consciously telling them to.

Clutching the sword to my chest, I pounded along the paved road, already breathing hard. I'd thought running through the humidity of a Maryland August was bad. That was nothing, it turned out, compared to running through the electrically charged air of a nor'easter with a medieval sword in my arms.

When I got to the main road, I was shocked by what

I saw. Branches had already been knocked down by the wind, and they dotted the road like track hurdles . . . or snakes. The leaves that were still attached to them were turned defensively upside down and gleamed a pale gray in what little light the thick black clouds overhead were letting through.

I took a deep breath and, never faltering in my stride, began running around the obstacles, hideously conscious of the fact that I was on a road not meant for pedestrian traffic. There was no sidewalk or bike path. I was running along open highway, dodging fallen tree branches, holding a big sword, and praying that if a car came along, it would see me in time and swerve.

No such luck. A car did come along.

But it was going at such a high rate of speed, there was no way the driver—a harried soccer mom, anxious to pick up her kids before the rain hit and soaked them—could turn in time to avoid hitting me. She came barreling right at me, only seeing me at the last possible minute, which is when she hit the horn and stomped on the brakes at the same time. . . .

Evil won't stand for any interference from the Light. It will throw insurmountable obstacles in our path—deadly obstacles.

. . . and I leaped off the road, as fleetly as that deer I'd seen at the edge of our driveway, and began tearing through people's lawns instead of sticking to the road.

This proved to be a lot more convenient than dodging swerving SUVs and fallen trees. Plus the grass was gentler on my shin splints than the asphalt. . . .

The powers of darkness—if they existed—didn't seem to like that any more than they'd liked me bringing along the sword. Either that, or it was simply time for the heavens to open. Because it was right about then that they did just that, unleashing a sudden curtain of hard, stinging rain, that soaked through my T-shirt and shorts in an instant and flattened my hair to the back of my neck.

I kept running, clutching the sword even more tightly to my chest, trying to ignore the fact that the rain was coming down so fast, I could barely see two feet in front of me, and was turning the grass beneath my feet into a river of mud. I had to be, I told myself, close to the Wawa by now. And the Wawa was halfway to the park. Just one more mile. Just one more mile to go.

And they had nothing more to throw at me. Lightning hadn't stopped me. Oncoming traffic hadn't stopped me. Rain hadn't stopped me.

Fear hadn't stopped me.

Nothing could stop me. I was going to get there. I was going to—

That's when the hail started.

At first I thought I'd kicked up a rock from beneath my foot. Then another one hit me. Then another. Soon ice pellets were bouncing off my head and shoulders, my thighs and calves.

But I kept going. I lifted the sword—safe from the hail in my dad's windbreaker—over my head, using it as a sort of shield against the worst of the hail. And I started dodging beneath trees as I ran, even though the meteorologist on the news had said that was the worst place to be during a storm.

And it was probably even worse to be under a tree while carrying a long metal object. . . .

But I didn't care. I wasn't district champ—back home, anyway—in the women's two hundred meter for nothing. I was too fast for them—too fast for the lightning that ripped through the sky, turning it a sickly teal green this time, instead of bloodred. Too fast for the deafening clap of thunder that followed it less than a second later. Too fast for the rain. Too fast for cars. Too fast for hail . . .

The storm was right above my head.

And it was furious.

The hail turned back to rain, but it still came down in torrents. I was so wet by then, I didn't even care. Especially when, through the thick gray curtain of it, the sign welcoming me to Anne Arundel Park—PLEASE, NO LITTERING—appeared.

I was there. I'd made it. I staggered toward the sign, not even aware, until that very moment, that I'd been crying, probably since the hail started. Me, who never cries.

And then the rain stopped.

Just like that. As if someone had turned off a spigot.

I paused only long enough to wipe the water from my eyes. Then I started running again—sprinting, really—

for the arboretum, while overhead, the sky rumbled in protest, as if there were giants up there, talking among themselves.

As I passed the dripping tennis courts and flooded lacrosse field, I saw a sight more welcome than even a dry towel would have been at that moment:

Will's car, sitting all by itself in the parking lot.

He was here. He was safe. . . .

Except that he wasn't in his car. I checked. It was locked tight.

And empty.

He couldn't have spent the entirety of that hailstorm in the arboretum. Not when he had a nice safe car to run to.

I was too late. I had to be. Marco had already come and gone. I was going to find Will stretched out dead on that boulder of his. I knew it.

But surely, if he were dead, the dark side would not have worked so hard at keeping me from getting here. . . .

Except that it had stopped. The rain had stopped.

Then I caught myself. What was I thinking? *Dark side?*

It was a storm. *Just a storm.*

A storm that had come from nowhere. A storm that had turned over trees and electrified a highway and sent my cat streaking for the safety of the inner recesses of the house. A storm that had sent a dog barking hysterically into the phone. Barking at me.

I turned up the pace, running all out now, the sword

clutched in one hand by its hilt.

Inside the arboretum, which I expected to be a mess—branches and even some trees down—everything was precisely as I'd seen it last. The smell of rain was thick in the air, but clearly no rain had fallen here. The trail was so dry, puffs of dust rose up from my feet as they pounded against it.

How that was possible, I hadn't the slightest idea. But I didn't really have time to think about it, either. Because finally I was in front of the ravine, cursing myself for not having brought a flashlight, because it was dark in those woods, with the storm clouds overhead. I crashed through the heavy bracken, trying to get a glimpse of the creek bed. I thought I could see someone down there, but it was hard to be sure. . . .

And then I saw him. Will.

But he wasn't sitting on his favorite boulder. He wasn't standing on it, either. Instead, he was stretched out across it, on his back, like . . .

Well, like a dead man.

CHAPTER TWENTY-FIVE

Under tower and balcony,
By garden-wall and gallery,
A gleaming shape she floated by,
Dead-pale between the houses high,
Silent into Camelot.

I didn't scream.

I don't think I could have uttered a sound if I'd tried. For one thing, I was breathing too hard from my run.

And for another, the cold hard fear that had been gripping my heart since I'd heard Cavalier barking—but which I had refused to let myself acknowledge—seemed suddenly to convulse, cutting off all the blood supply to the rest of my body.

I don't even know how I got to the bottom of the ravine. I suppose I stumbled there somehow. I do know that by the time I reached Will's boulder, my legs were covered in oozing scratches from all the brambles I'd apparently encountered, but hadn't felt.

Lifting my gaze to where he lay, his eyes closed, I could detect no sign that Will was breathing. But neither could I see any obvious bloodstains. Still, he had to have heard me coming. And yet he hadn't moved. . . .

My legs trembling uncontrollably—both from emotion and the endurance test I'd just put them through—I walked around the boulder and set down the sword, still safely wrapped in my dad's jacket. Then I placed the toe of my shoe into one of the footholds I'd used to climb Will's boulder the last time. . . .

And his face suddenly popped up above mine.

"Elle," he said. He reached up to pull off a set of headphones he'd been wearing. "You came. I knew you would."

And then he grabbed my hand and pulled me up onto the top of the boulder. . . .

. . . where I completely lost it. My limbs turned to jelly. All the blood in my body, which seconds before had been frozen, seemed to thaw at his touch and left me feeling as if I hadn't the strength to so much as stand.

Will must have recognized this, for just as I felt my knees begin to give, he said, "Hey—" and let go of my hand, throwing an arm instead around my waist. When my still-liquid limbs continued to sway, he caught me up against him with a laugh that ended abruptly as our bodies met, and my hands flattened out against his chest.

Then he said, "Hey," again—but in a different, much softer voice.

Staring into his swimming-pool blue eyes, just inches from my own much plainer brown ones, I finally found my voice.

"I thought you were dead," I whispered raggedly.

"Far from it," he whispered back.

And then he was kissing me.

And suddenly, my arms and legs didn't feel like jelly anymore. Instead, I felt as electrified—as if I really had been struck by lightning . . . only better. Much, much better. Because you can't wrap your arms around lightning. Or feel lightning's heart skip a beat beneath yours. Or taste the coffee he'd had to drink earlier, or smell the nice clean scent of his shirt. I could do all these things with Will, and did. . . .

. . . including press myself as close to him as I possibly could, and not just because I was so cold, after all that rain. Also to prove to myself that he was alive. *Alive.*

And he was kissing me.

And seemed to like kissing me. Very, very much.

"Now why haven't we done that before?" Will wanted to know, when we'd finally stopped kissing and his forehead was resting against mine.

"Because you already had a girlfriend," I reminded him. I was amazed that I still possessed the ability to speak. I would have thought, after a kiss like that, I'd have been rendered speechless. My lips were still tingling from it.

"Oh yeah," he said, still holding on to me. Then he lifted his head. "Hey. You're shivering." He rubbed my arms with his hands—his big, warm hands. "No wonder. You're all wet. How'd you get so wet?"

"Because it was raining," I said. And as if to confirm this, thunder rumbled ominously overhead.

"Not here," Will said.

"Obviously," I said.

"How can that be?" He let go of me, but only for a second, while he leaned down to lift up a jean jacket he'd left lying beside his iPod. He threw the jacket over my shoulders, then pulled me to him again. "Look, I'm sorry about what happened back there. At the school. With Marco. That was bad."

"Yeah," I said, loving the way his arms felt around me. "It was. I . . . I'm sorry, too."

"Nothing for you to be sorry for," he said. "You didn't do anything. I could have killed him when he pushed you."

"Yeah," I said. "About Marco, Will." I swallowed and then, placing both hands on his shoulders, I pushed him away a little, so that I could look up into his face. It was as darkly handsome as ever, his brilliant blue eyes ringed by thick black lashes.

"What?" he asked, gazing down at me. "He didn't—you haven't heard from him, have you? I lost him outside school—I drove around, looking for him, but I couldn't find him. I . . . I didn't want to go home." He glanced away from me then. "I tried calling your house a few times, but the operator kept saying all circuits were busy. I thought about coming by, but after what happened, I

255

wasn't sure—"

I grabbed his face between both my palms and turned it so he had to look me in the eye.

"You can't be serious," I said. "You think I wouldn't want to see you? Just because of what happened at school?"

That shadow I knew all too well flitted across his face, darkening his features, although his grip on me didn't loosen.

"It must be all over town by now," was all he said.

"Will, your mom called me. She's really worried. . . ."

He did let go of me then. He let go of me and turned his back, running a hand through his dark hair.

"Look," he said to the trees. "I just need a little time away from her. And my dad. To think things over." He looked back at me, his expression wry. "It's not every day a guy finds out his mom's not really dead, you know."

"I know," I said, again. "That's not why she called, though."

He grimaced. "I know why she called. It's Marco, isn't it?"

I nodded, not trusting my voice to speak. Overhead, thunder rumbled again.

Will sighed. "What'd Marco do now?" He was grinning, but not as if he found the subject a particularly amusing one. "Trash the Land Cruiser? Empty Dad's liquor cabinet? No, he's already done all that. Besides, none of that would hurt me, and I'm the one he blames for all this. Oh, wait, I know. He took the *Pride Winn* out and ran her aground."

"No," I said, and swallowed. "He's stolen one of your dad's guns. And I think he's going to try to kill you."

CHAPTER TWENTY-SIX

And as the boat-head wound along
The willowy hills and fields among,
They heard her singing her last song,
The Lady of Shalott.

"That's impossible," Will said flatly.

"Will."

I felt miserable. I'd come crashing down from the high his kisses had sent me to. It was almost as if they'd never happened. Had I dreamed them? Everything that had gone on in the past hour seemed like a dream, from the storm to . . . well, this.

"It's not impossible," I said. "Your father's gun case was broken into, and Marco is still missing. I know you didn't take it. Who else could have?"

"Oh, I believe Marco took the gun," Will said. "But kill me? Jean—I mean, Mom—is overreacting a little. Marco's not a killer."

This was exactly what I had said to Mr. Morton. Before I'd found out the rest.

"Um," I said. "Will. This may be a little more complicated than you think."

"More complicated than my real mother giving birth to me while her husband was overseas, and giving me to the man who'd actually fathered me to raise, so her husband wouldn't find out she'd been unfaithful? More complicated than having been told my whole life that my mother was dead, until today, when I was told she's actually the woman my father married after rising high enough through the ranks to be able to send his best friend—her husband—to his death?" Will's laugh was without mirth. "Believe me, Elle. I get the gist."

"Yeah," I said. "About that. I have something to tell you, and it might sound a little strange, but you know before, when you were telling me about how you sometimes get this feeling that you've been here before? Well, there's this group of people who believe you actually—"

"What's he want to kill me for?" Will interrupted, as he paced up and down the length of the boulder. Above our heads, his question was answered with another loud rumble of thunder. "My dad's the one who did it. Not me. I had nothing to do with it."

"Yeah," I said. "Well, see, remember when Marco attacked Mr. Morton last year? It turns out—"

"And it's not like my dad did it on purpose," Will went on. "I mean, yeah, he sent the guy into a hot spot. But it wasn't like he shot that helicopter down himself. They were under enemy fire. It could have happened to anyone."

"Will," I said, reaching out to grab him by the shoulders so he'd quit pacing a minute. "It doesn't matter why. The fact is, Marco wants to kill you. Now, don't you think you and I should get out of here, in case he shows up?"

"Here?" Will's dark eyebrows slanted downward. "But he doesn't even know about this place. I've never brought him here, much less told him about it."

"And the meeting today with Mr. Morton and your mom," I said. "Did anybody tell Marco about that? Or did he just show up?"

"No, nobody told him. He . . ." Will's expression changed from fury to confusion as he looked down at me. "How could he have known about that meeting? Unless . . . He must have been listening in on the other extension when Mr. Morton called."

"Right," I said. "Or . . .Well, there's one other explanation."

One side of Will's mouth quirked up. "What? That he's got ESP?"

"That, or he's an agent for the powers of darkness."

I said it fast, to get it out before I thought better of it. I still didn't believe it. At least, not completely. But I thought I had to give him fair warning, since Mr. Morton obviously hadn't.

"The powers of . . ." Will's voice trailed off as he stared down at me.

But instead of laughing it off or otherwise dismissing

it the way I'd half-expected him to, Will's gaze grew even more intense.

"What did you mean before, when you said that about my thinking I've been here before?" he asked. "And what was that about a group of people who believe . . . something?"

"You know what?" I gripped his shoulders more tightly than ever. "It's kind of a long story, and there's a good chance it may not even be true. But true or not, I still think we'd better go—at the very least to get out of the rain, if not away from Marco."

Will looked up at the ever-darkening mass of clouds overhead—what we could see of them, through the treetops. Funny how it had rained everywhere else but here.

But not ha-ha funny.

"Okay," he said, and started to follow me as I climbed down from his boulder. "But where do you want to go?"

The deep voice seemed to come out of nowhere.

"May I recommend Tahiti?"

I froze. The blood that Will had thawed with his kiss iced up again.

Because I recognized that voice. I knew who it was even before I turned around and saw him standing in the creek bed, the mouth of an ugly black gun trained on the center of Will's chest.

"I hear the Polynesian Islands are lovely this time of year," Marco said casually.

The two brothers stared at each other, Marco, down in the creek bed, and Will on the top of his boulder. It was so still, I could hear both of them breathing. At least until lightning coursed across the sky overhead, making me jump—even before it turned everything along the horizon a bright, cardinal red.

Then thunder crashed, and the red disappeared as quickly as it had appeared.

"Elle," Will said, in the sudden silence that followed these celestial pyrotechnics. He never took his gaze off Marco. "Go home."

"Yes, *Elaine*," Marco said, in a voice dripping with malice. "Run home to *float* some more. There's nothing you can do here."

I bristled. I knew what Marco meant. That there was nothing *Elaine of Astolat* could do here.

But that was fine, because I wasn't Elaine of Astolat, no matter what he might think. And there was plenty Elaine Harrison could do.

"I'm not going anywhere," I said.

Marco feigned that he was touched.

"Aw, how sweet," he said. "She's going to stay to defend her man."

Will didn't seem to think it was very sweet, though.

"Elle," he said, in the same voice he'd used that day with Rick, outside Mr. Morton's classroom—a voice that really did sound as if it might belong to a king, it was so filled with outrage over his wishes being disobeyed. "Go home. I'll meet you there later."

"Uh, no, you won't, Will," Marco said. "That's why she's not budging. She knows as well as I do that you won't be meeting *anyone* later."

Another jolt of lightning. Again the sky turned red. Then just as suddenly, thunder turned it gray again.

"Marco," Will said. "This is stupid. You don't want to do this."

"See, that's where you're wrong," Marco said. "I've been wanting to do this for a long, long time. You think I didn't get sick of it, back home? *Why can't you be more like Will? Look at Will, he didn't flunk shop. Look at Will, he didn't wreck the car. Look at Will, he's not skipping class to get high behind the Dairy Queen. Look at Will, the Golden Boy. The QB. Mr. Four-Point-Oh, Prom King.* I never got it, you know. I never understood why my mom was always harping at me about you. Until now." He switched off the safety on the gun.

"And then," he went on casually, as if we'd all bumped into one another down at Storm Brothers, or something, "she up and marries your dad. Lucky me! Now I get to live with you! Yeah, I get to see up close and personal what I could have been, if I'd applied myself. And as if that's not enough, guess what? Turns out we're brothers! Yeah, *brothers*! Like I didn't feel completely inadequate before. Now I have to deal with the fact that you and I share a significant amount of DNA. Oh, and that your dad was boffing my mom behind my dad's back? Yeah, nice one."

"Marco," Will said, in a low, even voice. "Our parents are screwed up, okay? But we don't have to take that out on each other."

"Don't we?" Marco laughed without humor. "Gee, that's big of you, Will. Considering my dad didn't kill your dad, the way yours did mine. The way I see it, there's only one way to even up the odds. An eye for an eye."

"If it's an eye for an eye you want, Marco," I said, my voice shaking, "kill Will's dad, not Will."

Will threw me a *Stay out of this* look. But I didn't care.

"I thought about that," Marco said. "But the thing is, I want the old guy to suffer. And what could hurt more than knowing that his precious golden boy died because of something he did? He'll have to live with that for the rest of his life, just like I'll have to live without my dad. That's what I call an eye for an eye."

"But what's the point, Marco?" Will wanted to know. "It's not going to bring your father back."

"No," Marco said, in a voice that sounded entirely reasonable. "It won't. But it will make me feel a hell of a lot better."

"And when you're in jail?" Will asked evenly. If he was afraid, you couldn't tell by looking at him. He was standing straight and tall, and his voice didn't shake a bit. He looked almost . . . well, kinglike.

And apparently I wasn't the only person who thought so. Marco couldn't seem to take his gaze off him.

Which was a good thing. Because it gave me the opportunity to slide down the back of the boulder and reach for the sword I'd left at its base.

"I'll only go to jail if I get caught," Marco was saying. "And I don't plan on that happening."

"Oh, right," Will said, with a laugh. "What are you going to do, go on the lam? You don't even have any money. You blew it all on that stupid Corvette of yours. Which I hope you're not planning on using as a getaway car, by the way. You won't get any farther than the Bay Bridge before the cops pull you over. They're already looking for you, after that stunt you pulled back at the school."

I couldn't see Marco's expression, since I was busy unwrapping my dad's sword from the windbreaker. But he sounded as coolly disinterested as ever.

"I'll just use your car, then," he said. "And whatever cash I dig out of your wallet after you're dead. Now come on down from there. You're giving me a crick in the neck."

"You've got problems, Marco," Will said, in a preternaturally calm voice. "You need help. Put down the gun and let's talk about this."

"It's too late for talking." Marco was starting to lose his cool. His voice had risen, and not just because the thunder overhead was growing even louder and more menacing. "Get down off that rock, Will, or I'll shoot your girlfriend in the head. What is she doing back there, anyway? Yo! Lily Maid! Get out from behind there. I'm not kidding. I'll blow a hole through him, I swear."

I scrambled back up to the top of the boulder, dragging my dad's sword behind me. No one seemed to notice.

"Marco." Will had spread his hands open wide, appealing to Marco's better nature . . . if Marco even had one. "Come on. We're brothers."

"Aw, now, see." There was real disappointment in Marco's voice. "Why'd you have to go and remind me? I'm just going to have to shoot you now. And I was going to wait and shoot your girlfriend first, and make you watch." And he raised the gun, closing one eye to take aim. "Oh, well."

"Will!" I cried. "Here!"

And when Will glanced my way, I threw the sword to him, hilt-first.

CHAPTER TWENTY-SEVEN

Out upon the wharfs they came,
Knight and burgher, lord and dame,
And round the prow they read her name,
The Lady of Shalott.

The gun went off, a muted pop in the deeply forested ravine that Will seemed hardly to notice. The bullet whizzed harmlessly past his head, because he'd stooped to catch the sword. Looking down at what I'd passed to him, confusion clouded his face.

"A *sword*?" He held the blade aloft, still staring at it in confusion, as if to ask, *How is this supposed to help me?*

He had a point. I mean, what good is a sword against a gun?

Except . . .

Except that when Will's fingers wrapped around the hilt, something seemed to . . . change. I couldn't put my finger on what, exactly.

Maybe because at that moment, *everything* changed. It was as if someone had hit the autofocus button on the world.

Because suddenly, everything seemed brighter— sharper—more colorful. The dark shadows beneath the roots of the trees and at the base of the boulders seemed . . . well, darker.

And the green of the leaves overhead seemed . . . greener.

The sword in Will's hand seemed actually to gleam, the rust spots nowhere near as noticeable as they'd been just a second before.

That's when I saw that the sky overhead had started to clear up. The massive black clouds were rolling away, revealing the dusty pinks and soft lavenders of an Indian summer sunset. . . .

So that was why. I mean, why the minute Will's fingers closed around that sword hilt, everything suddenly seemed so much . . . brighter.

Although it didn't quite explain why Will himself seemed taller, his hair glossier and darker than ever. His shoulders seemed broader, his blue eyes brighter. It was as if he were radiating some kind of inner . . .

Well, Light. There was no other way to put it.

I shook my head. No. That wasn't possible. It was just that the storm was passing. Or my love for him, candy-coating him in my eyes—

Except that didn't explain Marco's reaction when Will turned to face him again, holding the sword in front of his body as naturally as if he went around holding swords in front of his body every day of the week.

"Put the gun down, Marco," Will said, in a voice that, like everything else around us, was just slightly different than it had been before—deeper and more self-assured. More—though I didn't like to admit it—kinglike than ever.

Which is when Marco, his face as white as the tank top he was wearing, fell to one knee, as if his legs had simply given out beneath him.

Or as if he'd suddenly recognized who it was, exactly, he'd been waving a gun in front of.

"N-no," he said from where he knelt.

I had come to stand just behind Will. When Marco finally lifted his head, it was to glare at me with eyes filled not only with malice, as before, but also with something I'd never seen in them before. . . .

Fear.

"You're *not* the Lady of Shalott," he breathed.

I shook my head. None of this made any sense. Except that, in a strange way, it sort of did.

"I never said I was," I reminded him.

"I'll put the sword down when you put the gun down, Marco," Will said, in that same super-authoritative voice. "Then we can talk this over. Like brothers."

"Brothers!" Marco echoed bitterly. Then he jerked the gun—and his gaze—at me again. "Why'd you have to go and give him a sword?" he shouted. "Only one person is supposed to give him a sword. And it's not you. It *can't* be you! That's *impossible!*"

Only those in Arthur's closest circle can put an end to the dark side's reign.

"Drop the gun, Marco," Will said. "Now—before someone gets hurt."

I saw Marco's fingers loosen on the gun handle. It was almost as if he couldn't *not* do as Will said.

It was working. He was giving up.

Which was when a blue-jeaned streak burst from the thick woods beside him. A second later, Marco was flat on his back at the bottom of the creek bed, Lance Reynolds sprawled on top of him. Lance's fingers closed over the hand that clutched the gun . . . but Marco had let go of it before Lance ever hit him.

"The man said drop the—" Lance went to pull the gun from Marco's hand, and, seeing it lying harmlessly in a nearby clump of brambles, looked flummoxed. "Oh. Well. Good."

A second later, Jennifer delicately picked her way through the underbrush. She looked at Lance and Marco, then up at Will and me.

"Oh, good," she said, her tinkly little voice filled with satisfaction. "We're in time. See, Lance? I told you they'd be here."

Beside me, Will slowly lowered the sword, staring at it as if he had only just realized it was there.

Then he raised his dazzled gaze to meet mine, and I saw that his chest was rising and falling as if he had just run . . .

. . . Well, two miles through a raging nor'easter.

Then the next thing I knew, he'd wrapped an arm around my neck and pulled me to him.

"Thank you," he murmured into my damp hair.

"I didn't do anything," I whispered back.

"Yes, you did," he said, holding me closer.

Then Jennifer's tinkling voice cried, "Oh, look, Lance! Didn't I tell you they'd make a cute couple?"

Then her tone changed. "Wait a minute. What's *he* doing here?"

And I looked up to see Mr. Morton struggling toward us down the side of the ravine, trailed by several officers from the Annapolis Police Department.

CHAPTER TWENTY-EIGHT

Who is this? and what is here?
And in the lighted palace near
Died the sound of royal cheer;
And they cross'd themselves for fear,
All the Knights at Camelot:

"I thought you were leaving for Tahiti," I said accusingly.

"Ellie," my mom said in a warning voice.

"Well, that's what he told me."

I glared at Mr. Morton from where I sat on the couch, a blanket around me, even though I'd changed from my wet clothes into my oldest flannel pajamas, and drunk about a gallon of hot chocolate. I just couldn't seem to get warm, in spite of the fact that the storm was over, and the night air was a relatively balmy sixty degrees.

Mr. Morton gave my father an apologetic look.

"I did tell her I was going to Tahiti," he said. He looked very strange, sitting there in our living room. I don't think I'll ever get used to seeing teachers outside of school. "It was incredibly arrogant of me. You see, in my wildest dreams, I never imagined—"

"And how was making Will's mom tell him the truth about their relationship supposed to help things?" I demanded.

"Ellie," my mom said, again.

But I ignored her.

"It just made things worse," I said. "I mean, you had to know Marco was going to find out."

"Of course, of course," Mr. Morton said. There was a cup sitting untouched in front of him. He'd gratefully accepted my parents' offer of tea when he'd come through our front door, just minutes after my parents and I had gotten home from the police station. Having finally made it through the horrific traffic on the Beltway, my mom and dad arrived at our house only to find a message on the answering machine (the phone and power lines having come back on just minutes before they'd gotten home) asking them to pick me up at the police station.

Which hadn't caused them to freak too much . . . not.

They'd met me, shivering in my wet things, outside the room they'd taken my statement in. Will was still inside, giving his. I wasn't convinced it was sitting so long in wet clothes that had given me the permanent shakes, so much as having had to sit there under the stony and unforgiving gaze of Admiral Wagner, who'd shown up with his wife after Marco used his one phone call to call . . . well, them.

273

Which I thought was kind of ironic, considering the fact that he'd been all set to destroy their lives a half hour earlier.

In any case, Lipton, which is what my mom brewed up for Mr. Morton, apparently wasn't quite up to his exacting standards, since the cup had grown cold in front of him.

"But after you left my place this afternoon," Mr. Morton said, "I couldn't stop thinking about what you'd said, Elaine. About how Arthur would never leave me to die, the way I was leaving him. You can't imagine the effect those words had on me. I've spent my whole life, you see, trying to uphold the values that the Bear taught us, and there I was, acting as cowardly as . . . well, as Mordred. I thought that if perhaps I could clear things up within Arthur's family circle," Mr. Morton went on, "there was a chance they could come to terms with the situation, and with one another—"

"And break the cycle," my mom interrupted eagerly.

I couldn't help but roll my eyes. Mr. Morton, an actual member of the mystical Order of the Bear, showing up on our doorstep had been like a dream come true for my mother. She'd been hanging on the guy's every word ever since he'd appeared at the door and introduced himself to my parents.

"But I should have known the dark side would never allow it," Mr. Morton continued. "It must have signaled to Marco somehow that something was afoot at the school—the last place I would ever have expected to see him, considering his antipathy toward the place . . . not to mention the restraining order keeping him from entering it."

"But how did you know we were at the arboretum?" I asked him.

"Quite simple, really," Mr. Morton said. "The lightning."

"The lightning?" I stared at him. "What are you talking about?"

"You probably didn't notice, but the lightning was centered over an extremely small area . . . the distance between this house—your house—and the park, to be exact. I had only to follow the lightning to know that I'd soon find the Bear. Lightning is, of course, a weapon of the dark side."

I nearly choked on my fourth cup of hot chocolate. I glanced at my parents to see whether or not they were swallowing this malarkey. But my mom looked enrapt— I could tell she was itching to get to her office to start writing all of this down in her book. And Dad didn't exactly look disbelieving, either.

And they're the ones with the Ph.D.s. Go figure.

"What I don't understand," my dad said, "is why the sword had such an effect on Marco—and Will, too, if what you described to me is true. That sword isn't even from the right century to be Excalibur. Near as I can trace, the only king it ever might have belonged to is Richard the Lionheart, but—"

"Oh, it wasn't the sword itself that mattered," Mr.

Morton said brightly. "It was the person who gave it to him that made all the difference."

All three adults turned to look at me. I blinked back at them.

"What?" I said intelligently.

"Don't say 'what,' Ellie," Mom said. "Say excuse me."

"I don't care about Image right now, Mom," I said. "Why are you all staring at me?"

"I have wronged you, Ellie," Mr. Morton said, in his deep, rumbly voice. "I don't blame you at all for being annoyed with me. I incorrectly assumed you were Elaine of Astolat when I learned your name and realized your connection with the Bear. But of course you were never the Lady of Shalott."

"I know," I said, a little impatiently. "I told you that from the beginning."

"I ought to have seen that you were someone far, far more important," Mr. Morton went on. "And powerful. Though in my own defense, I feel it ought to be stated that never in the Order's history has the Lady of the Lake been recorded as having made an appearance—"

I looked at him in some alarm.

"Wait a minute," I interrupted. "Lady of the what?"

"The Lady of the Lake," Mr. Morton said. "I really think I can be forgiven for my error, however, since the Lady—begging your pardon, Elaine—is such an ambiguous character in Arthurian legend."

"Absolutely," my mother agreed. "Some scholars believe she never existed at all; others insist she was a

Celtic divinity. Most agree she was at the very least a powerful high priestess. . . ."

"My only comfort," Mr. Morton said, with a nod, "is that the Dark mistook your daughter for the Lily Maid as well. Had they known they were dealing with anyone as powerful as the Lady of the Lake, they would have attempted to eliminate her early on. Even Marco, as I understand, heard the name and put it together with her fondness for—"

"Floating." I swallowed. "Mom. Dad. Listen. You can't honestly believe all this . . . junk."

But my parents just looked at me like, *You've got to be kidding.* They'd fallen for it, hook, line, and sinker. Which, given how little they actually get out of the house, shouldn't have been so surprising.

"Oh, there's no question about it, Ellie," Mr. Morton said, with a smile. "I understand that the idea will take some getting used to. But there's no getting around the fact that you are, indeed, the reincarnation of the Lady of the Lake. It was she who gave Arthur the weapon that he used to defend himself and the realm. And only she could have kept his friendship with Lancelot and Guinevere from splintering, leaving him vulnerable to attack from his mortal enemy."

"I didn't do that," I protested. "I just told Will he'd better tell Jennifer it didn't bother him, you know, so people wouldn't go around thinking he was upset about the whole thing when he wasn't—"

"Like I was saying." Mr. Morton smiled at my parents. "You have a very impressive daughter, Professors Harrison."

My mom beamed modestly back at him. "I always did think she was destined for greatness."

It seemed like a good idea to change the subject, which was creeping me out, so I asked the room in general, "What's going to happen to Marco, anyway?"

"Jail," my mother said, in a hard voice. While the Arthurian stuff seemed to be thrilling her, the gun thing really wasn't. "Hopefully for the rest of his life."

"I'm afraid it won't be quite that long," Mr. Morton said. "He didn't in the end actually hurt anyone. But when he does get out, which will be fairly soon, he should be quite harmless. The power of darkness left him when Will triumphed over it."

Oh, *brother*. I rolled my eyes some more.

"Poor kid," my dad said, with a sigh. "He's had a tough life."

"He was going to shoot our daughter," Mom reminded him. "Forgive me if I don't cry."

"With proper therapy and rehabilitation," Mr. Morton said crisply, "he should become a properly functioning citizen in no time."

"And . . ." I hated to ask it, since it was bound to get them talking about the Lady of the Lake thing again. But I had to know. I hadn't seen him since the police had separated us for questioning. I had no idea what had happened to him since. " . . . Will?"

"The Bear?" Mr. Morton looked thoughtful. "Yes,

well, Arthur is at a crossroads just at the moment. He's been betrayed by his brother, it's true. But also by his parents. It will be interesting to see—"

"Will didn't get along with his dad before this," I interrupted. "I mean, Admiral Wagner wanted him to go to military school, and Will didn't want to. And now that he knows that his dad lied to him all this time about his mom, I don't think he's going to be any more willing to do what the guy says. And could you please not call him Arthur? Because it is truly creepy."

"Ah," Mr. Morton said. "Yes, sorry. And he mentioned as much to me—about his father, I mean—when we talked back at the station house—"

"You *talked* to him?" I practically yelled. "You *told* him? About the Arthur stuff?"

"Well, of course I did, Elaine," Mr. Morton said, a little testily, considering a minute ago he'd been telling me I'm supposed to be a high priestess of some kind. "The man has to know his birthright."

"Oh, God," I said, dropping my face into my hands. "What did he say?"

"Not very much, actually," Mr. Morton said. "Not surprisingly, I suppose. It's not every day a young man hears that he's the reincarnation of one of the greatest leaders of all time."

I stifled my groan in my hands.

"I'll be staying here in Annapolis, of course," Mr. Morton went on, "in order to help guide his next steps. And other members of the Order will be flocking here, as

279

well, in order to best facilitate his needs." It was all my mother could do, I could tell, to keep from clapping her hands with glee at the thought of dozens of members of the Order of the Bear descending upon Annapolis . . . just in time for her to interview them for her book. "College is the next obvious move, but it's got to be the *right* college. With Arthur's—excuse me, Elaine, I mean, Will's grades he can get in anywhere, of course, but the question is, what university is really best for molding the mind of a man who could well become one of the most influential leaders in modern history?"

Thankfully, the doorbell rang just then.

I threw off my blanket and said, "I'll get it," then hurried to see who it was, muttering, "It better not be any powers of evil . . . " only to have Mr. Morton call merrily, "Oh, don't worry. They've all been thwarted, thanks to you."

"Great," I said sarcastically. And threw open the door.

To find Will standing there, holding a gym bag in one hand, and Cavalier, on a leash, in the other.

CHAPTER TWENTY-NINE

But Lancelot mused a little space;
He said, "She has a lovely face;
God in His mercy lend her grace,
The Lady of Shalott."

"Hey," he said quietly, his eyes looking bluer than ever in the porch light—so blue, in fact, that I was swimming in them before I even managed to get out a greeting of my own.

"Hey," I croaked.

Moths beat at the door I was holding, trying to get in. Behind Will, the night-dark, rain-soaked yard was an orchestra of chirping crickets and cicadas.

"I'm sorry to stop by so late," Will said. "But Cav and I . . . we sort of need a place to stay. Do you think your parents would mind if we crashed here for a few days? Just until I find my own place. Things at home are . . ." He gripped the strap to his gym bag a little more tightly. "Not good."

I'd have given him my own bed to sleep in, and gladly taken the floor. But I didn't admit this out loud. Nor did I let any of my intense relief that he was still in Annapolis show. If I had been in his place, I'm not so sure that I wouldn't have packed up and left town, not wanting to see ever, ever again any of the people involved in what could only have been the most painful moment of my life.

Instead, I said, as casually as I could, "Come on in, and I'll check."

Will came in, Cavalier following close at his heels.

"Who is it, Ellie?" Mom called, from the living room.

Standing in the darkness of the foyer, I looked up at Will.

"Mr. Morton is here," I whispered.

One side of Will's mouth twitched upward. I didn't know if this meant he was pleased or the opposite.

"I'm not exactly surprised," he said.

"I can try sneaking you upstairs," I offered.

"No," he said. And this time both corners of his mouth went up. "Kings don't sneak."

My mouth fell open. "You're not telling me you *believe*—"

"Move it, Harrison," he said, and taking me by the arm, propelled me back into the living room.

"Uh, Mom, Dad," I said. "Will's here."

For a second, both my parents and Mr. Morton stared up at Will as if he were some kind of ghost. Then Mr.

Morton finally pried his jaw apart to whisper, "Of course. Of course he'd come here," as if he were speaking to himself.

Ignoring him, I said to my mom and dad, "Will needs a place to stay for a couple of days. Can I give him Geoff's room?"

My mom looked worriedly at Will.

"Oh, dear," she said. My dad was the one who asked, "That bad at home, eh?"

Will, still holding his gym bag, nodded. Cavalier, at his side, was eyeing Tig, who'd risen to her feet and was standing on the hearth with her tail puffed out to five times its normal size. Neither animal, however, made a sound. They just looked at each other.

"I wouldn't ask, sir," Will said to my dad, "if it weren't . . .Well, Jea—I mean, my mom is all right. It's my dad. I—" Will glanced at Mr. Morton. "The thing is, sir, I sort of told him I wasn't going to enroll in the Academy next year, and he blew up. I probably didn't pick the best time to bring it up, exactly, with Marco . . . well, with Marco where he is right now. But I felt like it was time—*past* time—we all started being honest with each other. And— well, long story short? My dad threw me out of the house. I was hoping I could stay here until I can find a place of my own. But if it's a problem—"

"Of course you can stay here," my dad said, to my everlasting relief. "Long as you need to."

"You must be exhausted," my mom gushed, jumping to her feet. "I know I am, and I haven't been through half of what you have today. Ellie, show him up to Geoff's room. Did you have supper, Will? Want me to heat up some ribs? You're hungry, I suppose?"

The smile Will flashed her could have electrified the Beltway all over again.

"Yes, ma'am," he said. "Always."

"I'll fix you up a plate of something," my mom said, and hurried into the kitchen, while my dad followed her, muttering, in a perfectly audible voice, "Kid's going to eat us out of house and home."

"*Dad*," I said, appalled. "We can *hear* you."

"I know," my dad called back.

To Mr. Morton, who'd risen to his feet and was standing a few feet away, looking awkward and deferential, Will said, "Hello again, sir."

"Sire," Mr. Morton said . . . and he actually gave a little bow.

I thought I was going to crack up right there in front of him, but Will grabbed my arm and dragged me out of there and back into the hallway before I could.

"Oh my God," I whispered, trying to stifle my giggles. "Is he going to call you that every time he sees you now? Like in school and everything?"

"I hope not," Will said. "Come on, show me where I can throw this thing."

So I took him—and a politely inquisitive Cavalier—to Geoff's room, which was really just a guest room now, Geoff being away at college.

All I could think the whole time I was going up the

stairs was, *He's staying the night. Maybe more than just the night. Maybe a few nights. I'm going to see him last thing before I go to sleep. And first thing every morning when I wake up. Like the rose he gave me.*

Nancy will *die* when she finds out.

Will threw his bag down onto the bed without even glancing around to see whether or not he liked the room. Instead, he just looked at me.

And suddenly I was aware of how very alone we were together. Well, with the exception of Cavalier and Tig, who seemed to have slunk up the stairs behind us. The two of them carefully touched noses, then both backed into separate corners to eye each other some more.

"There's a bathroom right next door," I said. "My parents use the one off the master, and I use the one off my room, so you'll have this one all to yourself. There are clean guest towels in it already." I was babbling. I knew I was babbling, but I couldn't seem to stop myself. "We usually have just cereal for breakfast, but my mom makes pancakes on special occasions, and, well, this is sort of special, so maybe she'll make them tomorrow if we—"

"Elle," Will said gently.

I blinked at him. Well, what else could I do? Every time he called me that, it made my heart seem to swell to twice its normal size.

"Yeah?"

"I don't care about pancakes," he said.

I blinked some more.

"No," I said. "I don't imagine you do. Sorry. I just—"

And then he pulled me to him and started kissing me.

And I realized something as we kissed. Something strange.

And that's that I was happy. *Really* happy. For the first time in . . . well, a long time.

And I didn't think that feeling was going to go away anytime soon, either.

"Hey," I said, a minute later, when he finally let me up for air. "That's no way for a king to behave."

Will said something decidedly unaristocratic about kings, and kissed me some more.

"Besides," he said, a few minutes later, his kisses finally having put an end to my shivering, "you don't believe all that stuff Morton was talking about, do you?"

"Hardly," I said, with a snort. Because it was easy not to believe in the powers of darkness when Will was holding me in his arms and my cheek was resting on his shoulder.

"Yeah," he said. I loved the way I could feel his voice reverberating through his body as he spoke. "Me neither. I mean, can you believe there's a whole organization of people who've just been waiting around for King Arthur to rise again?"

"No," I said. "Although there are worse things than being worshipped as a demigod by a bunch of people who are apparently perfectly willing to pay your college tuition."

"That's true," Will said thoughtfully. "What I can't

help wondering though is . . . I mean, you don't think—"

I lifted my head. "What?"

"Nothing. Just . . . Well, that was weird today, in the park. When you handed me that sword—"

"It had nothing to do with the sword," I said, laying my cheek back against his shoulder. "Not because of what Mr. Morton says, either. It was just . . . the circumstances. You know, of my handing it to you just when the sky cleared up, and the fact that we might have been shot down dead at any given time. Tomorrow, when the police give the sword back to my dad, you'll take a look at it and see. It's just an ordinary, rusty old sword."

"I know. That's what makes it even stranger. I mean, I'm not saying I believe it. What Morton said. Not all of it, anyway. But some of it—like how I knew you. That very first day, by the ravine, when you smiled at me. I'd never met you before, but I still . . . I *knew* you."

"You just *wanted* to know me," I said, giving him a squeeze. "Because I'm so cute, and everything."

Will shook his head, his blue eyes gleaming.

"Think you've got all the answers, do you?" he asked. "Well, riddle me this, Batgirl. What about how similar everyone's names are? Lance and Lancelot. Jennifer and Guinevere. Morton and Merlin—"

I gasped at this.

"No! You don't think—not *Merlin*."

"Hey," he said. "Is it any crazier than me being Arthur, or you being the Lady of the Lake?"

"I'm *not* the Lady of the Lake," I said firmly.

"Oh, you're not?" He was grinning now. "With the amount of time you spend in the water?"

"It's a pool," I pointed out. "Not a lake. And I'm not even on the swim team. Besides, what if it *is* true? If you really are Arthur, and I really am the Lady of the Lake . . . well, then this isn't how the story's supposed to go, is it? With us, I mean. Together. Like this."

"It is now," he said, with a grin. And kissed me again.

And I remembered something then that I had forgotten up until that moment—something I knew that Mr. Morton had also realized, downstairs. Something I decided not to mention to Will:

And that was that, in the legend of Camelot, the Lady of the Lake didn't just bring Arthur his sword.

No, she performed one other service for him, too.

When it was all over, she brought him home.

To Avalon.

AVALON HIGH

A sneak peek at Meg's first-ever manga!
Turn the page for a behind-the-scenes look at
Avalon High: Coronation #1: The Merlin Prophecy.

Just who was the real King Arthur?
Learn all about the medieval hottie.

The latest on all of Meg's books

Still not enough?

For even more about Meg Cabot and *Avalon High*,
visit www.harperteen.com/megcabot.

Behind the Scenes:
The Making of *Avalon High: Coronation #1:*
The Merlin Prophecy

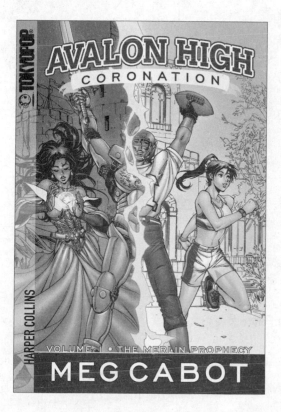

**First the artist read the novel
Avalon High and created character sketches. . . .**

Ellie   Will   Marcoς Morgan

Then Meg wrote a script for the new story in the manga. . . .

NARRATION: Certainly Mr. Morton believes it. Just like he believes that Jennifer, Will's ex-girlfriend, couldn't help falling for Lance, Will's best friend—any more than Guinevere could help falling for Lancelot.

(ARTWORK: *Show the police coming and taking Marco away while Mr. Morton and Jennifer and Lance and Ellie and Will stand there watching.*)

The artist read Meg's script and turned it into a rough sketch, called a thumbnail . . .

CERTAINLY MR. MORTON BELIEVES IT.

JUST LIKE HE BELIEVES THAT JENNIFER, WILL'S EX-GIRLFRIEND, COULDN'T HELP FALLING FOR LANCE, WILL'S BEST FRIEND — ANY MORE THAN GUINEVERE COULD HELP FALLING FOR LANCELOT...

And, finally, after everyone had seen and approved it, the final art was inked and the story was put in place!

Who was the real King Arthur?

"The Pendragons were way dysfunctional as far as families go. Jerry Springer would have loved them."
—Ellie Harrison, Avalon High

In *Avalon High*, Ellie Harrison discovers that she—along with her crush, Will, his best friend, Lance, and his not-so-steady girlfriend, Jennifer—are just like the characters in the legend of King Arthur. In fact, they may even *be* the kings and queens of the past—reborn and living in modern-day America.

But just who was the real King Arthur—and the rest of his crew at Camelot? Their identities are entwined with myths and stories, but historians have discovered some truth behind the legends. Here's a look at some of their discoveries.

King Arthur: A Uniter, Not a Divider

The real King Arthur lived around the year 500, when horrible wars and invading barbarians left England in shambles. Around this time, a strong king emerged and fought back the Saxons, Britain's biggest threat in the North, bringing peace and prosperity to the land for about forty years.

The real Arthur would not have had knights in shining armor, tournaments, or even stone castles in his day. His armor would have been made of chain mail and leather, and his castles would have been built with dirt and stones. Many of the embellishments that we know (like the tournaments and even the Round Table)

were added by later writers. The most famous of these are Geoffrey of Monmouth, a cleric in the 1100s, and Sir Thomas Malory, a former knight turned writer for the king, in the 1400s.

Guinevere: Queen of Hearts

Guinevere's identity is even more mysterious than Arthur's. Some historians believe she was a queen before Arthur married her—which explains her fierce independence. In fact, Arthur might have married her to gain land or form a political alliance. The legends agree that Guinevere was the most beautiful woman in the world. Some describe her as slender, with fair skin, dark hair, and a wreath of gold leaves around her head.

Guinevere was unfaithful to Arthur but not disloyal. She respected him, though she did not love him. She often ran his court in his absence. After he died, she became a nun.

Lancelot: Medieval Hottie

Lancelot first makes his appearance in a poem by Chrétien de Troyes, a twelfth-century poet hired by a noblewoman, Marie de Champagne. (Marie was the daughter of a woman who eventually married King Henry II.) Chrétien was influenced by Scottish legends, but mainly wrote to appeal to the ladies of the court. So he added lots of romance to Lancelot's adventures.

According to Chrétien's stories, Lancelot was raised by the Lady of the Lake, the same spirit who gave Arthur the sword Excalibur. Lancelot was the handsomest of Arthur's knights, and the most loyal. He was daring, strong, and even had his own kingdom in France. Of course, women loved him.

King Arthur knighted Lancelot, but Queen Guinevere presented him with his sword. By the rules of chivalry, Lancelot was then considered her knightly servant and defender. But soon Lancelot realized his love of Guinevere was beyond that of courtly love— and after saving her from a kidnapping, the two began a secret affair.

Mordred: Britain's Bad Boy

In some legends, Mordred was Arthur's son. (His mother was Arthur's half sister, Morgause.) In others, he was Arthur's half brother. But all versions agree: Mordred was a villain. Jealous of Arthur's success, Mordred wanted to take over the kingdom. He plotted with other knights to expose Guinevere and Lancelot's affair. When Arthur didn't believe the charges, Mordred gathered the other knights outside of Guinevere's bedchamber. Lancelot, who was, of course, inside with Guinevere, escaped by killing all of the knights but Mordred. Arthur vowed to find him, and soon Arthur and Lancelot's armies were embroiled in a terrible war. While his men fought, Arthur was toppled at home by the scheming Mordred.

Merlin: Wizard, Guidance Counselor

According to the legends, Merlin was a magician as well as an important advisor to Arthur and Arthur's father, Uther Pendragon. Merlin saved Arthur's life many times. He also helped Arthur draw the sword from the stone as a young boy, proving him to be the

EXTRAS

future king. Though Arthur didn't heed the warning, Merlin revealed that Arthur's end would be marked by tragedy.

The Lady of the Lake: Mystery Woman

Some historians believe the Lady of the Lake was a position, similar to president or team captain, which was occupied by several different women in different legends. One Lady walked on water, another was a mermaid who raised Lancelot, and yet another was an apprentice to Merlin.

In one story by Sir Thomas Malory, Arthur forged a special relationship with the Lady of the Lake. After losing one of his early battles, Arthur asked Merlin for a new weapon. Merlin, as mysterious as ever, brought him to the edge of a lake. As Arthur looked into the crystal-clear water, an arm appeared with a sword in its hand. The sword then disappeared, leaving a beautiful lady in its place. Arthur asked her if he could have the sword. The Lady of the Lake answered that he could, but that Arthur would have to give her a gift if asked. Arthur agreed, and the sword became Excalibur, with which he won the most famous battles of the Dark Ages.

Elaine of Astolat: Heartbroken Chick

Elaine was a noble lady who fell wildly in love with Lancelot. When her love was not returned, she didn't eat or sleep for ten days. After her death, her richly dressed body was sent down the river on a barge to Westminster, where King Arthur found it. She held a note in her hands for Lancelot.

Elaine is considered the embodiment of unrequited love. Alfred Lord Tennyson, a poet in the nineteenth century, wrote about her in his famous poem, *The Lady of Shalott*.

Want to learn more?
There are many books about Camelot. Here are just a few:

Nonfiction

Women of Camelot by Mary Hoffman

King Arthur and His Knights of the Round Table by Roger Lancelyn Green

Le Morte D'Arthur by Sir Thomas Malory

King Arthur by Norma Lorre Goodrich

The History of the Kings of Britain by Geoffrey of Monmouth

Fiction

The Crystal Cave by Mary Stewart

The Hollow Hills by Mary Stewart

The Last Enchantment by Mary Stewart

The Wicked Day by Mary Stewart

The Mists of Avalon by Marion Zimmer Bradley

Black Horses for the King by Anne McCaffrey

The Once and Future King by T. H. White

the mediator

Suze can see ghosts. Which is kind of a pain most of the time, but when Suze moves to California and finds Jesse, the ghost of a nineteenth-century hottie haunting her bedroom, things begin to look up.

THE MEDIATOR 1:

Shadowland

THE MEDIATOR 2:

Ninth Key

THE MEDIATOR 3:

Reunion

THE MEDIATOR 4:

Darkest Hour

THE MEDIATOR 5:

Haunted

THE MEDIATOR 6:

Twilight

Also by Meg Cabot:

1-800-WHERE-R-YOU

Ever since a freakish lightning strike, Jessica Mastriani has had the psychic ability to locate missing people. But her life of crime-solving is anything but easy. If you had the gift, would you use it?

Read them all!

WHEN LIGHTNING STRIKES
CODE NAME CASSANDRA
SAFE HOUSE
SANCTUARY
MISSING YOU

ALL-AMERICAN *Girl*

What if you were going about your average life when all of a sudden, you accidentally saved the president's life? Oops! This is exactly what happens to Samantha Madison while she's busy eating cookies and rummaging through CDs. Suddenly her life as a sophomore in high school, usually spent pining after her older sister's boyfriend or living in the academic shadows of her younger sister's genius, is sent spinning. Now everyone at school—and in the country!—seems to think Sam is some kind of hero. Everyone, that is, except herself. But the number-one reason Samantha Madison's life has gone completely insane is that, on top of all this . . . the president's son just might be in love with her!

Ready OR *Not*

In this sequel to *All-American Girl*, everyone thinks Samantha Madison—who, yes, DID save the president's life—is ready: Her parents think she's ready to learn the value of a dollar by working part-time, her art teacher thinks she's ready for "life drawing" (who knew that would mean "naked people"?!), the president thinks she's ready to make a speech on live TV, and her boyfriend (who just happens to be David, the president's son) seems to think they're ready to take their relationship to the Next Level. . . .

The only person who's not sure Samantha Madison is ready for any of the above is Samantha herself!

Girl-next-door Jenny Greenley goes stir-crazy
(or star-crazy?) in Meg Cabot's

TEEN IDOL

Jenny Greenley's good at solving problems—so good she's the school paper's anonymous advice columnist. But when nineteen-year-old screen sensation Luke Striker comes to Jenny's small town to research a role, he creates havoc that even level-headed Jenny isn't sure she can repair . . . especially since she's right in the middle of all of it. Can Jenny, who always manages to be there for everybody else, learn to take her own advice, and find true love at last?

Does Steph have what it takes?

HOW TO BE Popular

Everyone wants to be popular—or at least, Stephanie Landry does. Steph's been the least popular girl in her class since a certain cherry Super Big Gulp catastrophe five years earlier. And she's determined to get in with the It Crowd this year—no matter what! After all, Steph's got a secret weapon: an old book called—what else?—*How to Be Popular.*

Turns out . . . it's easy to become popular. What isn't so easy? Staying that way!

15

A hilarious new novel about getting in trouble,
getting caught, and getting the guy,
from #1 national bestselling author Meg Cabot

Pants on Fire

Katie Ellison has everything going for her senior year—a great job, two boyfriends, and a good shot at being crowned Quahog Princess of her small coastal town in Connecticut. So why does Tommy Sullivan have to come back into her life? Sure, they used to be friends, but that was before the huge screw-up that turned their whole town against him. But now he's back, and making Katie's perfect life a total disaster. Can the Quahog Princess and the *freak* have anything in common? Could they even be falling for each other?

Meg Cabot is also the author of the Princess Diaries series, upon which the Disney movies are based. In the books, though, Princess Mia has yield-sign-shaped hair, lives in New York, and Fat Louie is orange. And those are the least of the differences. The following is a complete list of the Princess Diaries books:

The Princess Diaries

THE PRINCESS DIARIES, VOLUME II:
Princess in the Spotlight

THE PRINCESS DIARIES, VOLUME III:
Princess in Love

THE PRINCESS DIARIES, VOLUME IV:
Princess in Waiting

Valentine Princess
A PRINCESS DIARIES BOOK (VOLUME IV AND A QUARTER)

THE PRINCESS DIARIES, VOLUME IV AND A HALF:
Project Princess

THE PRINCESS DIARIES, VOLUME V:
Princess in Pink

THE PRINCESS DIARIES, VOLUME VI:
Princess in Training

The Princess Present:
A PRINCESS DIARIES BOOK (VOLUME VI AND A HALF)

THE PRINCESS DIARIES, VOLUME VII:
Party Princess

Sweet Sixteen Princess:
A PRINCESS DIARIES BOOK (VOLUME VII AND A HALF)

THE PRINCESS DIARIES, VOLUME VIII:
Princess on the Brink

ILLUSTRATED BY CHESLEY McLAREN
Princess Lessons:
A PRINCESS DIARIES BOOK

Perfect Princess:
A PRINCESS DIARIES BOOK

Holiday Princess:
A PRINCESS DIARIES BOOK